Praise for
Fia Drake, Soul Hunter

Move over, Jessica Jones! There's a new boss bitch in town, and her name is Fia Drake.

If you want action, adventure, hot drummer dudes, and zombies that maybe aren't zombies, you are not going to want to miss this series! Pull up a seat and get ready to bag and tag escaped evil from Hell.*

* Crossbow lessons not included.

—Shannon McRoberts
USA Today **Bestselling Author**

Fia is a strong-willed female character who constantly breaks the boundaries of acceptability, doing as she pleases to the point of recklessness. As a reader, you want to understand what created this aloof, untouchable aspect to her. Jensen creates a vivid world, mixing good/evil, religion, and mythology to push the boundaries of what possibly exists in the dark alleys of our cities. Can't wait to enjoy the rest of this series.

—Finn O'Malley
Author, *Sessions with a Demon*

Fia is wonderfully authentic in ways that some current writers would not have bothered. She takes a splash of PTSD and mixes it with her alcohol and sex in a very real way. D. Gabrielle takes darkness and grunge and makes them beautiful.

—Consumer Review
Amazon

Whiskey and Ink is emotive, sometimes sexual, and as with its predecessor, packed with mystery.

—Rosie Wylor-Owen
***USA Today* Bestselling Author**

Fia Drake is the kind of heroine who punches you in the gut and you gladly ask for more. *Whiskey and Ink*, the second installment of the Fia Drake, Soul Hunter series, delivers that gut punch from beginning all the way to the end, which leaves you begging for book three.

—Theda Vallee
Author, *Stir Until Petrified*

What really stands out is Jensen's ability to breathe life into the gritty city street life that shapes her protagonist.

—Consumer Review
Goodreads

Rage and Release

Other Books by

D. GABRIELLE JENSEN

Fia Drake, Soul Hunter Series

Drummers and Demons
(Book 1)

Whiskey and Ink
(Book 2)

RAGE AND RELEASE

Fia Drake, Soul Hunter Series
Book Three

D. Gabrielle Jensen

BALANCE OF SEVEN

Dallas

For information, contact:
Balance of Seven, www.balanceofseven.com
Publisher: dyfreeman@balanceofseven.com
Managing Editor: tntinker@balanceofseven.com

Cover Design by Adam E. Mathews, Pikuled People Art
adammathews@gmail.com

Developmental Editing, Copyediting, and Formatting by TNT Editing
www.theodorentinker.com/TNTEditing

Proofreading by Amanda Mills Woodlee

French Language Consultant: Amanda Mills Woodlee

Publisher's Cataloging-in-Publication Data

Names: Jensen, D. Gabrielle. | Jensen, Desiree Gabrielle, 1980- .
Title: Rage and release / D. Gabrielle Jensen.
Description: Dallas, TX : Balance of Seven, 2021. | Series: Fia Drake, soul
    hunter; book 3. | Summary: When demons separate Fia Drake and her
    love interest, Max Hawkins, Fia is powerless to prevent his torture. In this
    conclusion to the Fia Drake, Soul Hunter series, Fia must ensure Max's
    release, find a traitor, and keep her end of a demon bargain.
Identifiers: LCCN 2021942494 | ISBN 9781947012172 (pbk.) | ISBN
    9781947012189 (ebook)
Subjects: LCSH: Demonology -- Fiction. | Interpersonal relations – Fiction. |
    Mythology – Fiction. | Solitude – Fiction. | Denver (Colo.) -- Fiction. |
    BISAC: FICTION / Fantasy / Action & Adventure. | FICTION /
    Fantasy / Dark Fantasy. | FICTION / Fantasy / Urban.
Classification: LCC PS36010.E57 R34 2021 (print) | PS3610.E57 (ebook) |
    DDC 813 J46R-- dc23
LC record available at https://lccn.loc.gov/20219424942020945579

25 24 23 22 21   1 2 3 4 5

For the women:

Stay loud. Take up space.

Raise hell and make 'em uncomfortable.

One

F ia Drake woke up swinging.

She reached the end of a heavy chain with a jerk, thick metal digging into the small bones of her wrists. Pain exploded from her left shoulder, sending fireworks through her nervous system, and she heard herself cry out, her voice sounding like it came from an adjacent room. It took several seconds for the fog to leave her vision, and when it did, it was replaced by a faint black ring around the edges, pulsing with her heartbeat. She thought the top of her skull might blow off like a bomb.

Where am I?

The floor beneath her was smooth, finished concrete and cold. For a second, she thought it might feel nice to press her cheeks against it, but she shook the distracted thought from her mind, renewing the throbbing at her temples.

A basement, she thought once the pain in her head was again reduced to a dull roar. *In someone's home?* She tried to focus on the last thing she could remember.

The accident.

Someone had broadsided the Scout. She searched her

memory for a culprit, only to be met with fuzzy darkness. She took several deep breaths and tried again, closing her eyes and working backward to the last thing she could remember.

She had left the safe house in the mountains, stealing away before the sun crested the horizon. She had stopped at her condo long enough to load her scooter into the Scout . . .

The throbbing cloud returned, filling in the rest of that sentence.

And then what? She tried again, reaching into the memory, trying to grab onto whatever details she could. She had been planning to come back. When it was over. Once the threat had been neutralized and the demons were back in their own realm, she had planned to come back. She had planned to stop off at the bunker to grab her second weapon.

Satisfied she could still access minute details, Fia tried to move forward. With the duffel in the passenger seat of the raspberry-red International Scout and the glittery red scooter wedged into the back, she had left the garage, heading north first, then . . . she hadn't decided. All she had known was she had a target on her back and that target had already drawn too much fire to innocent bystanders. If she took the target and left town, she had hoped her adversary would follow.

Even if they didn't, they wouldn't be using a houseful of nuns and children to get to her.

Max would be better off without her too.

She had been heading north to the bunker, turning right out of the garage.

The street had been quiet. She had thought it was the normal quiet of a residential area, but her presence here and her aching brain suggested otherwise.

What had happened? How had she gotten here?

More importantly, where was here?

The prospect of finding the answer to that question

anywhere in her memories seemed slim, but she might be able to narrow it down if she could just remember what had happened. The fog in her brain was lifting a little at a time, and she raised her hands to rub at her head, to help it along.

She saw then what could have potentially broken the small bones in her wrist. Iron cuffs, straight out of a medieval painting, encircled her arms below her hands, obscuring a two-inch section of the scarred flesh on the right one. They weren't tight; there was a sizeable gap between the metal and her skin. She stared at the arm, drifting into a vision of a dragon—a giant, winged lizard—shackled, while tiny villagers wielded torches and swords in her direction. Fia shook free of the image and tried to return to the last thing she should be able to access before being brought here.

One of the things Zari had taught her was how to hypnotize herself. It wasn't theatrical hypnosis, where a stage performer coerced a bunch of unsuspecting stooges to cluck like a chicken every time they heard a bell. Not exactly. This was more of a waking dream state, the ability to access her subconscious, memories she didn't know she had.

Closing her eyes, Fia blocked out her pulsating skull and the restraints at her wrists and focused instead on breathing deeply, steadily. She had to stop panicking before any of this could be expected to work. With each breath, she felt her heart rate slow and the fever in her cheeks lessen. Feeling more relaxed than she had a minute before, she raised her middle finger to her throat. Satisfied with what she found, she put herself back in her SUV, in her garage, in the city, letting the brick and concrete of the dank basement slip away.

Her arms rose instinctively to a driving position, her fingers wrapping around an invisible steering wheel. In her mind, it felt as real as if she were physically there.

She eased the SUV out of the garage, into the quiet street, giving only a passive thought to how quiet it was. It wasn't unusual not to see anyone out here. Everything for three blocks was residential, converted warehouses like her own. There was a tenant-run art gallery in one building, but they wouldn't open for another hour.

She pulled the wheel to the right as her front end touched asphalt, and to her left, she heard the squeal of a vehicle being urged to accelerate beyond its ability. Turning toward the sound, she saw an older-model pickup, probably about the same age as the Scout, blue with the emblem missing from its grill. Through the windshield, the eyes of a teenager met hers. She didn't think he could have had his license for more than a couple of months, and now he was going to throw it away on broadsiding her in her own driveway?

With barely a second to react, she slammed her foot on the gas pedal, cranking the wheel away from the impending collision. She couldn't get out of his way entirely, but she could avoid him hitting her directly. The screech of metal on metal tore through the serenity of the empty street as the back door and part of the front caved in. Something hit her head, and the street outside swam in front of her, her left shoulder screaming from the impact.

The teen in the blue truck climbed out and joined another man at the passenger side of the Scout. Dark, leathered skin. Dressed in black. The memory of the right side of her car was clouded from her concussion, and she searched old memories for the face staring at her through the glass.

Ariaz.

The seat belt release clicked, and she was vaguely aware of hands gripping her arm, hauling her free of the vehicle. The pungent, sweet smell of something meant to knock her out burned through her nose and throat, and she struggled against Father Ariaz's hand on her face. His black eyes were cold as she slipped away, but a satisfied smile spread across the Mayan angles of his face.

"That son of a bitch!" she swore, pulling herself back to the present. Shouting intensified her headache, but she no longer registered the pain. Now she was just angry.

"Ariaz!" she screamed, not even sure if anyone were around to hear her. She yanked against the restraints, rattling the chains as hard as she could. She looked around, searching for anything she could use to make a racket. Finding nothing, she dug into her core and screamed—wordless, cornered-animal screams—until her lungs revolted, sending her into a coughing fit. She thought she might vomit from the force. When she was able to breathe again, she swore, kicking her legs like a spoiled child.

"Miss Drake, so much fire, so much fury." His voice grated against the inner canals of her ears. His drawl feigned a pleasant demeanor; the words dripped disgust. Disgust, Fia knew, for a strong woman, and for her specifically. It had been there her entire childhood. The priests who sometimes visited the convent had chided Sister—now Mother—Agnes for not keeping Fia on a shorter leash. The idea had made Fia laugh. Agnes was the most unrelenting, hard-nosed person Fia had ever met. To suggest she keep any of the kids on a shorter leash would have meant handcuffing them to her.

"Come here where I can reach you, you son of a bitch. I'll show you fire."

He continued to lurk at the edge of the heavy shadows, the light from a window high in the basement wall reflecting off his predatory smile. The whole scene looked like a bad movie, meant to manipulate her into feelings of fear and dread.

All it really did was annoy her further.

At least there was a window in this place. She truly would lose her mind if she couldn't register the passing of time. It was a small window near the ceiling, but if she could get out of these shackles, she was sure she could escape through it. She began to work out the logistics in her mind: Just dislocate her thumbs, and the cuffs should slide right off. Ariaz hadn't made them exceptionally tight.

The priest must have noticed her sudden silence and stillness. "I must say, Miss Drake, I would be insulted if you weren't plotting your escape. But it really won't be necessary." He stepped forward, letting the dusty light wash over him.

She looked up at the sharp angles of his dark face, studying, looking for any indication of what he was going on about.

"Your presence here is only temporary. Much to my dismay, I have been given instructions not to harm one copper hair on your pretty, little head. I would break you as simply as a twig, but you've proven hurting you directly doesn't get the job done. You are too much the hero, the savior. The only real way to hurt you is to hurt someone you are meant to protect. You remember Ezekiel, don't you?"

Fia bit back a growl. The corners of her eyes twitched, but she tried to keep them from narrowing.

"Of course you do. So, as much as it would satisfy me to snap your neck or feel your throat break and collapse within my fists, you are to be returned whole and unharmed."

He crossed the concrete floor and lowered himself to his haunches in front of her, tracing the palm of one hand over her face. Her empty stomach twisted, and she pulled away from him.

"So smooth and delicate. Who would ever believe this face belonged to a cold-blooded killer?" He lowered his face until Fia could feel his breath on her lips. "Does he know? That man you have taken into your bed—does he know what you have done, the lives you have ended?"

He let his hand drift from her cheek to the side of her throat, fingers briefly gripping to cut off her air. A second later, he drifted farther down.

Fia let him drift, let him gather enough proverbial rope to hang himself with, knowing where he was headed before he got there. She turned her gaze from the predatory expression on his face to the hand that unceremoniously caressed the fullness of the top of her breast. When he covered her with his palm, squeezing as if he were hoping for milk, she swung her hand up from the floor. Her fist connected solidly with his jaw, wrenching her shoulder as she reached the end of the heavy chain. She bit down on the pain, swallowing a cry as he recovered.

"Bitch!" He swung the same offensive hand to deliver his own punch to her chin. Before she could recover, he wrapped both hands around her throat, squeezing, reigniting the pounding in her skull as he stole the oxygen from her brain. In his anger, she thought he had forgotten his orders to return her unharmed.

Return her to whom?

She drew her knees into her core and kangaroo-kicked him in the gut, sucking in air as her throat reopened. He landed on his back with a grunt and the jingle of a ring of keys on his belt, rage blazing on his dark face. Regaining his footing, he charged for her, only to meet the uplifted heels of her boots against his hips.

"Hey, maybe strangling me isn't the best way to return me unharmed?" Her voice was strained from the trauma to her windpipe, but she continued taunting him as he staggered back two steps. "What would the boss man have to say about these handprint-shaped bruises you're leaving?"

He took another threatening step toward her, reconsidered, and left the room, slamming the door without another word.

"Bring me a sandwich when you come back," she shouted. "Asshole." She worked her hands behind her back and pushed at the connective joint in her left thumb until she felt the familiar pop as it dislocated. She swallowed hard, choking down a pained cry, and worked free of the cuff. "And Max was appalled you could do that. It comes in handy sometimes. Handy? Get it?" She snorted at her own joke.

With her hands still behind her back, Fia grabbed her dislocated thumb in the other hand, took a deep breath, and jerked. The digit popped back into place with a nauseating surge of pain. She closed her eyes and breathed—in through her nose, out through her mouth, in through her nose, out through her mouth—until the pain ebbed to a dull ache. She hoped the keys she had heard rattle against the floor had a key for the other cuff because she didn't want to have to do that again.

One thing about dislocation: it hurt when it happened, it hurt to fix it, but in between and after, it was barely more than annoying. She reached her newly freed hand into the faux pocket on the leg of her pants, hoping to find the knife that should be there. Relieved that it was, she pulled it free of its sheath and secured the flap disguising the opening.

"Lucky for you, you didn't already stab him with it," she muttered, tucking it into her back pocket. "Of course, if you had stabbed him, maybe you wouldn't be in this mess." She hoped she could at least bury the blade in Ariaz's thigh if he got close enough. And she guessed the likelihood he would get close enough was high.

So much for celibacy.

Fia figured when a priest served a Hell demon, most of the vows he'd made to God went out the window, including, apparently, celibacy and that bit about deadly sins. He had lust and wrath covered, anyway.

Although, all things considered, maybe it was less about

ignoring his holy vows and more about who his true master was. How else would someone get into Hell on purpose?

Maybe his lechery could be used to her advantage. She unfastened her pants and scooted them off her hips, just far enough to make her suggestion clear, the lace of her underwear clearly visible in the open fly. Either he would take the bait or he wouldn't. She figured she didn't have a lot to lose at this point.

Now she just had to wait.

Fia leaned her still-throbbing head against the bricks behind her. "Asshole could at least bring me some water." She licked her dry lips with her dry tongue and took another look around for any clues to where she might be.

Now that the drug fog was mostly clear, she could make out the writing on the side of a nearby box. "Saint Anthony's. Of course he'd keep me in the basement of his own church." Thinking there might be someone else upstairs, she considered throwing another fit until they came to see what the ruckus was. She decided to wait, at least a little while, rather than antagonize Ariaz. He may have been given orders not to hurt her, but she wasn't sure he'd follow them if she pushed his buttons hard enough.

Thinking a little more clearly, she took a quick inventory. The bastard had left her her knife, so he hadn't searched her very thoroughly before locking her up. "Should I be insulted he didn't strip me naked while I was unconscious? I'm conflicted." Ultimately, she concluded he was as interested in her reactions as her body, and she couldn't react if she was incapacitated. She felt around, twisting to reach the opposite side with her free hand.

"No keys," she muttered. "Makes enough sense. He probably left them in the Scout. Also, no phone?"

She looked around what she could see of the room from ground level. To her left was a detached cabinet in the middle of the floor, a layer of dust scraped away between it and Fia's butt. The cabinet looked heavy, and even in the shadows, it looked like the back was slightly recessed. "To fit over an iron hook in the wall, no doubt," she muttered. Looking to the right, she spotted the boxes that had told her where she was several feet away. Atop one, she caught sight of the bright red of her phone's protective case. She suddenly recognized the benefit of the voice commands she had never set up. "Damn it."

Several minutes grew into what she estimated to be an hour from the change in the light from the window. She was beginning to think Ariaz wasn't going to come back for her when she heard a key turn in the lock. She grabbed the cuff with her free hand, keeping it behind her back so he would think she was still secured. She touched the handle of her knife with her fingertips, making sure she would be able to grab it as she let go of the cuff in one fluid motion.

Ariaz crossed the room, his eyes locked exactly where she had hoped they would: on the waistband of her pants. When he reached her, the toes of his shoes touching the heels of her outstretched feet, he stood over her for several long seconds, the predatory look in his eyes different than it had been before.

Once, she had thought he wanted nothing more than to kill her. This look confirmed he could and would be interested in a detour on the way to that goal. Not that he didn't still want to kill her, but satisfying his carnal desires might have been higher on the list. At least in this particular moment.

He's nothing if not predictable.

He took another step forward and lowered himself to his haunches, straddling her thigh. He traced a finger along the waist of her underwear, dipping in under the front edge and pulling them away from her body.

"I'll admit, Miss Drake, this moment has crossed my mind once or twice. I've heard stories of how you prefer to let off steam."

That was a wrinkle she hadn't expected. "Where would you have heard that?"

"Oh, Miss Drake, do you really expect me to believe you are that naïve? Would it not stand to reason among your conquests was at least one of the master's other human soldiers?"

He was right. She had to admit that. She had taken home more anonymous men than might be considered her fair share, thinking anonymous was better, thinking the less they knew about her, the better off everyone would be. She foolishly hadn't thought that one, or more, of them might have baited her into taking him home.

But why wouldn't they have? How satisfying it would have been for one of them to take her out in her own home.

Fia did her best to conceal her thoughts, wiping them from her face as quickly as she could, but not quickly enough.

"I see I have struck a chord. You really didn't consider that possibility, did you, you arrogant little bitch?"

He grabbed the top of her jeans with both hands and jerked them down, exposing her thighs to the cool concrete floor, before unfastening his own trousers. She steeled her jaw and swung her right arm, still cuffed, toward his face; she might have drawn him in, but she needed to put up at least a little protest to make it believable. He ducked her punch and dragged her to her feet, making her lose her grip on the cuff. He didn't seem to notice as he pressed his arousal against her, burying his face in her neck and inhaling deeply.

"I'm going to enjoy this." He forced his mouth against hers, pinching her lips between his teeth and her own.

Her empty stomach lurched under the priest's kiss, filling her throat with the sour taste of acid, and she swung her free arm out from behind her back, driving her knife to the hilt in what she estimated to be his kidney. The plan had been his thigh, to cripple him, but in that moment, tasting his violent, predatory kiss, she wanted to kill him.

He staggered back away from her, clawing wildly with both hands, trying to catch the hilt of the knife to remove it from its target. "You *bitch*!" he spat. "You stupid bitch. You'll never make it in time to save your lover. He's as good as dead. You deserve to watch him die, but you will never make it in time." He fell to the floor, out of her reach, still writhing and squirming to reach the handle of her blade.

She twisted away from him, toward her captive hand. With the taste of salt and bile still fresh in her mouth, she swallowed hard and pushed on the joint of her second thumb of the day. The pop buckled her knees, and she sank nearly to the floor before recovering.

She was scarcely free when he grabbed her by the ankle, ripping her leg out from under her. She grabbed uselessly at the air as concrete rose to meet her. Barely able to get her hands under her before her face smacked the floor, she rolled onto her back, kicking up to a squat before rising to her full height.

She stared down at the man, who had apparently used the last of his strength to pull her over, watching him for a moment before stepping over him. Reaching down, she removed her weapon from his organ, instantly soaking the concrete around him in dark red blood, and wiped the blade clean on the back of his shirt. She grabbed her phone on the way out the door.

On the other side of the door was a utilitarian concrete staircase, incongruent with the rest of the hundred-fifty-year-old building. She climbed the stairs two at a time, her eyes on her phone screen as she ascended, digging Max's number out of her contacts list. It didn't even ring, just bounced her straight into voice mail.

"Son of a bitch!" She kicked a pew at the front of the sanctuary before realizing she wasn't alone. Another priest was speaking with a young couple at the back of the room, and all three turned. She didn't care; she redialed the number, with the same results. She thought about throwing the phone but, deciding better of it, called Father Scott instead.

"That bastard priest has Max!" Her voice broke as she shrieked, barely giving Scott a chance to answer the call. She was outside the church by now, taking the stone steps two at a time to the sidewalk at their base.

"What? Fia, where are you?"

"Downtown. Saint Anthony's. Ariaz's church. He crashed the Scout, drugged me, and brought me here so someone else could kidnap Max while I couldn't move to stop them. They're going to kill him. If they haven't already."

She looked around, taking in her surroundings, trying to decide the best way back to her apartment. At the end of the block, she spotted a rack with e-bikes for rent.

"Can you meet me at my apartment?"

"I'll be there in a few minutes."

Two

Fia docked the electric bicycle in the return carriage a block from her building and sprinted for the door. Her mind flashed to the blue pickup jumping the curb and smashing into the side of the Scout. The SUV was gone; only a few scattered bits of glass and tire treads on the sidewalk indicated anything had happened there.

She jabbed her access code into the panel beside the door to the building and took the steps two and three at a time to her third-floor condo. Waiting at the top of the stairs in the hallway separating the condo from the garage was Father Scott McGregor, her employer of nearly eight years and her recent confidant. He was dressed from head to toe in black and was smoothing out his shoulder-length brown hair with his fingers. An electric hum in the air told Fia he had arrived only moments before her.

She retrieved a spare key from a box hidden on the other side of the door to the parking garage and flung open the door to her condo. She stormed through, surveying the space for anything missing or that didn't belong. If they had the Scout, they had her keys, which meant access to the condo.

Piled in one corner was the only thing she could see that was out of place: a stack of mismatched round, black drum cases—some soft and made of canvas, some hard leather like her guitar case, and each marked with a blue star so Max could identify it quickly—had been tucked into the corner barely twenty-four hours earlier.

The longest twenty-four hours Fia had lived through in a long time, maybe ever.

Scott's eyes panned from the single sofa and coffee table near the balcony door over the wide, empty space that might have been a dining area for anyone else but for Fia was just space. He looked over the exposed brick walls, devoid of any art or other decorations, toward the kitchen.

"It always looks like this. Did they take my car?" She considered all that had been in the Scout when the young man hit her. Clothes could be replaced with little trouble. And she had a spare crossbow in the bunker.

That damned crossbow. She had barely gotten it back, and now it was gone again.

"You were leaving. Where were you going?"

Fia shrugged, pacing the open space. "None of that is important now. We've got to find Max." A knot had formed in her throat, the size of a walnut. She tried to swallow it, but it refused to budge, burning repugnantly in response. "Uhlpir, we've got to find Max."

The priest's pale-blue eyes shone sadly, and he gripped her shoulders to halt her movement. "What did Ariaz say to you?"

She gave Scott a quick rundown of everything that had come out in the church basement, from Ariaz revealing she hadn't been the real target to the cabinet with the false back she assumed he had used to cover the shackles. "Ballsy son of a bitch, I'll give him that."

"He didn't give you any indication who might have kidnapped Max or where they might have taken him?"

"Not outside of whoever he's been working with. I think we can safely rule out his thug and the Scandinavian woman since we know where they are. My money is on that younger blonde. Can't you do that omniscient thing and find him? I'm sure I have DNA around here somewhere. Not as fresh as it could be, but there might be a fresher sample at the safe house." She wrenched free of his grasp and turned toward the back of the apartment, heading for her bedroom.

Scott grabbed her hand on the back swing, dragging her to a stop. He turned her back around to face him, a strange mixture of shock and confusion on his face. "DNA? No, Fia, I can't—"

He took a deep breath, encouraging her with his hands to do the same. She refused. "Fia, I need you to slow down and think. I may be able to track him, the way you are suggesting, but if you are right about Ariaz's connection to the demons—"

"Oh, I'm right about that. My guess is, that's what he used those shackles for; having them handy to lock me up was just a bonus. He called Irzelen his master. Said there were others like him, that I might have even brought one or more of them back here."

"Fia, do you mean—"

"That woman last night—it *was* just last night, right? That bastard didn't have me for more than a few hours, did he?" She rubbed hard at her forehead with the tips of her fingers. "The blonde woman, the leader. She was the one I said has been following me—well, one of the women who have been following me—"

"Fia?"

She barreled ahead, unwilling to allow time for questions. Her heart raced in her ears; even Scott's suggestion of a deep breath had felt like it would take too long. "It was her all along. She must be the one who summoned the demons. But why? I thought this was personal." By the time she reached the end of the sentence, Fia was talking more to herself than to Scott.

"That doesn't connect Ariaz—"

"That big guy. The one Max took out? He is—was—Ariaz's bodyguard or thug, hired muscle. And he was with her when they killed that bounty you left me when Max was out of town. It was the two of them and—"

"Wait. You told me about a man when we spoke yesterday, but you didn't mention that was a bounty. Fia, I haven't given you any bounties since the cave explosion. How many have you received?"

She staggered, falling back against one of the steel stools beneath the bar of the island that separated the kitchen from the rest of the space. She pulled it out and was climbing onto it when Scott gripped her arm, guiding her across the room to the couch instead. Then he returned to the kitchen and, as if he had been here before, pulled a glass from the first cupboard he opened. He filled it from the tap and carried it to Fia.

"Tell me more about—"

"Of course they weren't from you. They were setting me up. How could I be so careless? I just thought . . . the one I got after the explosion, when I thought you were dead? That one didn't have your seal. And that made sense if it was a new handler." She stood and resumed her pacing. "And I guess it just made sense when I got the one I used to catch you."

"Fia, please sit—"

"I knew. I knew from day one, when he saw that stupid bird—you were here that night too, weren't you? That's why Max found that feather. Were you spying on me? But if you were here, that means—"

Scott rose from the couch and gripped Fia by the shoulders. She pulled free and backed away from him.

"No. Don't touch me. You have known all along. About Irzelen, about—what else do you know? Do you know who's behind all this? Do you know where Max is?" The fever returned to her ears, anger, shame, and realization flooding her senses.

"I do not. Fia, please let me—"

"Let you what? Explain? Explain how you knew I had spoken with the demon? Did you know what was in that cave?"

"I suspected. Fia, we already talked—"

"And you led us in there anyway?"

"I did not anticipate what happened. Or that you would climb out the way you did. I am sorry, Fia, but you must understand. Given what we found, I could not have deterred you from trying to climb to safety without explaining why I knew it would be safer for you to stay—"

"You let me get blown up and dislocate my shoulder. I thought you were dead." She shook her head. "I can't hash this out with you. I need to find Max before I lose anyone else." She elbowed her way around him.

In her bedroom, Fia reached into the small trash can beside the bed and pulled out the condom Max had used the last time he'd been over. It was old by now, but she didn't have time to drive back to the safe house. She carried it to the kitchen and looked around. "Zipper bag or box?"

"I'm sorry?"

She held up the condom for Scott to see. "Do I put it in a bag or a box?"

The priest furrowed his brow, quiet for a moment. "Box?"

"Perfect." She fished a small food storage box from a cabinet, placed the sample inside, and secured the lid. "If you won't help—"

"I did not say I wouldn't help—"

"I'm going to take this to Zari. Are you coming?"

The muscles of Scott's face worked as he visibly weighed options. "I think, in the interest of time, it might be best if I return to the safe house, let the others know what has happened."

Fia froze. "Are you sure? I think someone there is behind—"

"I know, Fia. But I believe the best way to draw them out is to act as if we don't suspect them."

"So . . . you believe me?"

"I never doubted you, Miss Drake. That someone in the safe house is responsible for the demons is the most logical explanation. I have not discounted that they may be working with someone else, but if this is a personal attack against you, as the demon claims—"

"I believe him. He seems . . . he's too interested in retrieving—and too indifferent to everything else—I don't . . . I just don't get the feeling he's deceiving me."

"Your instincts are strong. If you don't think he is deceiving you—and I am not suggesting he is, either, not entirely—then it seems unlikely someone would go to this level because of your capacity as a hunter. It feels personal."

"Well, abducting Max to get at me sure as hell feels personal. What do you mean, you're not entirely suggesting he's deceiving me?"

"I think there may be details he has left out."

"You think, or you know?"

"Fia, if Max is being held by demons, time is of the essence. If pressed, they will be able to inflict a great deal of psychic damage in a short amount of time. Hours alone could mean the difference between what he can and cannot recover from."

"Then let's get to it. What can you do to help me find him? Can you help me find him?"

"In the interest of time, it may be better if you ask what Ms. Dacius can do for you."

Fia raised an eyebrow. She had been going to Zari on a hunch. She had never had more than suspicions that Zari could do more than read tarot cards and make cookies out of weeds. "Do you know something I don't?"

"I recommend you visit Ms. Dacius, see what she can offer you. I am going to head back to the safe house. You were intimate with Max yesterday before the attack?"

"What else do you think I did with your whiskey?"

"There may be enough residual energy in your space for me to do some tracking of my own. I fear, however, that the presence of the demons in or around Max's mind—"

"In?"

"Yes, in. While I am discouraged from invading a mortal's thoughts without permission, it is not impossible, and the demon kind are . . . rebellious, at best."

Memories of Irzelen thundering around in her head made Fia shudder. "Yeah, I kind of picked up on that. Do you mean in, like physically? Like some kind of parasite?" The pressure of the demon's thoughts had certainly felt like he had smashed his entire eight-foot frame and wings into the space of her skull.

"No, I don't. Though there have been cases . . . I think it is best to say no for now."

Fia's skin crawled. "No, tell me."

"It is rare, I believe, but there have been cases where a demonic attack left a shadow of sorts. I don't have a more accurate word for it. That's what I have heard other priests—and practitioners like Zari—call it. It makes healing from these kinds of attacks incredibly difficult."

Fia watched Scott's face, wondering if he would say more. When he didn't, she pressed again. "What causes the . . . shadow? Is there a way of knowing?"

Scott offered only a slow, reluctant shake of his head. Fia ground her teeth together. He was telling her there was no way to predict the presence of such a shadow in Max's mind, but she didn't know if she believed him.

Fia imagined there were things in the divine realm she could never hope to understand, and she had mostly accepted that. But this? If Scott had an answer for this question, she hoped he wasn't holding out on her or Max.

She sucked air deep into her gut and released it in a gust. "If you really think it's better, for time, for me to ask Zari, I guess that's the next step. You're headed back to the safe house?"

He nodded.

She took a few steps toward the door and, realizing he wasn't following her, left him alone in the middle of the living room. She considered telling him to lock up before he left but decided it was a moot point, given the unknown fate of her keys. In the hallway, she pulled out her phone to call a cab before remembering Max's car in the garage.

She walked around the little white car, trying to decide the best place to look for a hide-a-key. She started with the back bumper, then the fenders. She rounded to the front passenger side, mentally shifting gears to assess the possibility of breaking in and hotwiring it when she found the little tin box.

"Bingo!"

Fia gave the interior a quick look to see if there was anything he might not want her dragging around the city and climbed in. Even though Max was only about six inches taller, she had to adjust the seat considerably. She took stock of the locations of everything she might need—the speedometer, specifically, was positioned over the center console—and checked the mirrors. Once she was comfortable, she started the car and left the garage.

THREE

Armed with her plastic food container, Fia sprinted up the sidewalk and burst through the door of Zari's shop with such force, the wooden pipes that signaled patrons weren't able to keep up. "Zari?" she called out through what appeared to be an empty shop.

When Zari Dacius moved to Colorado, she had converted a small Victorian house, complete with all its ornate trim, into a crystal shop. She had kept what was originally the kitchen and dining room as an apartment, converting the original storm cellar into bedrooms, and moved all her mystical trinkets into what would have been a parlor. Glass shelves were packed tightly with a myriad of bits and baubles, pieces Zari had once told Fia "spoke to those who needed them most." Fia had walked out of that conversation with a tiny dragon carved from howlite.

Inside and to the right of the shop door was a display case where Zari kept more valuable items, like geodes and athames. Even with the small collection of blades in the case, Zari had been unable—or possibly unwilling, Fia wasn't certain—to sell the Scandinavian woman a quartz ritual blade when the woman had insisted Zari should be the person to have such a thing. When the woman had returned later, Fia wondered if what she had really been shopping for was Fia.

Behind the counter was a heavy curtain concealing Zari's card room. It was mostly for show, set up to provide tourists with the experience they expected, but Fia had had more than one tarot reading in that room reveal things she couldn't have otherwise explained. She peeked through the curtain and found the room empty. The absence of her former mentor made Fia's heart pound even harder, until she thought it might rip through her chest. "Zari?" she called out again, her voice nearing a shriek.

Fia darted to the back of the shop, swinging her shoulder to narrowly avoid upending a small, empty curio case, and pushed through the beaded curtain into the apartment. She nearly tripped over one of a pair of handmade rocking chairs—the mate to which could be found in the basement— and crossed hastily to the kitchen.

Giving the kitchen a quick pass to see if anything had been disturbed, she took to the iron staircase spiraling down into the basement, to the bedrooms. The door to Zari's bedroom stood open, and everything inside looked like it should. The door to the adjacent room was closed. Fia tried the knob to find it locked, then checked the bathroom. Though part of a renovation, the bathroom looked like it belonged in the original home, with a claw-foot bathtub and pedestal basin in matching white porcelain.

Returning to ground level, Fia called out again, her voice screeching. "I should have never come back here," she scolded herself, crossing back into the crystal shop. "Zari!"

Ariaz hadn't said anything about abducting Zari. Or worse. Had he lied about Max? Had it been Zari—

"*Chérie?*" Zari's sweet, warm voice called back to Fia from the second floor.

Fia pushed through another heavy curtain at the bottom of the stairs, getting tangled in it in her haste. She swore, swatting at the fabric. She took the stairs two at a time, nearly colliding with Zari on the landing; the sweeping hem of Zari's brightly colored skirt coiled around Fia's ankles. Zari's dark face showed spots of white dust, and her silver-gray braids were tied up in a scarf that bore no fewer colors than the skirt but also didn't match the skirt.

"Fiammetta, what is wrong?"

"Zari, I need you to level with me. Is there anything to all this?" She waved her hand toward the shop.

"This?"

"The crystals, the cards—Zari, do you remember the woman who was in here looking for a knife? Blonde woman, Scandinavian? She, that creepy priest, Ariaz, and one of the nuns—they kidnapped Max. Well, not her, she's locked up in the mountains. And that priest is probably dead by now."

"*Chérie*, slow down. Begin at the beginning."

"They took Max. Because of me."

"Because of you?"

"To get at me. To hurt me. Ariaz told me—"

"Ariaz, the priest? You said he was dead."

"I think so. He had me in chains in the church, in the basement—"

"There are chains in the church basement? Fiammetta, please, slow down. Breathe and begin again. What happened with the woman?"

Fia buried her face in her hands, forcing herself to inhale deeply. With her palms still pressed to her cheeks, she complied with Zari's request, starting with the attack on the safe house the night before and ending with finding herself shackled in the church.

"It looked like he had them behind a cabinet. I think he's been keeping demons there, right out in the open. I knew he was a creep; he's tried to make a move on me a couple of times. So, I let him think—and when he tried, because I knew he would try, I stabbed him."

As the words left her lips, Fia thought she should feel something. Remorse, guilt, even anger. But the fall of Armando Ariaz to her blade made her feel nothing but numbly indifferent. She had felt more emotion hunting hosts.

She watched Zari in silence for a moment, trying to gauge her response. The woman's gold eyes flashed, the eyes of a wildcat protecting her kitten. Fia couldn't remember ever seeing this level of anger in Zari's calm eyes. She even thought she could feel heat radiating from Zari's skin.

Zari took a deep breath and held it for several long moments before speaking. "You said your Max had also been abducted?"

Fia nodded as the fever along the edges of her ears burned down into her jaw and cheeks. She thought she might be able to read by the light of the fever in her face. "Ariaz told me the only way to hurt me was—he even knew what happened to Zeke, what happened after . . . when I couldn't face you for—so they took Max. They have demons, and Uhlpir—I know this is a lot to dump on you all at once, but most of it came about in the last twenty-four—well, thirty hours now."

Zari's face shifted from angry mother lioness to sad concern. The knot tried to reform in Fia's throat, but she pushed it down, this time forcing it into her gut.

"And Max is gone, that disgusting excuse for a priest is bleeding out in the church basement . . ."

Tears burned at the edges of her vision. Maybe it hadn't been her fault Zeke got killed. He had followed her on his own. But Max . . .

"*Chérie*, your Max made a choice—"

"You *are* reading my mind! I always suspected . . . Zari, tell me you can find Max. Uhlpir can't. He said he couldn't for the same reason he doesn't know who is behind all this."

"Uhlpir? Who is—"

Fia took another deep breath. Another piece Zari was missing from the puzzle. Although, this piece was one Fia had intentionally held back. The rest had been oversight. Or just too much to tell. But the feather—feathers—and where they had come from, that had been intentional. She had promised to keep the angel's secret. Now Zari needed to know.

"Father Scott, the priest in charge of my bounties, he's . . . the reason he got out of that cave . . . his real name is Uhlpir, and he is an angel." She gave Zari a moment to digest this information and formulate questions, which Fia was certain Zari would have after that bomb.

"I have heard stories of hunters who were . . . I am not certain *employed* is the right word . . . perhaps attended to by the angels. As I understand, many have been rogue, same as you. Solitary but gifted. I never knew, myself, if I believed the stories, but now . . . you said there was a reason he couldn't help?"

Fia outlined the explanation the angel had given her for not being able to find Max. "I brought DNA." She presented the box to Zari. "It's old, but I thought . . ."

Zari glanced at the proffered box, then met Fia's eyes. Fia studied the woman's face, taking in every out-of-character line and crease. It was the same face it had always been, but the furrows this conversation had dug made it harder, more resolute.

With a heavy sigh, Zari motioned for Fia to return the way she had come. At the bottom of the stairs, she crossed to the front door and locked it, turning the sign from *Open* to *Closed*. She scribbled something about a family emergency on a piece of paper and taped it to the door. Then, she returned to Fia, taking ownership of the box.

"I think this may work better in a place I can feel his energy. Where were you last together?"

"At the safe house. In the mountains."

"You can take us there?"

"Of course." Mother Agnes might not appreciate Fia showing up with yet another outsider, but in that moment, Fia didn't care.

Outside, Zari ran her hands over the body of Max's car, inside and out. "This is Max's, *oui*?"

Fia nodded. "Can you feel him? Can you tell where he is?"

"I can sense his energy, *oui*. It is a strong energy, warm, comforting. I can understand why he means so much to you. But I cannot see him. I need more room; there is a ritual." She held up the box. "Blood would have been better for tracking, but sexual magic is quite powerful. Do you know, every time you release, you produce a trace of magic?"

"Does it linger?"

"*Oui*. It depends on the release, certainly, but if you made love to Max in the safe house recently, it may be enough to form a bond. With a bond, I may be able to locate him."

They rode in silence to the edge of the city before Zari spoke again. "I must warn you, Fiammetta. I have seen the damage a psychic attack can cause. There is every chance your Max will come out of this experience a very different person."

"What do you mean?"

"If he is, in fact, being held by the demons, they could

invade his mind and corrupt his memories as though they were files on a computer. Take things away, insert new memories. His captor—his human captor—may use the demons to insert themselves into his memories, to turn him against you. They may try to make you the villain. Convince him you are behind the abduction and the attacks." Zari fell silent for a moment. "If they are truly attacking you *through* him, that would be the most likely path. I simply need you to be prepared."

"Can you . . . can something like that be fixed?"

"*Oui*, eventually. It may take days; it may take months. It will come down to how strong the attack is and how strong Max is."

"He's strong." Fia wasn't prepared to allow any other truth. Max *was* strong. And stubborn. It was what had kept him with her.

After a few minutes on the interstate, Fia pulled off at an unmarked exit. She followed the narrow road until it forked. To the right, the paved road continued north into the woods. Fia turned left onto a narrow dirt road barely wide enough for two cars to pass each other safely.

She had gone far enough into the heavy growth of green and blue evergreens they could no longer see where they had come from when Zari reached across the center console and gripped Fia's hand on the steering wheel. "*Chérie*, can you safely stop the car?"

Fia glanced around to find the widest place she could to pull off the road. It was a private drive in and out of the safe house, so they shouldn't meet anyone coming or going, but she wanted to be as far out of the way as possible. Just in case. She climbed out after Zari, leaning against the front fender to watch.

Zari paced along the road, a dozen or so yards in each

direction, slowly zigzagging toward the other side. When she reached the edge, she looked down into the trees, then up to the sky.

Fia joined Zari after a minute, not wanting to break her concentration. Off the side of the road, Fia could see a few broken trees and mashed vegetation. She looked to the left, then the right, seeing a lot of the same scenery. Broken trees were not uncommon in the area, especially saplings and the frailer aspens. They would collapse under the weight of heavy snow in the winter or break in the wind. However, something about the scene felt weird to Fia, though she couldn't put her finger on it.

What Zari said, when she finally broke the silence, didn't help. Her words came out choppy, in fragmented sentences, as though she were speaking without really thinking about the words first. "Something . . . violent . . . sudden . . . an impact . . . forceful. I smell . . . sweet. I don't know if I smell or taste—it is here." She rubbed her hand over her throat.

Fia pointed into the trees. "Do you think Max is down there?"

Zari looked around, turning in a full circle. "I hear pain. Someone is hurt, whimpering softly . . ." She touched her fingers to the side of her head. "A crack, ringing, then black silence." She stopped moving, stopped talking, and stared back the way they had come.

"Zari?" Fia said after another minute of listening to the sounds of the forest.

"I am sorry, *chérie*. Whatever it was I had, I have lost it."

Fia wondered what *it* was but guessed it defied explanation. She waited for Zari to move back toward the car before moving herself.

They rode the rest of the way in tense, electric silence. Zari had something brewing, and it filled the car with palpable energy, though on a different frequency from the energy of the angel and demon. By the time they reached the house, it had built up enough that Fia was out of the car almost before it completely stopped, rubbing furiously at her arms to stop the tingling.

Looming before them was a structure Fia considered closer kin to a hotel than a house. Built mostly of the same dark wood she knew they would find inside, the structure covered three stories and, Fia wagered, close to five thousand square feet on one level alone. The end closest to the drive was made almost entirely of glass. Fia had originally assumed it to be a greenhouse, but she'd learned later it was a full library.

Scott stood on the step outside the front door. He held the door open, gesturing for the women to enter ahead of him.

Mother Agnes stood waiting in the cavernous foyer, the black of her habit contrasting starkly with the white granite floor. The elder nun's face, which was normally long and solemn, seemed especially drawn and gaunt. The tingle returned to Fia's limbs. A pall hung in the air, but more than that, Fia sensed something else had gone wrong in her absence.

"Where is Annabel? Where is Rebecca?" she asked, suddenly deeply uncomfortable with Agnes's solitude in the immense space.

"I'm here," Rebecca answered from the front door. She stepped around Fia and up beside the elder nun, speaking to her directly. "No sign of her."

"I am afraid Sister Annabel may have met the same fate as Max." Agnes's delayed response to Fia's question felt heavy in the air between them.

Fia narrowed her eyes. "What do you mean?"

"Fia," Scott said softly, gripping her by the shoulder. "Sister Annabel is missing as—"

"And your first assumption is that she was abducted, not that she was responsible?"

"Fiammetta, why would—"

"Someone with an idea who I am," Fia cut in, not letting Agnes finish, "summoned a horde of demons to 'deal with me.' Annabel transferred here because of 'my reputation.' Now Max is missing and—"

"Fia may be right," Rebecca interrupted. "I didn't know what it meant at the time, but I overheard Annabel on the phone a week ago, maybe a little longer, ordering someone to get something done, no matter what it took."

"See?" Fia waved her hand at Rebecca. "I heard that too. Where did you hear it? I went looking for the source—I didn't recognize the voice because she was angry and sounded almost like she was hissing or growling—but I found the secret passage instead."

Rebecca nodded. "I was in the kitchen. She was in the back hallway; that's where the passage comes out. That's probably how you heard it."

"Fiammetta," Zari whispered gently but urgently.

Fia swallowed hard. "We can finish sorting this out when we find Max. It sounds like our chances of finding him with Annabel are pretty high. I brought Zari to help. She is going to do . . . something and said it would be easiest if she were in the last place we are sure Max was."

Agnes stepped forward, her hand extended. "Ms. Dacius, I am sorry we are meeting under these circumstances."

"*S'il vous plaît*, Reverend Mother, you may call me Zari. And Fia and I have only just reconnected ourselves. A tragedy in Fia's life separated us. But we are meeting now, and that is what is important. Now, I must insist we get to work. What was left behind is fading by the minute. Fia, *chérie*, please show me to the room you shared with Max."

FOUR

In the dark bedroom, Fia took the box Zari had been carrying from the woman's now-extended hand. After a moment of consideration, however, Fia skirted the edge of the bed to check the small trash can beneath the bedside table. Hopefully Rebecca's efficiency had been slack that morning following the harrowing adventure of the previous night.

Relieved to find the trash had not been emptied, Fia exchanged sample for sample, placing the more recently used condom into the box for when Zari was ready for it. Turning back to meet the gazes of the two nuns, Fia tried to smooth a blush away from the apple of one cheek with the heel of her empty hand. Behind Agnes, Max's black hooded sweatshirt was slung over the back of a small armchair opposite the door to the room, reminding Fia how hastily Max had left. It was still ninety degrees in the city, but up here, the chill of early autumn was already present in the evenings. Max had brought the sweatshirt with him and, in his anger, left without it.

Fia placed the box on the edge of the bed and began to open the blackout curtains covering the nearly floor-to-ceiling windows, but Zari shook her head. "No, *chérie*. I think I would like them closed."

She flipped on the bedside lamp, then sent Rebecca to the kitchen with a list of supplies she would need for the ritual. She pulled back the covers, moving the box to the bedside table, and climbed onto the bed, drawing her legs under her into the lotus position. She switched the lamp off again and began to meditate while she waited for Rebecca to return.

Fia stepped out into the hallway, leaving the door unlatched, so she could bring Rebecca in quietly. The young nun pushed through the swinging kitchen door into the hall, her hands full of a large can of salt and five long, thin, white emergency candles balanced on a stack of small dessert plates. Fia put a finger to her lips to signal the nun to stay quiet and motioned her into the room, drawing the door closed behind them.

Back in the room, Fia found the others focused intently on the woman in the center of the large four-poster bed. Zari's eyes were wide open, but she didn't look like she was seeing anything the rest of them could see. Her lips moved, forming words, silently and too quickly for Fia to read her lips, though she guessed it might not matter if Zari was speaking in another language, which was likely.

After a moment, Zari spoke aloud. "Fiammetta, you were imbibing before the intruders came? From the crystal on the bureau?"

"Yes? Do you want . . . ?"

Zari unfolded herself from the bed and stepped toward the dresser. Fia watched, unsure if she was still in her trance, as Zari picked up the glass closest to the bed. She ran a long, dark finger around the rim, then touched the finger to her lips. She licked her lips as if tasting something from the glass.

As Zari moved from the dresser to the bed, Fia cringed

slightly. Zari was playing out one of the last scenes to occur in this room the day before.

"Fia, might Max have left anything behind last night? A personal possession?"

Fia gathered the sweatshirt from the chair. Disturbing the garment sent a waft of Max's musk up to Fia's nose, and she inhaled the comforting aroma of mint, leather, and black pepper. She handed the sweatshirt to Zari.

"Thank you, *chérie*. This will be perfect. Anything to bring me closer to him."

Zari took the garment and laid it on the foot of the bed. Then she took the supplies from Rebecca. She placed the candles on the floor around the bed, chanting over them as she lit them. Each candle had its own small base, an aluminum cup designed to both keep the candle upright and catch the wax as it dripped, but Zari placed each cup in the center of a plate, most likely for even more stability.

Zari then climbed back onto the bed and pulled Max's sweatshirt into her lap. She surrounded herself with salt. Removing the sample from the box, she cupped it in her hands, along with more salt, and whispered into her cupped hands. She shook her hands as if she were holding dice, then vigorously rubbed them together. A whiff of blue smoke drifted out between her fingers, and she added the contents to the rest of the salt on the bed. The new addition was blue, and the condom was gone.

Fia pulled out her phone, thinking she might want to see what was happening now and again later, and set the phone to record.

Zari was chanting almost inaudibly, drawing intricate patterns with her fingers in the air over the salt ring.

Fia glanced down at the phone screen to make sure it was not only recording but also picking up what she was seeing.

Tiny tornados swirled the salt crystals. First, they swirled in place; then the swirls started to combine, until they swirled together around Zari. Each individual crystal moved on its own, but the section of blue stayed together as it spun around the woman, as if it were contained in a transparent chamber.

As the swirls climbed higher off the bed, they formed shapes. The shapes came together to form a scale model of a house, one of the gingerbread Victorian houses prominent south of downtown, like Zari's.

Soon, the salt crystals stopped moving, finding their proper places in the walls of the house. The image looked like a 3D computer drawing that showed the inside and outside of the house at the same time.

The house contained two stories and a basement. The ground level showed a large space—the living and dining room—a smaller room Fia guessed was the kitchen, and two even smaller rooms, likely a bathroom and a pantry or closet. Four distinct rooms made up the upper floor, and the base-ment appeared to be one open space.

What caught Fia's attention, though, were the blue salt crystals. Beneath the basement, beneath what Fia had labeled the kitchen, the blue crystals formed the shape of a tiny person lying on their side.

Fia's breath caught in her throat. The edges of her vision blurred red, and her ears started to burn. She wanted to ask if the salt model was more like a snapshot or video footage of the scene, but she couldn't risk breaking the spell before it was complete.

She agonized over what she was seeing, forcing herself not to speculate, forcing herself to wait for Zari to finish.

Zari held the spell for a few more minutes—Fia thought it felt like an eternity, but according to the video timer, it wasn't more than three minutes—before letting the salt model collapse back to the sheets.

"I apologize for the mess, Reverend Mother, but I hope it was at least helpful."

"Zari," Fia said softly, shutting off the video.

"What is it, *chérie?*"

"There was a person. He wasn't moving . . ."

"You want to know if he was alive. I can only say his energy would not be so strong if he were not."

Zari meant the words to be reassuring, but Fia didn't love the noncommittal way she presented them. "He was so still . . ." Fia barely recognized the small voice coming from her own throat. She swallowed hard against the lump that had returned and tested her voice. "Do . . . do you know any more than what we saw? Did you learn anything more than we did?"

"I am sorry, *chérie.* I do not."

"Does anyone have any ideas for how to find one house out of a potential thousand?" Rebecca asked. Her voice sounded as unsteady as Fia's felt. "Assuming, of course, they have him in Capitol Hill."

"I might say the subbasement could be a clue," Scott offered. "Though I would wager 'torture chamber' is not something anyone would have filed for a building permit."

Fia turned to the priest, wide-eyed, her eyebrows knitting together over her nose. She snorted out a mirthless laugh. "No, I don't suppose it would be. So how are we going to find this place?"

"Zari," Rebecca said, "are you certain what we saw was definitely Max?"

"I am inclined to say, Sister, with the connections I have made here, that it was. Though it is not inconceivable for the demons to have manipulated the situation to deceive us; the divine are quite adept in the art of deception. More than we, as mortals, could ever hope to achieve. Though they rarely deceive with the kind of malice we find in human deceptions."

Zari let the end of her statement drift off. Fia thought she was finished but left the words hovering on the air for a moment.

"So the body—the little blue person—could have been one of the demons?" Fia liked that idea even less. She had already been lured into a cave full of those things, a cave she now assumed she wasn't supposed to have walked away from.

If this was another trap, she didn't think whoever set it would let her be so lucky a second time.

Assuming whoever set the trap wasn't lying in a pool of his own blood.

If there were still demons and they were right about how to banish them, Ariaz either hadn't been responsible or wasn't alone. And while it was plausible Zari could be mistaken, Fia couldn't figure out any logical way both the demon in charge and the angel would be wrong about something like that. Even with Ariaz dead, someone was left controlling the demons. Possibly someone in this room.

Or someone conspicuously missing from the group. Fia glanced around at the four other candlelit faces.

The flickering candlelight threw long, dancing shadows around the room, and each face Fia found in the darkness suddenly looked wrong. Zari was almost completely shielded from the light by the edges of the bed, and her dark features now resembled those of the demon's. With a shudder, Fia turned her eyes to Rebecca at her right elbow. The shadows cast by the candles dug deep hollows into the young woman's already chiseled cheeks. The white of both nuns' wimples glowed golden in the strange light.

She turned to Scott, who had positioned himself at the back of the room, far from the reach of the candlelight. Even so, Fia detected a faint haze extending from his shoulders. She thought back to the hours following her discovery of his secret, to a clandestine conversation in the woods behind the safe house, and how the sun had highlighted a void in the dancing dust motes.

She turned back to the bed and took in a lungful of hot candle-scented air. "Zari," Fia said, her voice still soft, quiet. She knew her next words would not be well received by anyone in the room. "How can I call the demon?"

"*Chérie*, do you mean you want to speak with Irzelen?" Zari replied after a long moment.

"Fiammetta, you cannot be—"

"Yes, Agnes, I am. Maybe more serious than I have ever been. Zari, I cannot thank you enough for . . ." Fia waved her hand at the bed. "But I need to be sure. I need more information."

"That is to be expected, Fia, but . . . seeking out the demon?" Rebecca asked.

Fia set her jaw, unwilling to discuss her plan further. The truth was, she didn't really have a plan. She wasn't even sure having a plan would help. But Uhlpir couldn't help, and Zari had helped as much as she might be able to. It was time to confront the demon.

"Do you have a better suggestion?" she shot back after a moment.

Rebecca recoiled, the startled look on her face distorted by the candlelight. "Well, no, but—"

"Then the demon is my next course of action." Fia stepped toward the bed, reaching for Max's sweatshirt. Scott was at her elbow in only a handful of long strides.

"Fia, may I have a word?" Scott asked thoughtfully, taking a step toward the door.

"Not if that word is going to be no."

"Fia. Please." He pulled at her elbow before letting it go and striding out of the room.

"Fine." She followed the priest into the hall. "All right, out with it. Convince me this is a terrible, dangerous, and unpredictable idea. Tell me how I should sit on my ass—"

"I am not going to say any of those things, Fia."

She flinched, quickly blinking a couple of times. "You're not?"

"No. I am going to discourage you from seeking out the demon but because you may need his help later. *Max* may need his help later. If Max is being held by someone in control of a horde of usurped, Earth-bound demons who is using them against him, the damage—"

"Yeah, Zari mentioned something—you think the damage will be something Irzelen can repair?"

"I think if you discover neither Zari nor I are able to help, you may need an ace up your sleeve."

"I guess I can see that. But what do we do in the meantime? The damage is all theoretical until we find him—them. Those Victorian houses around Capitol Hill all look the same. And we can't even connect the house—"

"I may have a solution to that problem. Give me time to make a few phone calls."

"Phone calls? That's what you've got for me? Phone—"

"Fia, please, you must understand I am in your corner, but I have physical limitations on what I am capable of doing in this Earth-bound form. If I am honest, I have done far more in my true form here than I ever should have. I—Father Scott has a few human contacts I can consult regarding where the demons may be hiding. Let me connect with them, and we will reconvene shortly. No longer than half an hour. Promise me you will stay put until we know a little more."

It wasn't a request. Fia's mind flashed to a vision of

turning onto one of the residential streets in Capitol Hill, only to find an angry angel standing menacingly in the middle of the street, wings unfurled to block out the sun, arms crossed over his chest. Probably even tapping his toe like some kind of caricature.

"Fine. I'm not going anywhere." She looked at her phone. "Maybe I'll watch this with Zari to see if she can see something we didn't."

"Thank you, Fia. I will return shortly." The angel wearing a priest disguise turned and retreated toward the kitchen and the office that lay beyond it.

Fia kicked the wall and swore before returning to the bedroom.

She crossed to the bed, where Zari and the nuns were doing their best to clean the salt up from the sheets. She picked up the sweatshirt from the chair, where someone had folded it neatly, and threaded her arms into the sleeves. She pulled the zipper up over her chest, surrounding herself in Max's scent.

"Can I get you a vacuum?" she asked, watching the women scrape salt off the bed. They had acquired a broom and dustpan—Fia guessed from the room's closet—while she was in the hallway. Rebecca held the dustpan against the edge of the mattress while Zari swept, standing in the center of the bed. She assumed they had chosen to improvise instead of interrupting her conversation with Scott.

"I'll get it." Rebecca dumped the dustpan's contents into a nearby wastebasket and pushed by Fia and out into the hallway.

A few moments later, a crash came from the foyer, accompanied by a pained cry from the little nun.

Fia, with Agnes on her heels, hurried out to see what had happened. She found Rebecca doubled over, the relic of a

1960s canister vacuum in a pile at her feet, surrounded by a variety of other cleaning supplies. "What happened?"

"I don't know," Rebecca groaned, pulling herself back upright. She held a hand to her chest, rubbing at it firmly. "The vacuum caught on something, and I lifted it to get it free. I got hit last night, and it must have been harder than I thought."

"Do you think you are injured, Sister Rebecca?" Agnes asked, gripping Rebecca by the elbow to guide her free of the wreckage. "Should we go to the—"

"No, I think I will be fine. I'm sure it is just a bruise. But, Fia, would you mind . . . ?" Rebecca waved her free hand at the vacuum.

"Not at all." Fia gathered up the heap of appliance, righted it, and dragged it back to the bedroom.

She remembered using it a few times as a kid when she had spilled or broken something. It had been horrible for regular vacuuming, but she thought the hose setup would be ideal for this project.

She flipped it on, and Zari stepped aside, climbing down from the bed. Fia sucked up the last remnants of the salt, returned the machine to the hall closet, and reentered the room.

"Zari, I filmed your ritual—I hope that's okay—and I thought if we watched it again, we might see something we missed before? If nothing else, we can stop it and look things over more slowly."

"I think that is a wise plan, Fiammetta. Sister, Reverend Mother, might you have a way of enlarging what Fia has on her phone screen so we all might benefit from another look?"

"There's a projector in the classroom," Rebecca answered. "It can connect to a computer wirelessly."

"Great." Fia headed for the door. "Let's go."

FIVE

In the lowest level of the glassed-in library that took up one end of the massive cabin, the four women filed into a small room outfitted with four old-fashioned school desks—the kind with the seat attached and a top that flipped up to hold a few supplies—and a larger desk at the front of the room.

The classroom was formed by two lightweight false walls and two permanent walls of the house. On the permanent wall at the back of the room hung a giant whiteboard that Fia guessed, watching Rebecca set up the projector to face the board, doubled as a projector screen.

"Fia," Rebecca beckoned after a few moments of fussing over the machine. "It's ready to pair with your phone."

Within a few seconds, the back wall of the room was filled with the scene from the bedroom, Zari seated on the bed, surrounded by salt. They watched closely, hoping to find anything they might recognize in the model of the house, each of them asking for the video to be paused at various points so they could get an even closer look.

"The problem," Rebecca said, examining a single frame

of the video, "is that there is not a lot of detail. I know it's one of those gingerbread houses downtown, but that's really all I've got."

Agnes stood and approached the board. Using a marker, she drew a circle around a shape near the back of the house. "It looks like this might be a cellar hatch."

"That may help. In a few ways," Zari said thoughtfully.

"How's that?" Fia asked. "I mean, I see how it would narrow the search, but how else would it help?"

"By providing an alternative entrance. It would make it easier to create a diversion if one is needed." Zari stood and joined Agnes. "Reverend Mother, may I?" She held her hand out to request Agnes's marker. Once Agnes had handed it over, Zari drew on the board over the projection as well.

"You three—Fia, Sister Rebecca, Reverend Mother— could go in through the front,"—she drew an arrow through what would be the front entrance—"while Father Scott and I go in through the rear." She drew another arrow through the presumed cellar entrance. "If the three of you make as much of a commotion as possible, we may be able to get in here"— she drew a circle around the blue human figure—"and rescue Max with little trouble."

"Why you?" Fia asked, her question coming out more curtly than she would have liked. "I don't mean . . . why would you and Father Scott rescue Max and not me?"

"Because, *chérie*, if Max is being held by demons, we have no way of knowing what he might think or believe. He does not know me and therefore has no memories of me for them to corrupt."

"But he knows Father Scott," Rebecca replied.

"*Oui*, that he does. But I think there may be a way around that. No, I think it is best if it is the priest and I who bring Max to the surface."

"Do you really think they would have corrupted his memories of me enough that—"

"Fia, I think this is the best way." Zari's voice was stern, resolute.

Fia wanted to argue, but something in Zari's uncharacteristic tone told her to keep quiet. She didn't like the idea of anyone else carrying Max out of wherever he was, but something told her there might be more to Zari's plan than she was revealing.

"Fine," she acquiesced. "But if I think for a minute you are in trouble . . ."

Zari smiled, her face gentle and caring. "Fiammetta, do you not believe I can take care of myself?"

"No. I mean, of course I think you can. But—"

"The priest and I will be fine."

As if on cue, Father Scott slipped through the classroom door, letting in as little light as possible to avoid disturbing their projection. "Well," Fia prodded. "Did you find the house?"

Scott shook his head. "Sadly, I was unable to learn any information. I would like to make another contact—"

"Can't you just—"

Fia's breath caught in her throat, as if someone had choked it off. She flashed a startled look in Scott's direction.

His jaw was set, his eyes looked cold, and he shook his head, only enough for her to see it because she was watching for it. *I know you are upset, Fia, but you must continue to watch what you say.*

She rubbed hard at her temples and shook him out of her mind. "There's got to be something we can do more immediately."

"I am afraid, for the time being—unless Zari has an idea—we are stuck where we are."

Zari made a thoughtful noise in her throat and stroked a hand over her chin. "I may be able to do some intuitive work on the ground from within the neighborhood. Fia, I would like to scout out the situation a little before we go in. If we could go back to the city . . ."

"You don't have to ask me twice. Should we all pile in and head—"

"For now, I think it is better if I work alone. In fact . . ." Zari turned to the priest. "Father, if you wouldn't mind, I think you mentioned making some contacts in the city? I would like to discuss something with you. May I impose on you for a ride?"

"Wait. No, I'm not—"

"Fiammetta. *S'il vous plaît, chérie*, I am not keeping anything from you. All will be revealed in time. But I need a few moments, unencumbered, with Father Scott."

Fia narrowed her eyes, pinching her brows together over the bridge of her nose. She felt a wave of realization as she figured out it wasn't Scott Zari wanted to talk to but Uhlpir. She nodded and disconnected her phone from the projector. "I'll be right behind you."

"I would expect nothing less."

The three of them made their way toward the classroom door when Rebecca caught Fia by the elbow. "Before you go, Fia, I wanted to talk with you a moment."

"Can it wait? I need—"

"No, I think it's important we talk now. Before you leave."

Zari had paused when Rebecca stopped Fia and now looked at the two younger women questioningly. "Fia, do you want us to wait for you?"

Fia shook her head. "No, I . . . go on ahead. I'll be along shortly."

Zari nodded, and Father Scott held the door for her to pass through ahead of him. When they were gone, Fia turned back to Rebecca. Agnes stood a few feet away and moved to join them. She gestured for Fia to sit down and took a seat as well.

"What's going on? I'm feeling ganged up on."

"Fiammetta, we are simply worried about you. Father McGregor said you were also abducted?"

"Is that all? I handled it. It wasn't about abducting me, anyway. It was a distraction so Ann—whoever did this"—she waved a hand at the now-blank whiteboard—"could get to Max without me being in the way. I handled it."

Agnes kept her eyes firmly on Fia's face, long enough that Fia thought they were going to burn holes into her skin. "I handled it," Fia repeated, turning away. "Is that all you wanted? I need to get—"

"Fia, you've gone through a horrible few days. If you would like to stay—"

"No, thank you. I need to get back to the city. See what Zari finds out."

"If you insist."

"I insist."

Fia left the nuns in the classroom and headed for the stairs out of the library.

Halfway up the stairs, Rebecca caught up to her. "Fia, wait. I want to talk to you."

"Rebecca, I don't have—"

"Annabel left in the middle of the night."

Fia stopped and turned back to face Rebecca. "What do you mean?"

"After you went to bed. She took the car and said she was going to look for Max. That must have been when she . . ." She looked around suspiciously. With Agnes still in the classroom, cleaning up the projector, Fia wasn't sure what Rebecca expected to find. "Maybe we should talk upstairs."

Rebecca skirted Fia and headed for the main level of the house. Fia followed the young nun through the foyer, through the hallway, and back into the bedroom. Rebecca closed the door behind them and motioned for Fia to sit in the chair facing the bed. The nun backed up to the carved wood post at the corner of the bed and leaned against it.

Fia took stock of the state of the bed and wondered how long it would be before Rebecca couldn't stand it being so disheveled and started putting it back together.

"After you went to bed, Annabel said she wanted to go look for Max, that she was afraid for him out there with the potential of big cats. She took the car and left."

"I'm guessing Agnes doesn't know?"

"Oh, no, she does. But where I agree with you that her absence implies her involvement, Agnes believes she was likely taken with Max. Or murdered in the process."

Fia bit back shock at Rebecca's bluntness. "Murdered? Did she say that?"

"She implied it."

Fia mulled over the possibility. It *was* plausible that if Annabel had been with Max, she could just as easily be dead as responsible. As Fia considered Rebecca's statement, there was a knock on the door.

"Sister Rebecca, are you in there?"

Fia opened the door to find Agnes on the other side. Her face was ashen and drawn with the same deep concern she had worn when Fia and Zari had first come into the house. "Fiammetta, I thought you had left. Is Sister Rebecca—"

Rebecca joined Fia at the door, stepping around her to face Agnes. "What is wrong, Reverend Mother?"

Agnes shifted her gaze from Rebecca to Fia and back.

"No," Fia blurted, sensing Agnes was about to call Rebecca into a private discussion. "I don't care if you need to discuss bowel movements. No more secrets."

"Fia's right. If something is wrong, she needs to know."

Agnes sighed. "Very well. Sister Rebecca, have you checked on our prisoners since locking the door last night?" Fia had heard that tone more times than she cared to think about. Agnes had the noose in hand; she wanted Rebecca to put it around her own neck.

"No, Reverend Mother. Not explicitly. I did not feel safe opening the door. I took them breakfast, and the door was locked just the way we—Fia and I—had left it."

Fia cocked an eyebrow. "You took them food but didn't open the door?"

"There is a trap door in the bottom of the main door," Agnes explained. "Which was open when I went down to check on them just now."

"Apologies, Reverend Mother. I must have—"

"Rebecca, the cell was empty."

"What?" Fia and Rebecca asked in unison.

"How is that possible?" Rebecca added.

"That is what—"

"Reverend Mother?" Scott's voice cut through from the kitchen.

The three women followed the sound to find Zari and Scott standing in the middle of the expansive, gleaming commercial kitchen, a few feet from the door to the rest of the house.

"Father McGregor," Agnes started. "I am afraid we have a situation—"

"The prisoners are missing," Scott announced.

"Is that why you're back?" Rebecca asked, her fingers fidgeting with the edge of her wimple.

"In fact, it is. As we were leaving the property, Zari urged me to pull off the road—"

"A dozen or so yards from where I had you stop before, *chérie*. I believe I may have misread what I was sensing. This time, I was pulled to the north side of the road, and we found a man. He had been shot in the back of the head." Zari's voice was strained but not panicked. Fia knew Zari had seen her fair share of horrific sights in her time, but she was still a kind, caring woman, and the idea of a man being shot and left on the side of the road would shake anyone.

"He was one of the intruders from last night, so we doubled back," Scott added. "I went straight around to the basement."

"You must have come around the corner as I was coming back inside," Agnes replied. "I had gone to check on them and found the cell empty. I was just discussing the details with Sister Rebecca."

Fia heard a soft, shuddering breath to her left. She tried to look at Rebecca to see if the nun was crying without letting on that she had heard the sound.

"I am certain the door was locked tight when we left them last night. Fia watched me check it."

"I did. I actually thought she was being a little over-careful."

"And then I went down this morning with some break-fast for them. I checked the lock again. I didn't open the door to look inside. Even the women in the cell were big enough I could not have defended myself had they blindsided me. Never mind the two men."

"Rebecca, please be calm. You did nothing wrong," Scott offered softly. "I would not have expected you to open the door to check on them with the door padlocked from the outside. I am honestly surprised the Reverend Mother chose to do so alone."

After watching Agnes in guerilla-warrior mode the previous night, Fia found herself doubting Scott's last statement. If anyone could be confident enough to open the door on a potential ambush, it was the woman who had put a bolt point-blank through the neck of one of their attackers without batting an eyelash.

"It makes no difference, now, who did or did not check on the prisoners, or when," Agnes replied. "The important thing right now is finding Max and Sister Annabel."

Finally, something Fia could get on board with. "Right. And how are we going to do that? Wait, what did you do with the man? For that matter, what did you do with the other bodies from last night? Tell me they're not just marinating in the garden shed."

"It has been taken care of," Scott replied flatly.

Fia cocked an eyebrow at the angel's façade before stealing a glance toward the nuns. She really wanted to know what he meant, but she also knew better than to press in mixed company, should the answer in fact involve divine magic. And what had he told them?

"And Theresa?"

He nodded solemnly. "It has been taken care of."

"Fine, don't tell me." She didn't know if she was doing enough to bait him into a telepathic connection, but if she was, he wasn't taking the bait.

"I think we need to stick to our original plan," Zari said. "I will return to the city with Father Scott, and we will touch base with you when we have some answers. But in the meantime, *chérie*, I want you to rest. Meditate and recenter. I have no reason to think we are not going to need every ounce of positive energy we can employ. I need you focused on healing, not vengeance."

"I concur," Scott said with a nod. "Fia, I know your plan was to follow us back to the city, but I think you would benefit from some rest."

"You're benching me?"

"If that is how you choose to look at it, yes."

Fia opened her mouth to protest but yawned instead. Betrayed by her own physiological response to more than twenty-four hours without real, restful sleep, she gave in.

"I promise, Fiammetta, we will be back with an answer sooner than you know." Zari wrapped long, dark fingers over Fia's cheeks and pressed a kiss to her red head. "It will all be okay."

"Thank you, Zari."

With that, Zari and Scott cut through the garage to get back to the driveway, leaving Fia alone with the nuns.

"Fiammetta, would you like something to eat? I imagine you haven't had anything in quite some time."

Fia looked at her phone to check the time but didn't really need it to tell her the greasy-spoon lunch she had shared with Max on the way home from Kansas the day before had been the last time she had eaten. "Shit. Sorry, yeah, yes, I can just make a sand—"

Before Fia could finish the sentence, Rebecca flew into action, digging food from the refrigerator. "It is nearly dinnertime, and we missed lunch," she explained as she worked.

"At least let me help," Fia offered.

"Fiammetta, I think Sister Rebecca has it under control. I suggest you go upstairs and try to get a little sleep. We'll come find you when it's time to eat."

Lacking the energy to argue, Fia turned and left the kitchen. She climbed the stairs toward the second level of the enormous cabin. Halfway up, she stopped. A dark stain marked the place where Max had stopped a large man whose head seemed to sit directly on his shoulders from beating Fia to death with a baseball bat.

Another couple of steps up, another stain had been left by the Scandinavian woman's wounds. Annabel had tended them while Fia had argued with Max. When Fia and Rebecca had taken the Scandinavian woman, along with three others, to the basement, the woman had been weak but alive. There had been no mention that she had expired while the others escaped, so for now, Fia had to assume she had left with them.

When Fia and Rebecca had come back up from leaving the prisoners in the basement, Scott had told Fia Annabel insisted on tending to the casualties, which had left her alone, unattended, outside. For all anyone knew, she could just as easily have snuck into the basement after they finished locking up the prisoners and let them out. They may have been gone all along.

Fia wasn't sure how long she had stood staring at the bloodstain on the stairs before turning and going back down to the granite floor of the expansive entryway. With a quick glance around the space, she decided to clear her head with a walk outside.

She pushed through the glass-paned French doors, taking extra care to stay as quiet as possible.

As she passed through the garden Rebecca tended with the now-absent children, Fia inhaled deeply, filling her lungs with the aroma of roses, tomato vines, and spruce trees. She crossed the stone circle where a Middle Eastern fakir had set up camp only days before, armed with rose thorns and wood ash to mark Max and four young hunters with protective runic tattoos that would keep them from being possessed by the souls they hunted.

For fifteen years, those souls had been the worst of Fia's worries. When she had accepted this mantle, she never could have guessed she would be facing demons and human kidnappers as well. Even after a host had shot and killed her friend Zeke, Fia hadn't expected to see anything worse.

Now, she had stood toe to toe with the demon responsible for everything she had trained for—not once but three times—and she had angered someone badly enough they had summoned an army of demons. Even that she could have—and had—written off as an occupational hazard.

But abducting Max? Ariaz had told her that was personal.

On the other side of the garden, Fia passed into quaking aspen and fragrant spruce trees. The path ended at the shed Fia guessed was filled with gardening tools—and possibly dead bodies. She skirted it and hiked deeper into the trees. She breathed in the bouquet of the Colorado mountains. Soil smelled different from dirt as it mingled with fallen pine needles, animal waste, dead leaves, and thin, cool air.

She marveled at how much cooler it was here than in the city. It always was, but as summer grew closer to autumn, the chill set in sooner up here. Shady patches of snow refused to let summer defeat them, and a countable handful of leaves were a lighter shade of green than the others around them, beginning their annual phoenixlike transformation.

Fia found a patch of dry ground and sat, leaning back against the tree there. She leaned there for several minutes before sitting upright, not allowing sleep to overcome her. She pulled her legs into her body in a meditative pose and took several breaths deep into her lungs, holding each for a four count before exhaling slowly.

She closed her eyes and continued breathing, deep and heavy, filling her lungs each time. As she focused, the air around her changed. She was sure it grew warmer, still, stale. She could smell dead dust in place of nutrient-rich soil. The dusty smell carried with it something she identified as concrete. And blood. She smelled blood, and the hair on her arms prickled with the electric energy of a divine presence.

She wanted to withdraw, pull herself out of whatever was happening, but she forced herself to stick it out.

After what may have been seconds or hours, she registered a new sensation. It was the feeling of security and safety that simply exuded from Max like part of his aura. The field behind Fia's eyelids flooded with swirls of blue in varying shades. The color waved and twisted like the wax inside a lava lamp.

Thin snakes of black weaved in and out of the layers of blue, and Fia's heart began to race.

She struggled to fill her lungs as the black overtook the blue, dominating the image. Still, she forced herself to remain in the moment. Fever reached the tips of her ears, her cheeks, made her scalp itch.

The itch spread down to her neck, arms, legs. The scars covering her right arm prickled like new. She felt like her skeleton was trying to escape her body.

She jumped at the press of a hand on her arm, feeling like someone had slammed her soul back into her body. She opened her eyes to find Rebecca standing over her, her face drawn with worry.

"Fia? Are you okay?"

Fia blinked several times, suddenly not sure where she was. Trees and undergrowth had replaced the blue-black swirls, and soil and pine needles had replaced the sensation she had been sitting on concrete.

She was in the forest, behind the safe house.

Fia's head throbbed, and she quickly checked herself, looking for visible injuries. She ultimately decided yes, she was okay, and told Rebecca as much.

"I thought you were having a seizure. You were thrashing, and . . . well, I'm just glad you're okay. Although I might not have known to look for you back here if not for the commotion. Dinner is ready. I thought we'd have something homey. Do you like spaghetti?"

"Huh?" Fia still felt disoriented and took a moment to process the nun's question. "Oh, spaghetti, sure." She moved to find her feet, stumbled, and tried again.

Rebecca gripped her elbow and helped her stand. "You are certain you are okay?"

"Yeah. A little light-headed. Just hungry. Let's eat."

SIX

The gold dome of the state capitol loomed ahead of the Sherpa when Scott pulled off the busy main drag into a residential neighborhood at Zari's instruction. Soon they were surrounded by the tall silhouettes and scalloped trim of the Victorian-era gingerbread houses that marked the early days of the city.

Following more instructions that seemed to come to Zari in spurts, Scott pulled into a parking space next to the same park where he had revealed his true form to Fia. The park—more to the point, the pavilion toward the center of the park—was rumored to be haunted after an early, largely unmarked graveyard had been buried beneath it.

"There are many souls here," Zari mused, climbing out of the vehicle before Scott had even gotten it completely stopped. "Perhaps one of them can tell me something. This is where I will leave you, Father Scott."

He stepped out to join her. "You don't have to keep calling—"

"Nonsense, that is the honorific you have chosen for yourself in this form. It is not my place to sully that reputation by ignoring it. I am certain in the time you have worn it like a badge, you have done more than your share to earn it."

Scott dipped his chin. "Very well. You will be fine here alone? Would you like me to wait?"

"*Mais non*, I will be fine. It is not a far walk home from here. You have your own work to attend to. You are going to find more like Fia: teens—children—living on the streets?"

Scott chuckled. They had talked at length on the way back into the city, but how he planned to find the house they were looking for had not been part of that. Of course, he had known, even before Fia, all that Zari was capable of, though he had not expected her to be capable of reading his mind in his human form. That level of telepathy was rare, and he was, for the moment, humbled by it.

"Aye, yes. They are harder to locate now that the warehouses where they congregated have been demolished, but I think I know where to look for a few of them."

It was Zari's turn to nod in acknowledgment. "Then I bid you farewell until we have both completed our tasks. I trust you can find your way back to my shop?"

Scott nodded and climbed back into the cab of the large vehicle. He left Zari in the park and headed toward downtown.

Downtown was easy for transients and runaways. There was plenty foot traffic for them to make some extra money panhandling or busking. Capitol Hill was harder, though there was a good crowd there too. But the younger group Scott was looking for would be closer to the mall and farther north even than that.

He had spent a fair number of years, even after Fia had gotten off the streets, watching out for the transient teens and twenty-somethings. Zari had been right about him earning his priestly honorific, even if he had never attended seminary. He had earned it on the streets.

In that time, he had developed a few tricks for picking them out—none of which involved invading a young tramp's mind without their consent—and it wasn't long before he spotted exactly what he was looking for.

Four young men had gathered around a flattened cardboard box in the middle of the open-air mall. Surrounded by shoppers and concrete planters, three of them took turns dancing on the box, entertaining the small crowd with their trademark spins and acrobatics, while the fourth provided music with nothing but his hands, mouth, and throat.

Buskers were only allowed an hour in one place, and while no one enforced it to the minute, many of them remained vigilant about not going over their time. They didn't want to do anything to lose the privilege to perform for tips, which was sometimes the only option they had if they wanted to eat. Scott took up residence on a nearby bench and waited for the men to finish up their show and start packing their things to move on to a new spot. He stood and closed the gap between them, resting a hand gently on the beatboxer's shoulder.

"Excuse me, my son," Scott said in his best mortal-priest voice. "May I have a word with you and your companions? Perhaps buy you some dinner?"

The young man, who had deep tawny skin and tight black curls, edged away from the priest. "I don't—"

"Dre, chill, bro," one of the others said, stepping in. "Ain't like he's gon' . . ." He looked Scott up and down, golden-hazel eyes taking in everything he saw. "I mean, look at him. He look like one of us. He look a little like Marcus with that long hair. Sure, Preach, what you want to know?"

"If I may start with your names?"

"'Course. I'm Jax; that's Dre. White boy over there is Marcus, and that's Cal." Scott nodded and offered his own introduction. "Father Scott? See?" Jax turned back to Dre. "Told you he was straight up. You mentioned dinner, Preach?"

"Of course. Anything you like. In exchange, hopefully, for some information."

"Anything we like?" Jax shrugged. "I mean, I ain't had lobster in . . ." He made a show of counting on his fingers. "Ever?"

"Cut it out, Jax," Marcus said, stepping in. "I'm sure we would all be fine with sandwiches or a burger."

"And fries," Cal added.

Scott smiled. "Seems we might want somewhere with some variety. I know just the place." He led the young men, whom he estimated to range between sixteen and twenty, to a diner a couple of blocks off the mall.

"Hey," Dre said. "Ain't this place been on TV?"

"What do you know about TV?" Jax scolded. "You been on the streets since you was in diapers."

Dre pointed at a sign in the window. "Yeah, see? This is cool. Like the people here are celebrities, yeah?"

"I am glad you approve," Scott said, ushering them through the door.

Once they were seated and waiting for their orders, Jax took another opportunity to talk with Scott. "So, what you lookin' for from us, Preach?"

"I need some information, and I know if anyone knows what's going on in the underground, it's the youth."

Jax polished his fingernails dramatically on his shirt and laughed as if it were the funniest thing he'd ever thought to do. "Yeah, I mean, we hear things. People pretend we're not here, so we can hear a lot."

"I know. What I'm looking for is someone who might be using a house in Capitol Hill, or somewhere similar, for dark rituals."

"Dark rituals? Yo, Preach, you mean like Satanists or something?"

"Or something. I am looking for a young man who has been abducted by . . ." He hesitated, suddenly unsure how much he wanted to unload on these young men. As he considered his next words, their server, a redheaded girl named Tracy, returned with their orders. "I'll let you eat first."

"Nah, that's cool, Preach," Jax said. "We can talk and eat too. Ain't nothing you can say gon' make me lose my appetite."

"That's not exactly . . . I am looking for a house someone may be using for—"

"Dark rituals. Yeah, you said that. Hey!" Marcus slapped Cal on the shoulder. "What about that creepy priest from that place on Broadway. Didn't you say he was offering people a place to stay? Had a house in that area?"

"He was approaching people who were alone. Yeah, said he had a place. Clark Street, I think he said."

"Creepy . . ." It was the same word Fia had used to describe someone whom Scott assumed was the same person. "Do you mean Father Ariaz?"

"Is that his name? Yeah, I guess so. Seemed pretty sketchy."

Scott chewed on that for a few seconds. *What would be the objective of taking individual street kids to this house? Unless . . .*

"Did you see anyone take his offer? Have you seen them since?"

The young men exchanged glances around the table. After a long pause, Jax offered a reluctant response. "Dillon. Dillon disappeared a couple days, maybe a week ago. Last I saw him, he was headed for that church."

"Didn't really think anything of it. You know how it works on the streets, right, Preach?" Marcus added. "Sometimes people just bounce. Come back after a few days, ain't saying where they been. An' Dillon was Catholic, as Catholic as you can be out here. He'd slip into a church now and again."

"But you haven't seen him in a few days?"

"Nah. You think that other priest did something to him?"

Scott remained quiet for a long moment. He didn't know what, but he did think Ariaz had something to do with the young man's disappearance. He thought of the bounties Fia had received following the explosion in the cave.

"I am sorry to say there is a distinct possibility. I would ask you to remain vigilant in the coming days. Don't go anywhere alone with anyone you don't know. Can you promise me that?"

All four men told him they would.

Even though Scott knew the young men no longer had any reason to fear Ariaz—or his hired muscle—he didn't know who else might be involved. Enough blood had been shed because of those misguided mortals; he wanted to prevent more if he could.

A heavy silence hung over the rest of their meal. On their way out the door, Scott stopped at the counter to pay the bill and again urged vigilance from the young men.

"Ain't no one sacrificing Jackson Marshall to pay a demon." Jax pounded a fist against his own shoulder and held it up for Scott to see. "Hope you find what you're looking for, Preach."

SEVEN

She's sleeping." Rebecca's voice drifted into the hazy realm between waking and sleep, bringing Fia out of what must have been a deep slumber. "She had some kind of episode in the woods behind the house."

Fia sat up in the oversized bed and worked the muscles of her mouth, trying to create enough saliva to wash away the taste of leftover garlic. Rebecca's spaghetti had been delicious; Fia could have gorged herself on it. She had wanted to stay awake a little longer, let the heavy but comforting meal settle some before lying down, but exhaustion had gotten the better of her.

She wriggled free of sheets she barely remembered getting between and padded on bare feet out of the bedroom. She found Rebecca with her back to the door, blocking Fia's view of Scott on the other side.

"I'm fine. What's going on?"

"Fia, are you okay? What is this episode Rebecca—"

"Nothing. I fell asleep and must have had a nightmare or something. She's making more of it than it was." Fia decided, without a lot of thought, to keep exactly what had happened in the woods to herself for the time being. She thought she'd ask Zari about it, maybe run it by Scott, but not now. She didn't want to share too much with anyone she didn't know unequivocally was on her side.

Scott raised an eyebrow, indicating he was onto Fia's lie but willing to let it slide for now. When Fia asked her question again, he said, "I know where Max is."

Fia responded with a handful of rapid blinks. "Well, let's go get him," Rebecca said, stepping around the priest.

Scott blocked her passage with his forearm. "I think a little preparation may be prudent. We do not know what we might find in a house full of demons."

"A little preparation and a full night's sleep." Agnes stepped into the hallway from the foyer. "Apologies for eaves-dropping, Father McGregor. I couldn't help—"

"Not at all. I agree. Perhaps we should convene somewhere more comfortable to strategize. Fia, do you still have the video of Zari's ritual?"

Fia shook her head, trying to clear the remaining fog from her nap. "Sorry, I didn't—yeah, it's on here." She pulled her phone from her pocket. "That salt model was so primitive, are we sure we can use it to make a plan?"

"Fia," Rebecca interjected. "I am surprised you, of all of us, are willing to sit around here strategizing when we know where Max is. I would think you—"

"And three hours ago, you would have been right. But the adrenaline that was keeping me awake is gone."

Agnes rested an uncharacteristically gentle hand on Fia's shoulder. "Fiammetta, I believe it took a lot for you to be able to say that."

Fia pushed a stray lock of hair out of her eyes and sighed.

"Hey, I know my limits. Sometimes the only option is to ignore them and push forward. This doesn't feel like one of those times."

"But, Fia, the damage those demons are doing to Max's mind—"

"I have enough faith in Zari to let that be an acceptable risk." She turned to Scott. "Where do you want to set up?"

The house that had manifested in Zari's salt spell was in an old part of the city, near the capitol building and the old, haunted park. As Fia maneuvered the little white race car toward the peachy glow across the eastern horizon, she snorted a laugh through her nose.

Rebecca leaned forward in her seat to ask what Fia was laughing at.

"Not laughing so much as reveling in the irony."

"Irony?"

"We're headed to possibly rescue Max from actual Hell, and we're surrounded by dozens, if not hundreds, of lost souls. Story is, when people were coming here looking for gold, they just buried their dead kind of wherever, but in that general area." She nodded toward a concrete structure visible in the park from the street. "When the government took over, when the state became a state, something, they built that pavilion over the old graves. And you can probably figure out the rest."

"Oh."

"Yeah. And then over there"—Fia waved indistinctly in the other direction—"is the home of that lady from the *Titanic* movie—"

"*Titanic* movie?"

"Sorry. Convent. Not really important. The point is, they made her house into a museum, and it's supposed to be haunted too." She stole a glance to the side, trying to gauge Zari's thoughts on the subject. The older woman's face was blank. She appeared to Fia to be in a trance.

Turning onto one of the narrow one-way streets of the residential neighborhood, Fia recognized the house from the spell. Even though all the houses on both sides of the tree-lined street—as well as those on the next block and the two to the right and left—looked virtually the same, the one they were looking for may as well have been on fire. The demonic energy emanating from it seemed to blur the air around the house.

There was no question they were in a part of the city that had been governed by affluence during its creation. Many of these homes—Victorian-era houses with corbels and ornate molding—stood three stories high, four counting the basements. The rooms on the top floor would have slanted ceilings: maybe servants' quarters, maybe a nursery for larger families. Each home featured a porch nestled into an alcove, and every porch was dark, shadowed in the early dawn light by the thick growth of trees that created the well-manicured urban forest.

The shadows on the front of this house *felt* almost sentient; Fia thought the shadows shifted as the car approached.

"If we get separated, Zari and Fia need to be together. They are the most important links in the chain."

Just as they had planned, Fia drove around one block, then another, following the annoying One Way signs back and forth through the neighborhood until she got to a place she could park unnoticed. She cut the engine and waited. Scott would be waiting in the alley behind the house with Mother Agnes in the gold sedan that hadn't disappeared with Annabel. Despite Agnes's protests, Rebecca had insisted on riding with Fia and Zari.

"I can provide backup at a sword's length."

In this scenario, Fia was the muscle. And the distraction. The kicker down of doors. She planned to do just that: kick in the front door and shoot whoever she found there with the little nine mil she had picked up from her apartment on the way into the city. Make as much noise doing it as she could manage while Scott and Zari moved into the subbasement through the cellar entrance.

From the video of Zari's spell work, it had looked like the space where they would find Max was directly beneath the cellar door. The challenge at that point, Fia thought, was going to be finding the entrance to that area.

Uhlpir wasn't going to access Max's mind unless he had to. He suspected the demons had done enough of that, that it wouldn't do either of them any good. He didn't expect to find anything but twisted memories and fear if he did.

Rebecca and Agnes would follow Fia into the main house. Rebecca had brought along her sword—*"We don't know if bullets will hurt them, but I'm guessing cutting off their heads will slow them down."*—and Agnes had her ruthless little crossbow pistol. Between the three of them, they could hopefully make enough noise to draw Max's captors out of hiding and give Zari enough time for her extraction—*"Ten minutes. Start timing as soon as we're all at the house."*

Fia's phone buzzed with a text saying Scott and Agnes were in place two blocks over. She set the timer to ten minutes . . . ten minutes and ten . . . thirty seconds. Ten minutes and thirty seconds. Fia gave Rebecca's sword a long look—

"Two nuns walking into the house shouldn't draw a lot of attention, especially if the neighbors are used to seeing Ariaz."—and snorted a joyless laugh through her nose.

"So much for not drawing attention. Is there anything you can do with that?"

Rebecca also took stock of the weapon and maneuvered it and her arms inside her robe. "Better?"

"Some. Maybe the shadows will work to our advantage." Fia nodded to her companions, and they split; Zari moved to the west, carrying a pack filled with whatever she might need to make Max trust her enough to get him out of the cellar, and Fia and Rebecca moved to the south. Fia still felt conspicuous in her black hooded shirt, cargo pants, and heavy boots but was less nervous without the glint of Rebecca's blade catching the rising sun.

As they approached the front of the house, Fia's gut twisted, and her breath caught in her throat.

She—they—were going in blind. There hadn't been time for proper surveillance, for staking out the house or its possible residents.

What if they were walking into an ambush? What if the house was full of homeless teens Ariaz had lured there? Bile burned in her throat, and she doubled over, suddenly sick from the uncertainty.

"Fia?" Rebecca laid a hand on her back. "We're going to get Max out of there."

Fia turned to meet Rebecca's amber eyes, which glistened with concern for her friends. "It's not—we don't know what's in there." She waved a hand toward the house.

Agnes, who had caught up to them, exchanged looks with Rebecca. "Fiammetta, you need to pull yourself together. How many times did I remind you as a child that sometimes circumstances are not ideal but you must do what needs to be done?"

Fia looked at the woman's weathered face and, for a moment, wondered if she was looking for Fia to give her an actual number.

"You hadn't the chance to surveil this house as you would have a bounty, making sure that everything, that you, that Max, would remain safe. And that scares you. Am I correct?"

Damn that woman. "Yes, Reverend Mother." Fia wiped her mouth with the back of her hand, then her hand on her pants before righting herself. "You're absolutely right. We have no idea what, or who, is in that house. Do we know for certain we're not storming in on two-point-five kids and a dog just casually enjoying their pancakes?"

Another glance at the dark house told Fia it was more likely she'd find two-point-five demons and a hellhound, but her concern remained untouched.

Agnes's steel eyes burned into Fia's. Eyes that had always made Fia feel small, no matter the circumstance. Eyes she had not missed in the time that had passed since her teens. But the stare was enough to reignite Fia's determination.

That stare had been the catalyst for at least 75 percent of Fia's rage-filled rebellion from the time she was nine to the age of sixteen. Today, she was fighting alongside Agnes, not against her.

Fia waved a hand weakly toward the door of the house. "Into the fray. I hope we're right."

Three steps up to the deep shadows of the porch. As Rebecca freed her arms, Fia took one final glance over her shoulder to make sure the others were on her heels and to check the street for passersby. Certain they were alone and before she could consider neighbors watching from their windows, Fia pulled the firearm from her holster and aimed it at the doorknob.

Rebecca squeaked and shoved Fia's arm down. "You don't use that thing a lot, do you? Trust me; that won't do anything but create sparks and alert whoever's inside to our presence."

Fia's cheeks warmed under Rebecca's firearms safety lesson. "The point of this exercise was to make as much noise—"

"Perhaps . . ." Agnes reached for the knob, turned, and pushed. The hinges whined as the door glided open into a dark foyer. She raised her eyebrows at Fia, who pushed the rest of the way inside.

Fewer than five steps through the door, a staircase ascended to the second floor. To the right was a pair of folding doors, opened to reveal the parlor that made up the L of the porch. Scant sunlight through the large window revealed enough dust that Fia initially thought all the furniture was covered in white sheets.

To the left was darkness. Heavy drapes were drawn over the smaller windows of the room. The only light came from the parlor window, but it was enough to show Fia where the tripping hazards might be. A set of Queen Anne–style furniture—a sofa with one broken leg and two chairs—served as a divider between the entryway and dining area. Fia was able to make out a rotted hole in the center of the dining table, and the chairs each looked like something enormous had used them for toothpicks.

Beyond the dining area was a small closed-off kitchen. Through the opening, Fia could see what had once been white ceramic tiles and a cupboard door dangling from one hinge.

The electricity and acrid stench of sulfur Fia had come to

associate with the demons filled her senses, burning her lungs and tingling across all her nerves. From the corner of her eye, she saw Agnes rubbing her hand over her arm as she moved into the parlor. Fia guessed she felt the energy too. Rebecca covered her nose and mouth with the sleeve of her robe.

Aside from the subtle hum, the house was silent, dark, eerie.

The silent stillness gave Fia a different kind of uneasy feeling. She understood now that she wasn't going to murder children, but what she could feel but couldn't see might be worse. Her memory flashed back to the cave; it seemed like a lifetime ago.

"You two get out of here."

Just as Rebecca opened her mouth to protest, Agnes—who had rejoined them from her quick scout through the other rooms of the lower level—drew the little crossbow and fired. The bolt whistled past Fia's ear and found its target with a thump. Whatever the Mother Superior had hit shrieked and hissed, the smell of hellfire intensifying.

Fia wheeled around. One of the midsize demons, the ones that had been careening around the city dressed up—badly—like humans, was shrieking and struggling to remove the little six-inch bolt from its ocular cavity. One thing about those little bolts: If they hit right, they buried themselves deep. They didn't leave much to grab onto, especially if one didn't have thumbs.

Rebecca stepped up to the plate and swung her sword like a baseball bat, removing the thing's head from its shoulders with a *crunch-squelch-crunch* as the blade passed through exo-skeleton on either side of soft tissue.

No one said anything. Fia could feel the *I told you so* hanging on the air like diesel exhaust, black and suffocating. She moved to holster the handgun, but Agnes stopped her. "I'd rather you put that against mortal flesh if it comes to it. I believe Sister Rebecca was correct about the demons not being fazed by your bullets, but they will be quicker against a human."

The smugness in the room shifted, replaced by grief. Fia knew they were all thinking the same thing: she was going to end up shooting one of their own.

The conspicuously absent Annabel still seemed the most likely culprit.

Ariaz was out of commission. His thug was, too, thanks to Max. Of the ten soldiers who had attacked the safe house, only three remained that Fia knew of. But how many did that leave? Around the world, thousands, maybe millions. But here in her city? Another hundred? A thousand? Or was it a small, isolated sect that had been all but wiped out in that one strike?

She deeply doubted the latter.

There was at least one more.

Fia's skin prickled, and she froze, scanning the room as much as she could without moving her body. "Something's not right," she hissed through clenched teeth. "That thing was either in here alone, which I think is unlikely, or it was cannon fodder. Why haven't any of its friends come to see what the screaming was? Unless they already knew—"

"You are absolutely correct, Fia."

The familiar voice cut through the darkness from behind them. Fia spun again, back toward the front door, her handgun ready to fire. Fia's eyes met Annabel's, and the muzzle blast lit up the room.

The woman—whom Fia barely recognized dressed in plainclothes with a heavy blonde braid hanging over her shoulder onto the chest of her white t-shirt—didn't flinch as the bullet passed through her shoulder and into the wall behind her.

"What the . . . ?" Fia looked into the barrel of the gun, not sure what she expected to find.

The surface of Annabel's skin shimmered, and a sound like smashing a mutant cockroach filled Fia's ears. As she watched, the veil fell away, and the defrocked sister returned to her natural form, covered in inky-black chitin, with razor-sharp claws extending six inches from webbed hands and feet.

"Fia?" Rebecca whispered. Fia turned and looked at the young woman, whose face was pale, frightened. Fia reached for the hilt of Rebecca's sword, which the stunned nun gave up easily. Fia raised the blade to her shoulder and, following Rebecca's example, cleaved the being's head from its body. It rolled and bumped against the toe of Rebecca's sneaker.

"Was that one of the demons? It looked like . . ." Rebecca let the end of the sentence dissipate into the thick darkness.

"One of. There are the little carrion ones too, the ones that eat the hosts. They're about . . ." Fia waved her hand between her knee and hip. "Have you never seen them transform? None of the ones in the cave?"

Rebecca shook her head, her eyes wide. Fia stole a glance in Agnes's direction. The elder's face remained stony, but her steel eyes flickered even in the darkness, betraying her surprise. Returning the blade to Rebecca, Fia checked the timer on her phone.

"Should we check upstairs?" Rebecca asked quietly. "That thing must have come from there. Maybe there are more."

"That is not what we came here to do, Sister."

"Besides, we don't have time." Fia held up her phone so the others could see: two minutes, thirty-five seconds.

"So we're just going to stand here and—"

Rebecca had regained her composure with a vengeance,

but her indignant protest was interrupted by a small piece of plaster falling onto her shoulder from the ceiling above. Chalky-white dust showed bright against her black robe.

The joists above them creaked, moaning like a porn star, and Fia raised her eyes to the source of the sound. A spider-web of jagged black cracks worked outward from the dust-laden ceiling fan. Fia dove, a breath before it all gave, knocking Rebecca out of the way. With a bone-rattling crash, they were buried in dust and rotten wood, a swarm of the little piranha demons circling them like rabid coyotes.

Agnes reached out a hand to pull Fia free of the rubble as Rebecca and her sword righted themselves, swinging even before she had fully regained her footing. In one sweep of the shimmering steel blade, she bifurcated three of them and knocked a fourth off its feet. The air raid siren Fia had chosen to alert them to the end of their ten minutes—ten minutes and thirty seconds—blasted through the chaos.

Suddenly wishing she had a shotgun instead of the nine mil as she imagined bits of demon splattering against the wall with the force of the blast, Fia unloaded the remainder of her magazine into what she could of the demon swarm. Agnes improvised, employing a rotten two-by-four from the ruin to golf-swing chitinous black bodies into the side of the stairs. She did little more than stun them, but it served to keep them occupied while Fia moved toward the door, ushering Rebecca ahead of her.

Fia looked back to see Agnes still fighting off the monsters and, shoving Rebecca through the front door, turned back to her mentor. "Reverend Mother, we need to go." She grabbed the weathered, old nun by the arm and tried to haul her out of the house.

Agnes wrenched her arm free of Fia's grip and reached into the pocket of her robe. From it, she drew out a box of wooden matches. Without a word, she met Fia's stare with the cold steel of her own. She struck one match across the strip on the outside of the box, dropped it back in with the others, and slid the whole box across the hardwood floor toward the kitchen.

EIGHT

Only then did Fia recognize the subtle mingling of scents in the house. The demons emitted a smell like a dozen matches lit at once. Dying, their scent grew stronger, as if whatever equated to their souls was dissipating back into the atmosphere to return to Hell. But now Fia was aware of a new smell: the smell of an unlit gas range dispensing fumes into the air.

Agnes pushed Fia toward the door, closing it behind them and urging Fia to a run. They had barely reached the other side of the street when a series of small explosions toppled the old, rotten house in on itself. The collapse created more noise than the explosions. Fia looked up and down the street, panicked, expecting neighbors to come swarming out of their houses to inspect the commotion.

"Go!" Agnes pushed her again, and they ran around the block to where they had left Max's car.

Fia climbed in and started the engine, pulling away from the curb as calmly as she could with her heart pounding in her ears. She guided the car toward the busy avenue a few blocks away. All she had to do was get there and blend in with traffic.

From where they were, Zari's shop was west, left. Instead of risking a left turn across the busy street, however, Fia merged into the eastbound lane and drove cautiously for a couple of miles, just as they had planned. She reached the abandoned shell of a fast-food restaurant and pulled into a space facing the building. She cut the engine and slammed her fists into the steering wheel, screaming.

"Fiammetta, please remain calm."

"Calm?" Fia shrieked, not bothering to control her voice. She felt hysterical, and she didn't feel like hiding it. "You want me to be calm. You blew up a *fucking house*! Possibly with the closest things I've ever had to parents inside. Not to mention Max, whose rescue was the whole point of going in there. Or have you forgotten all that?"

Agnes's leathered face flashed with the sting of Fia's words, but she wiped away the expression quickly. "I have not forgotten, Fiammetta."

In the moment, Fia had thought Agnes had gone rogue, ad-libbing her own solution to the problem of a house so thoroughly corrupted by darkness. But as she had driven away, putting more and more space between herself and what had happened, Fia realized it must have been part of the plan, something Agnes and Scott had decided without her. From the look on Rebecca's face in the rearview mirror, Fia guessed she hadn't been filled in on that final step either.

"This was all part of the plan from the beginning, wasn't it? Just one more thing Fia doesn't need to know. Keep her in the dark. Only give her her own lines in the script. I should make you walk back to the safe house."

The silence in the car was palpable, suffocating, with no one knowing how to break it.

The next step of the plan—as far as Fia knew—was to wait in this parking lot until they heard from Scott.

She had seen him walk away from a cave-in, but what if he hadn't been able to this time? He had had some warning in the cave. If he hadn't known Agnes's plan, he might not have had time. He was immortal, but how well did immortals hold up against crushing injuries? And even with all that, Agnes wouldn't have known she was blowing up an angel.

Fia suddenly remembered what Scott had told her about only staying in one place for a short time before moving on, before anyone could notice he didn't age. Being crushed beneath a house would be a convenient way to disappear, wouldn't it?

Rebecca reached between the seats and tapped on Fia's shoulder with a handkerchief. Fia looked at the linen square, confused, until the sister pointed to the rearview mirror. Tears had washed streaks through the dust coating Fia's cheeks from when the ceiling caved in. Fia eschewed the handkerchief, choosing instead to wipe her face with the heel of her hand.

She looked at the clock in the center of the little car's dashboard, nestled beneath the speedometer, though she didn't know what she expected to learn. She didn't know when they had left the . . . demolition site. She had just decided to give the others five more minutes when her phone buzzed, making her jump in her seat high enough to jam her thighs into the steering wheel.

We are safe. On our way to Zari's. Give us twenty minutes.

She dropped the phone in the cup holder between the seats and, without looking at either of the other women, started the engine.

"Was that Father Scott?" Agnes asked, perhaps more softly than Fia had ever heard from her.

"They need a few minutes."

"Where are we going, then?"

"Right here. I just need to . . ."

Fia reached for the center of the dashboard, and with the push of a button, the cabin filled with a screaming guitar, followed by a heavy-handed drummer abusing her snare drum. Soon the gravelly voice of the singer was telling them a story about a girl who'd grabbed him by more than just his attention.

"Fiammetta, I do not—"

Mother Agnes stopped herself midsentence. Fia closed her eyes, tapping out the basic rhythm of the song on the edge of the steering wheel, shaking and bobbing her head along with it.

Three and a half minutes later, she lowered the volume, turned it all off, and climbed out of the car. In the parking lot outside an abandoned fast-food restaurant, Fia Drake doubled over, one hand on the hood of the car, the other on her knee, and vomited.

Fia pulled Max's car into the alley behind Zari's shop, and the three of them piled out. Father Scott leaned against a low retaining wall beneath the kitchen window, his arms crossed tightly over his chest, his mousy-brown hair coated in white dust from Agnes's explosion.

As Fia approached, he stood and blocked the door. She tried to sidestep him, and he countered. "Fia, you can't go in there."

She stepped to the other side. "Get out of my way." He countered again. "Don't make me—"

"Fia, you cannot go in there. Zari has him under deep hypnosis right now, but he displayed an extreme panic response upon seeing me. She was right in keeping you away. If he is that afraid of me, I can only imagine his response to seeing you."

Fia chewed on that information for a moment before rejecting it outright. "He's nervous around you anyway. The whole . . ." She waved a hand in front of him, indicating his priestly façade.

"No, Fia, this was fear. True fear. Whatever was done to him, he truly believed I was there to hurt him."

Fia narrowed her eyes. "Hurt? Is he okay?"

"Physically, it looks like he will be fine. A few cuts and some bruises but nothing permanently damaging. One deep cut on the bottom of his foot that I think can be healed without too much trouble. The rest should mostly take care of themselves by the time Zari is finished with her work. I have to wonder if whoever had him captive wished to harm him more extensively but couldn't for whatever reason, so they left everything to the demons."

"So, you're saying it was someone who might have cared about him?"

"Likely more than they realized. I think perhaps in trying to get to you, they learned more about him than they had intended, making it more difficult to harm him physically."

That someone could do that—care about him and still use him as a pawn to get to her—made Fia's blood scorch. "How could—I need to see him."

"I really don't think that is wise, Fia. He is truly terrified of us. Well, of me. I cannot imagine—"

"You said that. You said Zari hypnotized him. I'll just peek. I won't say anything or touch anything."

Scott sighed heavily. "Just one minute." He turned away to head into the house. Fia stepped to follow him, and he spun back to her. "Stay. Put."

Fia surprised herself with a low growl but stepped back, waving Scott into the house. She stood with her back to the nuns for another long moment before kicking a rock with the toe of her boot, sending it skipping into the side of the house. She paced back to the car, where Agnes and Rebecca stood waiting for her.

"Fiammetta, is there anything—"

"How the hell am I supposed to know?" Fia snapped, kicking a tire on the car. "I should be in there," she grumbled. "I need to fix this." She rubbed at her eyes with the heels of her hands, pushing back the threat of tears.

"You have grown to trust Zari, is that not correct?" Agnes asked, her tone gentle but firm.

Fia shrugged. "Yeah. Yes, I trust her. What does that—"

"Do you believe part of that trust is accepting she has your best interests in mind?" Fia didn't answer, and the elder nun pushed forward. "And do you trust Father McGregor?" Fia nodded. "Do you accept he has your best interests in mind?"

"I do, but—"

"But nothing, Fiammetta. If you trust them and accept they would not do anything against you, you must do—"

"Do as they say. Yeah, I've heard all that before." Fia paused, thinking back over the previous few weeks. "I wish I had never gotten involved with any of this. With Scott, with you, with Max. But I did, and now . . ." She let the sentence crumble and turned back toward the house.

"Father Scott said you shouldn't go in," Rebecca reminded her.

Fia covered the space between herself and the younger nun, stopping with her face inches from Rebecca's. "I will do what I want. It's my fault he's in there. Don't tell me what to do."

Rebecca took a step forward, closing the small gap left between them and held Fia's stare without saying a word. They held the challenge for several seconds before Agnes stepped in.

"Ladies, please. Fiammetta, you are angry; that is understandable. But if Father McGregor believes it is better for you, and for Max—"

Fia threw up her hands and stepped away from the nuns. "I'm fine. I'm fine."

Before she could say anything else, Scott returned. "Fia, could you come here, please?" She crossed the space to stand in front of him. He rested his hands firmly on her shoulders and placed his body between her and the door. "Zari said you may come in, but you must be positively silent. Can you do that?" She nodded. "Fine, come with me. Remember. Silence." He moved to let her into the house.

To the right of the door was a round hole in the floor. A spiral staircase in lacquered black iron led down to the lower level, where Fia knew they would find two bedrooms and a bathroom. One bedroom was still, years later, decorated for small children. A set of bunk beds rested against one wall. In the opposite corner sat a handmade rocking chair, the mate to which sat in the living room on the main level of the house. A quilt hung over the back of the chair. Fia had stayed in that room the first night she had met Zari, with fresh burn scars stretching from her fingertips to her elbow.

The other room was Zari's. It was in that room Fia had learned she and Zari had the same past. At least in part. Zari had been a hunter as well, trained in a small village on the island of Haiti. She had immigrated to New Orleans later in life and hunted there for a short time before moving herself and her crystal shop to Denver.

Fia had also suspected from their first one-on-one

conversation that Zari's intuition was more than just expert guessing skills. Without being told, Zari had addressed Fia by her full name. She had also mentioned Fia was being hunted by demons. Fia had tried, in the moment, to convince herself Zari had said haunted instead, but she knew, ultimately, that hadn't been the truth.

In the last few weeks, Fia had wondered if that had been a prediction rather than an assessment. Had Zari known somehow that someone was trying to bring demons into the world?

Zari met them at the door to her bedroom. Her face was dark and drawn, with deep shadows crossing her forehead and eyes. "Fiammetta, I am sure Father Scott told you what is required of you in this moment?"

"Absolute silence."

"*Oui*. Max's condition is volatile, and I am not sure what might happen if he hears your voice. I want to keep you separated to be sure your presence won't set us back. But I also understand you need to see for yourself that he is whole. Please follow me."

Scott hung back in the hallway, while Fia followed Zari into the bedroom.

The walls of Zari's bedroom were painted red, with runic symbols painted one shade darker. Just as she had the first night she'd known Zari, Fia placed her left hand over one of the runes, letting its warmth seep into her flesh. She touched her scarred right hand against a similar symbol on her shoulder. The magic the symbols had been imbued with comforted Fia.

She turned away from the wall and saw the center of the floor had been pulled away, leading into a subbasement. The soft glow of candles emanated from beneath the floorboards, and the smell of charred sage and rosemary filled her nostrils.

"There is not much room below," Zari explained. "Even you, I think, will need to be mindful of your height."

Fia followed Zari into the small room beneath the floor. She had been right; there was barely room for Zari and Max, let alone one more body.

Zari—or maybe Scott—had laid Max out on the dirt floor, fully nude. "Flesh to earth," Zari explained, as Fia looked at his bare body. "It helps keep him connected as we reach back through the trauma and attempt to reassemble his shattered mind."

Fia nodded. The fakir who had tattooed Max had said something similar. Not about the trauma but about the connection of flesh to earth. She wanted to tell Zari but forced the words back, keeping her promise of silence.

Fia knelt beside Max, studying him. His lips were swollen and cracked, white from dehydration and caked with blood. The deep hollow of his left cheek was purple black, stretching down his jaw. The same color decorated his right bicep into his shoulder. Several jagged cuts in groups of four—claw marks—streaked his pale torso in red black, welts and scabs and dried blood. One set, near his still-fresh runic tattoo, was blistered, as if the claws had been made of molten steel.

She reached out a hand, letting it hover over his damaged cheek, scalding tears threatening the edges of her vision. "What have I done?" she whispered.

Max's body jerked, as if he were trying to pull away from something, from Fia. She could feel his temperature rise in the small space, and the unmarred skin of his cheeks turned red.

Zari looped an arm around Fia's waist and pulled her away from him. "I told you absolute silence." Her usually sweet, kind voice was harsh, angry in a way Fia had never heard. "You have seen that he is whole physically. His reaction to your whispered words only reinforces my suspicion that your voice alone is enough to cause even more damage. I need you to leave. Focus on finding out what happened from the other side. Find the summoner. Make right with your own guilt. I will find you when it is safe for you to be near him again. For now, he trusts me because he had no memories of me for the demons to have corrupted. But I am the only one. I cannot risk having him near anyone else. Please go."

Zari gestured toward the ladder that led back to the bedroom. Fia hesitated. She wanted to say something, but Max's reaction to just her whispering told her Zari was right. She had to go occupy herself with other things until Zari was finished. She climbed the ladder.

She slipped past Scott, who stood in the doorway to the hall, her heart heavy with guilt. She had known, from the beginning, that Max didn't belong in her world, that being near her was going to get him killed or worse.

This looked worse.

Scott followed her quietly back to the surface, back to Max's car in the alley behind the house. Without a word, she climbed into the car and started the engine. She flipped the stereo from radio to CD, and a sad smile crept over her face. Max had had his own band's CD in the player the last time he had been behind the wheel. Fia closed her eyes, focusing on the bright cymbal chimes and the sharp snare beats, imagining him on stage, his handsome face obscured by long, golden-brown hair, his arms flailing with maniacal precision.

When the song finished, she turned down the volume and rolled down the windows. "All aboard who's coming aboard. I'll take you back to the safe house."

"I am going to stay here, in case Zari needs something," Scott said, his face twisted in a suggestive grimace.

Fia assumed he was trying to suggest *in case Zari needs something from Uhlpir* and again urged the nuns into the car.

NINE

Fia reached to turn off the music. Agnes, who sat in the front passenger seat, put a hand over Fia's, pushing it away from the stereo. "Is this Max's band?"

Fia furrowed her brow, thrown off by the informality of Agnes's question. "Yeah, how did you—"

"A hunch. Based on the way you were listening to it. You may leave it playing, if it is soothing to you."

"Turn it up," Rebecca added from the back seat.

"Really?"

Both nuns nodded, and Fia turned the volume dial slightly, though not nearly as much as she would have had she been alone. The bright, sharp snap of Max's snare drum introduced the next track on the disc, a dark, heavy song about the dangers of hero worship, one Fia realized, with a pang of guilt, she hadn't heard. She pushed the feeling aside, forcing absolution.

No one said anything until they reached the spot where Zari had asked Fia to stop the car the day before. She stopped again without being prompted and climbed out. She left the door open and the engine running and crossed the road without a word.

Something drew her to the edge of the road. She looked down into the ravine, surveying the broken branches she had seen before and written off as downed by snow and wind. On a whim, she grabbed a branch on a nearby tree for support and started down the steep incline.

"Fiammetta, where are you—"

"I don't know, Reverend Mother, but I think there's something—"

Fia slipped, tumbling a few feet down the side of the mountain before regaining her footing. She chose not to finish her sentence and continued down the gradient.

At the bottom, she found a creek. Nose down in the creek was the light-gold sedan.

Fia looked back up the incline to where she had left the nuns. She didn't doubt they could get down to where she was, but could they get back up? She wasn't fully confident she was going to be able to. She decided to investigate alone and let them know what she found when she returned.

The back, passenger-side fender was crushed like aluminum foil, with black paint along the creases in the dent. The driver's door of the sedan was open, wedged against a tree. Fia guessed, from the angle of the car in the creek, that the door had fallen open when it was unlatched.

She looked inside. The driver's seat belt had been cut, and there was blood on the window of the door. Lightning-bolt cracks divided the windshield into several jagged pieces.

Fia looked around for more signs of what might have happened to the occupants of the car and found nothing that explained anything. But she guessed this was what had gotten Zari's attention the first time. She looked back up the hillside again.

She couldn't quite see where she had come over the side. Down had gone a lot faster than up was going to. She looked down at the ground, hoping for footprints, but found none.

She looked in the water, hoping not to find a body, and to her relief, she came up empty there too. Though that didn't prove there wasn't one downstream. She followed the water for what she guessed was about one hundred feet. The creek wasn't deep—chest high in the center, she guessed—so a body should have been easy to spot.

The blood on the car door had likely been the result of Annabel—or whoever was driving—hitting her head. Though it would have been easy enough to climb out the way they had gone down, a concussion might have caused enough disorientation to make that impossible. Fia made her way back to the car, still scanning the ground at her feet for footprints, anything that would tell her what had happened.

When she felt she had explored all she could, Fia climbed back out of the ravine, using roots and brambles to help pull herself up. When she reached the road, Rebecca asked what she had found.

"The car," Fia replied, catching her breath.

"Fiammetta, do you mean the car Annabel took to find Max?"

"I didn't check the VIN, but I can't imagine a reason for there to be a different gold land yacht down there." She paused, considering her own statement. "Can you?"

Agnes shook her head. "No, I cannot."

"The windshield is shattered, and there's blood on the driver's window. I think someone hit them from behind; the back fender is all crunched."

"Did you find Sister Annabel?"

"I looked downstream to see if she fell in somewhere. I

didn't go far; it's pretty shallow. But I didn't see footprints or anything to tell me where she might have gone."

"Based on what you saw, do you think she's alive?" Rebecca asked.

Fia shrugged. "I really don't know. She's not anywhere near the car, and whoever was driving definitely went over in the car. They cut themselves out of the seat belt."

"Do you think you can track her? Figure out where she might have gone?" Agnes asked.

"Not without somewhere to start. She got out of the car. And since she didn't come straight back to the house, I'm guessing she didn't climb directly up where she went over. Judging from the broken glass, she probably has a decent concussion. She might be totally disoriented, staggering around in the creek. If you know someone with better experience tracking in the wilderness, you should call them."

"Come, then." Agnes motioned them back to the car.

As Fia pulled the car out of the trees into the clearing in front of the house, Agnes reached across, resting her hand on the steering wheel. "Fiammetta," she whispered loudly.

"I see it." Fia eased the car back under the cover of trees.

The front door to the safe house stood wide open.

Fia pulled the little handgun from the floor beneath her seat, and the three women climbed out of Max's white coupe, leaving the doors open as they proceeded toward the house.

"Fia, would you like me to take the lead?" Rebecca held out her hand, her eyes on Fia's firearm. "You don't seem as confident with that as with your bow."

"Um . . ." Fia followed Rebecca's gaze and turned the weapon to hand it to the nun, butt first.

The nun accepted Fia's offering and let the little gun lead the way through the gaping front entrance. With a deft hand,

Rebecca flicked the gun's safety lever, her stance shifting from defense to offense in a breath. Only a step behind her, it didn't take long for Fia to figure out the cause of the shift.

Annabel stood facing them in the center of the granite floor, covered in mud and forest debris and smelling of wet wool. Streaks of dried blood coated the left side of her face from a walnut-sized knot near her temple. Under the blood, her skin was a rotten shade of blue green. She scanned the room and the women standing before her as if unsure what she was seeing.

Mother Agnes stepped toward her charge, reaching out to take her hand. "Sister Annabel, are you okay? Do you know where you are?"

Annabel's blue eyes spun in her head as she struggled to process the Reverend Mother's questions, and she shook her head. She opened her mouth, and her voice betrayed her, cracking as she tried to speak. "W-where is Max?"

Fia felt the blood in her cheeks boil, creating a red haze at the edges of her vision. Before she could contain herself, she was on the nun, her hands full of the heavy fabric of Annabel's habit. She drove the nun backward several staggering steps. The momentum caused Annabel to trip over her own feet and topple to the stone floor, Fia on top of her.

"What did you do?" Fia growled, lifting the nun's shoulders from the floor. She shook Annabel hard enough to whip her head back and forth, and Annabel cried out in pain. "Did you have anything to do with any of this?"

Wrapping one long arm around Fia's ribs, Agnes hauled her off Annabel. Rebecca stepped into the place where Fia had been. Fia expected Rebecca to help Annabel to her feet, but she didn't expect Rebecca to pin Annabel to the closet door with her forearm across Annabel's chest. She thought she could hear low growls from both women.

When Agnes returned Fia to her feet, Fia dove again, reaching for Annabel's throat. She didn't make it far before Agnes had secured her in another crushing bear hug, pinning Fia's arms to her sides.

"Fiammetta." The word alone was a sentence and carried enough force to make Fia stop struggling. Rebecca also turned to face the elder nun.

When Agnes spoke again, her tone was softer though no less firm. "Fiammetta, perhaps allow Sister Annabel a chance to recover before employing the thumbscrews."

"What for?" Rebecca's frigid voice sliced through the cavernous space.

"Excuse me?" Agnes asked, a genuine question. Even Fia was taken aback by the venom Rebecca had packed into just a couple of words.

"What are we giving her leniency for? You want to give her a chance to work up a lie?"

"Sister Rebecca, do you not believe if Sister Annabel were planning to lie, she would already have her story figured out? Letting her get her bearings is not going to change what she tells us."

"All right, then. What do we do with her in the meantime?"

Agnes reached out and took Annabel's arm from Rebecca. "We start by treating her like a human being."

Fia tensed, each of her muscles tightening of its own volition, her short nails digging hot crescent moons into her palms. She had been prepared to beat Annabel to a pulp when she saw her, but now she wasn't sure.

Annabel looked and smelled like she had been through the wringer, but that didn't mean she hadn't been involved in all that had happened. Someone had shot one of the intruders and left him as a snack for the big cats. It wasn't out of the question that they might have shoved Annabel off into the creek at the same time.

None of that absolved her of planning the siege. It just meant her henchmen had turned on her at the end. As far as Fia—and probably Rebecca too—was concerned, there was too much pointing toward Annabel to ignore.

"First thing," Agnes continued, "is to get her cleaned up." She nudged Annabel toward the stairs, motioning for Fia and Rebecca to follow. In the upstairs hallway, Agnes guided Annabel into her quarters, then turned back to face Fia and Rebecca. "Sister Rebecca, I would like you to tend to Sister Annabel. I'm sure she can manage showering and dressing herself, but I ask that you stand guard. There is only one way in and out of the bathroom, but I don't want her sneaking off when no one is looking."

Fia's brow furrowed. *I don't want her sneaking off . . .* It almost sounded like the elder nun was accepting Annabel's guilt.

"Fiammetta, I would like to see you in my office." Agnes turned on her heel and strode away from Fia. Fia followed, leaving Rebecca alone outside Annabel's room.

"It would be inappropriate for you to assist, should Sister Annabel need assistance," Agnes explained, standing aside for Fia to enter the office ahead of her.

Fia looked around the room. It might have been in a different structure, but it was the same office Fia remembered from childhood. There was nothing on the stormy-blue walls but an oil painting of the Virgin Mary, a crucifix, and painted in a darker shade of blue, the sigil Agnes had tattooed somewhere on her body.

They all had them. Fia's was on her left shoulder. Max's—the last one to have been done—was in the hollow at the base of his sternum. Fia had never known the location of the nuns' markings. It had never been appropriate to ask.

Agnes had even replaced the utilitarian furniture Fia assumed had been lost in the fire with nearly identical matches. The only thing that had been added since Fia was a child in the convent was a certificate Agnes had received along with the title of Mother Superior.

Agnes unlocked a cabinet behind the desk and produced two simple glasses and a bottle of amber liquor. She placed the glasses on the desk. "I think, after the last couple of days, we could both use a drink."

Fia eyed the glasses, expecting them to be some kind of trap. After a long moment of contemplation, she accepted the proffered drink. The familiar burn in her throat was comforting, and she had to stop herself from gulping it down in one shot.

Agnes motioned to one of the chairs facing the front of the desk, taking the other for herself. "Fiammetta, I wanted to talk to you about what I found in that house today."

"Oh?"

"In a room off the kitchen, there was a bank of monitors, television screens, each showing a different location. I am not sure of all of them—I would guess they were positioned in and around your home—but one, I am certain, showed the room you have utilized during your stay here. Fiammetta, whoever is behind this plot against you has been surveilling you quite seriously. And I cannot imagine, from the locations of the cameras, that they have not been privy to the more intimate details of your time with Max."

Fia huffed through her nose in frustration. "Great, so not only is she a vengeful monster, she's also a pervert."

Fia had not always exercised the most discretion in her

sexual encounters and had engaged in them in public spaces more than once. But the violation of Max's privacy made her queasy. She had considered a lot of the potential risks he faced staying with her, but spy cameras had not been on the list.

For that matter, neither had abduction or torture by demons.

Agnes took another sip of her own whiskey, her eyes steady on Fia. When she didn't say anything else, Fia shrugged, defeated. "What do we do next?"

"Once Sister Annabel has had a little time to recover from her ordeal, we will talk with her. Find out where she has been, what she remembers."

"Trust her not to lie."

"I think you have developed some decent instincts regarding what is true and what is not."

"I don't know that I have. Until recently, I spent most of my time alone. I haven't been around people, at least not in circumstances where I'm called to determine truth from lie."

Fia shuddered, thinking about the other men Annabel had watched her bring through her apartment. She wasn't embarrassed, but she did feel violated. *Would it not stand to reason among your conquests was at least one of the master's other human soldiers?* Ariaz's final taunt echoed in her head.

Had one of them been responsible for planting the cameras? She had made a point of never letting them wander off without her. But it would have only taken a second if they were good.

Fia studied Agnes's face, looking for any sign of what she might be thinking. Her demeanor told Fia she was not as strongly in the corner of her underlings as she had been previously.

"What do you know, Reverend Mother?"

"I am not prepared to cast stones until I am certain who

I am targeting. Is it not possible that our fallen sister, Theresa, might have also been responsible? That she had arranged all of this before her death?"

"It's absolutely possible. But we know her death didn't get rid of the demons, and neither did killing Ariaz. Do you think she might have been working here alone? Or with Annabel?"

"That is what I mean to find out." The nun finished her drink and nodded for Fia to do the same. "If you don't mind, Fiammetta, I would like to make a phone call. Please close the door on your way out."

Fia drained her glass and followed Agnes's instructions. Outside the office, the hallway was empty. Fia assumed Rebecca had gone into the bathroom to help Annabel with something and headed toward the stairs.

As she passed the bathroom door, something she heard made her stop short. ". . . put my child in danger."

Child? It was definitely Rebecca's voice cutting through the heavy quiet of the nearly empty safe house, carrying enough venom to take down a lion.

"Sister Rebecca, I don't know what you are talking—"

"Save it. It's bad enough you summoned an army of demons to kill Fia. She's an adult. She can handle herself. But what you did here the other night—you endangered *my* child."

"Who? Rebecca, please, I don't understand." Annabel was crying. Fia looked around, weighing her options. Stay and listen and risk getting caught? Confront Agnes with the information? Head downstairs and pretend she had heard nothing?

She turned back to the office, deciding to confront Agnes, but heard the latch click on the bathroom door. She dove forward, then turned, as if she had only just come from the office. She met Rebecca coming out of the room.

"Is she . . . better?" Fia asked, coating her words in salt

so the nun wouldn't know she had been eavesdropping.

Rebecca rolled her eyes and rubbed her knuckles. "She's fine. I don't agree with the Reverend Mother's insistence that we mollycoddle her, do you?"

Did she? Fia decided she didn't. "What do you suggest?"

Rebecca turned her eyes to the floor. "We have an empty jail cell."

"Let's go."

"Where is Agnes? We can't get caught."

"On the phone."

"We'd better hurry, then." Rebecca opened the door to the bathroom and ushered Fia inside.

Annabel was dressed from crown to hem in a fresh, clean habit. Fia hadn't expected her to already be wearing her wimple over wet hair. Fia must have been in Agnes's office longer than she thought. She reached for one of the nun's arms, Rebecca took the other, and they led her quietly from the bathroom.

Outside Theresa's vacant room, Rebecca jerked her head toward the door. "Should we take the passage? Might be easier to avoid Agnes."

Fia considered the suggestion and shook her head. "I think it will be easier to avoid her out in the open. My memory of the Reverend Mother has her waiting for us when we come out the other side."

Rebecca nodded and shoved Annabel, possibly harder than she needed to, to get her walking again.

They marched their prisoner down the stairs to the main level and back through the kitchen to the recessed entrance leading to the basement. Fia considered, for a moment, that Annabel wasn't fighting them, wasn't resisting in anyway, and wondered what that might mean. Her stomach tightened, remembering the genuinely frightened tone she had heard through the bathroom door, and she loosened her grip on Annabel's arm. If the nun noticed, she didn't react.

Rebecca unlocked the padlock and swung the steel door open. She nodded to Fia. Fia lead Annabel through the doorway into the cell, and Rebecca followed, pulling the door closed behind her.

"All right, Annabel, let's talk."

Ten

Rebecca stepped toward the other sister until the toes of their shoes bumped. "Where have you been? You really expect me to believe you've just been wandering around in your own front yard and didn't know how to get back?"

Fia pulled Annabel away from her interrogator and sat her on the cot against the back wall. The accommodations looked medieval, but at least there was a cot. Fia glanced at a set of shackles on the wall and suddenly wondered why everyone in her world had shackles. She turned back to Rebecca and pointed at them.

"What's the deal with the shackles? Ariaz had them too. Did you all time travel here from the eighteenth century?"

"Ariaz had shackles? That priest you thought was involved in summoning the demons?"

"Yeah. I assumed he was using them to keep the demons put. And that made enough sense. Though the audacity of having them in the church basement was pretty incredible. Especially since it seems like everyone else around this city has some kind of hole dug beneath their basement. But what does a group of nuns and children need with shackles? Was Agnes expecting to have to lock up a demon?"

As she talked, Fia convinced herself the heavy iron might be necessary to contain the strength of an ancient immortal.

It still didn't explain why they had been installed. And Rebecca hadn't used them on the prisoners from the siege. She had simply shoved them into the box of a room in zip ties.

Rebecca shook her head. "Agnes wanted to be prepared for any contingency. Did you not know there was a cell in the convent?"

Fia's eyes widened. "I did not. Where?"

"In the basement. Far north corner. It's where the fire started."

"Was there someone in there? A prisoner?" Fia's head swam. For all the trouble she had caused as a child, she was suddenly indescribably grateful for the privilege of kitchen duty, knowing now that an actual prison cell had been a possible alternative.

"There was a demon in the cell," Annabel offered quietly.

Fia turned to face her. "What? Agnes caught a demon?"

Annabel shook her head and pointed to Rebecca. "I wasn't there, but I heard the story."

Fia turned back to Rebecca. "*You* caught a demon? Why?"

Rebecca's eyes grew wide, as if she had been caught doing something wrong. "I didn't . . . I didn't know it was a demon. These things we've been tracking—they've been around longer than you realize."

Suddenly, Fia's head throbbed as a memory she hadn't considered in years came sweeping back to her.

In it, she had been treating Zeke to their first real meal with the money from her first bounty. They had passed one of the graffitied alleyways of downtown, and something had caught Fia's attention in a way she couldn't escape.

She watched heavy shadows in the alley shift and undulate, moving as if they were alive, beckoning to her. Something like static electricity forced the remaining hair on her arms to stand at attention beneath her shirt sleeves. An electric buzz hummed in her ears, and she took a step into the alley. And another. And another. Looming over her, a comic-book-style woman with blue-and-black hair had been spray-painted onto the bricks, her eyes closed, her too-red lips parted gently, waiting for a kiss from an unseen partner.

As Fia watched, the dark shadows stretched clawed fingers over the woman's face until the paint was almost completely obscured. But before that, Fia thought for sure the painted woman had grimaced, her painted face twisting in agony.

Fia realized then that the sounds of the mall—the bell on the free bus, the conversations of shoppers, Zeke's voice—had been replaced by the buzzing that had grown louder in her ears and all around her.

Fia shook herself free of the memory. "Yeah, I know. I didn't know what it was at the time either, but I encountered them long before seeing the one Ariaz had in the mall."

"I found this person roaming the forest behind the convent, so I grabbed him. Agnes didn't know I knew the cell was there. I stashed the guy there and was on my way to tell Agnes, or anyone else, when the fire broke out."

Fia looked back at Annabel. "Did Agnes tell you all this?"

Annabel shook her head. "Terra."

"Terra? Like, Terra who I grew up with, Terra?"

"The same."

"How did she know? Father Scott said she was gone by the time the convent burned down."

"No, she was still here," Rebecca replied. "I mean, she still lived in the convent but was gone. At the time of the fire, she had gone, I believe, to New Mexico; she was looking for a place to live, I think. Or that was the story." They both looked to Annabel for confirmation.

Annabel shook her head. "I don't know about any of that. The way she told the story, I thought she was here—at the convent, I mean—physically present when it happened. She seemed so certain of the events."

"Your memory seems to be recovering," Rebecca said, shifting the attention back to Annabel. "Maybe you are ready to tell us where you've been?"

Annabel shook her head. "I really was just out in the woods. I had gone to see if I could find Max and was bringing him back to the house when someone ran us off the road. It was a black SUV, newer model, and it was coming from this direction. We passed them—"

"You should have known there wouldn't be anyone coming out of here," Rebecca scolded. "Why didn't you follow them? Try to stop them?"

"In a car with half a horsepower? I'm sorry I don't have your taste for reckless adrenaline, Rebecca. Of course I knew that SUV didn't belong on that road, but they were leaving, not coming. Whatever threat they might have posed—whatever threat they had posed—they were moving on. Or so I thought."

Annabel took a deep breath. "They doubled back and bore down on us. I didn't even have time to try to outrun them—not that I would have had anywhere to go if I had—before they smashed into the back of the car. I lost control and spun off the road. The man—it was one of the men and one of the women you two brought down here. Not the leader, the other one, the one the big guy fell on. The man came and punched me in the head." She gingerly touched the fading bruise along the side of her face. "The next thing I knew, I was stumbling out of the car into the creek."

"They killed their partner. Why did they leave you alive?" Rebecca wrapped her hands in the folds of Annabel's robe, pulling her up off the cot and bringing their faces within inches of each other.

"Rebecca, stop." Fia pulled Rebecca off the other woman and pushed her toward the door. "I believe her. I don't believe she's innocent, but I believe she doesn't know what happened to her. Let's leave her here and go back to the crash site. See if we can find anything else. You up for a climb?"

Rebecca started to push around Fia but stopped and turned her eyes to Fia's. "Yeah, maybe. Maybe there's something else there." She stepped aside and motioned for Fia to leave the room ahead of her.

Fia pushed the door open and stopped short, causing Rebecca to collide with her from behind.

Agnes had staked a claim to one of the metal folding chairs, positioning herself directly beneath the single bare bulb that illuminated the outer room of the basement. She sat with her hands crossed over her knees. Fia thought she could have held that pose for days if she had needed to.

"Ladies." Agnes stood and crossed to push past them into the cell. "Sister Annabel, I trust you are feeling more yourself?" Agnes pulled the younger nun from the cot and guided her out of the cell. "Whose idea was this?"

Fia lowered her eyes, feeling like a child who had broken something valuable. *Tell Agnes it was Rebecca's before she assumes—*

"It was mine, Reverend Mother," Rebecca said, interrupting Fia's thoughts. "After what she has done, I disagreed with your choice to treat her with kid gloves. She is a criminal; she should be kept like a criminal."

"And why, Sister Rebecca, are you so certain Sister Annabel was responsible for the attack we endured?"

"Because she's still alive." Rebecca set her jaw, folding her arms over her chest like an indignant child.

Fia remained silent as Agnes and Rebecca studied one another, their eyes locked in a silent challenge. She started inching toward the door, hoping no one would notice. She wanted to run through a few channels back in the city, and the sooner she could, the better.

"The fact she is still alive is all the proof I need," Rebecca continued after a long moment. "The demons are still here, the intruders who took Max killed one of their own but not her—"

"Not for lack of trying," Annabel interrupted.

Rebecca took a threatening step forward, meeting with Agnes's hand against her chest. "What did you say?" she growled.

"They just didn't shoot me. The woman said something." Annabel screwed up her face, trying to remember what she had heard. "She was at the passenger door. She must have drugged Max. He just fell into her a few seconds after she opened the door. Before they came to the car, I heard the gunshot. They must have shot their third when he got out of the car. I was trying to figure out what to do; I knew we were trapped. I thought about getting out and taking my chances over the side, but I hadn't had time to tell Max when she opened his door. Then the man opened my side. She said . . . she said, 'Leave her; he's the one she wants.'"

"You're lying!"

"Sister Rebecca!" Agnes practically shouted.

She? So it is *a woman behind all this.*

Fia took advantage of the tension between the other women and slipped free, leaving the basement door open behind her. She took the stairs to the surface two at a time and headed back inside through the commercial-grade kitchen.

She paused outside the door to the first-floor bedroom. There was at least one spy camera in there, trained on the bed. Agnes had destroyed the monitors, though, so Fia decided the camera could wait.

Right now, Fia had a new suspect who made more sense than anything she had heard yet. Annabel had known Terra before coming here. At least that's what she had said. Fia had no idea how to confirm that story, but she did have an idea of how to figure out if Terra was behind any of this. First, she had to get back to the condo.

Fia made her way out the front door and across the clearing to where she had left Max's car. "Shit," she hissed, realizing the doors had been left open in the interest of stealth. "It's a good thing I came back."

She pushed the passenger door closed, then walked around to the driver's side, kicking closed the back door, from which Rebecca had exited, on her approach. She climbed back into the little subcompact and put it in reverse, hoping the driveway was steep enough the car would roll backward far enough she could start it without anyone inside the house hearing.

When the house was out of sight, she turned the key, bringing the engine to life, and turned around on the narrow dirt road. Not wanting to end up in a predicament similar to Annabel's, she kept her speed down until she reached the end of the driveway and eased the car onto the pavement that would lead her to the interstate that cut east to west across half or more of the country.

Pulling into traffic on the interstate, Fia took a deep breath, holding it in her lungs for an eight count before letting it go. "You've been looking for someone in the present. You didn't think about looking for someone from the past," she scolded herself. "Maybe Terra caught more hell than anyone realizes. Or wants to talk about."

Agnes would know the answer to that, but would she tell Fia? Cecilia would too, but Fia had no way of asking her, not now. "Talk to Agnes. You need to talk to Agnes. And ask her about what Rebecca said, about her kid."

The drive back to the city felt like it took forever. By the time Fia pulled into her garage, all her nerves were firing, and she was certain anything sudden might give her a heart attack.

Fia hadn't taken much when she left the convent. It hadn't been an experience she wanted to remember, and she had had very little she considered her own.

One thing she had taken, for reasons she hadn't understood at the time, was a photo with the other orphans. It was the only thing she still had from that time, and she had stashed it in the same safe where she usually kept her little handgun.

She had actually forgotten it was there until Annabel brought Terra back into her thoughts.

She crossed the condo to her master suite. In the bathroom, a line of lights just above the foot molding was on a motion sensor, giving the expansive room a warm glow as she entered. She pushed on a knee-level section of the short wall encasing the vanity, triggering the release to pull out the gun safe. She removed the sculpted foam that had held the weapon and found the photo right where she expected it to be.

Fia flipped on the lights surrounding the vanity mirror, flooding the space with enough light to land an airplane, and held the photo where she could study it closely.

And dropped it into the sink with a gasp.

Eleven

Fia took a couple of deep breaths and retrieved the photo from the sink, her shaking fingers struggling to grip the paper on the first try.

It had been taken in City Park, with a fountain in the near background and the city skyline's signature Cash Register in the far background. On the far left was Meredith's round face and curly, brown hair. Next to her, his arm tight around Fia's waist, was Felix with his gelled coif of blond hair and toothy grin.

On the opposite side was another girl, close to Fia's stature. She wore a flat expression, though slight creases at the corners of her brown eyes betrayed her true emotions. What had caught Fia's attention, however, was her dark sandy-blonde ponytail, pulled tight to the top of the girl's head and reaching well past her shoulders.

It had been more than a decade since the photo was taken, but Fia couldn't erase the image of that same ponytail swinging down the stairs ahead of Rylan barely six weeks ago. All she had seen of the woman in the bar had been her hair.

"It's a coincidence," Fia muttered to the empty room. "Ten years? What are the chances Terra still wears her hair like that?" Fia looked up at her reflection, a memory dancing in the mirror before her.

Fia ran her fingers back through her dark copper hair, catching them in what could no longer be called just a tangle. Her fingers still tangled, she pulled the beginning of a dreadlock forward to examine it.

Shaking free of the wad of hair, she fished the small knife she had bought for protection from its sheath in her backpack. The black blade was short enough to wear concealed on her thigh, and in place of a handle, it had three finger holes. She gripped it the best she could and began sawing at the matted hair.

"No, it's a coincidence."

Still not convinced, Fia pulled the gun she had been packing from the holster at her hip and returned the gun to the safe and the safe to the wall. She flipped off the vanity lights and carried the photo out of the room.

It was a long shot, but she had an idea.

Back in the garage, she climbed into Max's little boxy white sport car. In all the chaos, she hadn't even thought to ask Scott again if he knew what had happened to the Scout and her scooter. She had been tunnel-visioned on finding Max.

Fia pulled the car into the lot outside the Catholic outreach center where she had seen Annabel with the priest she assumed to be Father Donovan. She cut the engine and watched the entrance for a few minutes. She wasn't certain what she expected to learn, but she also didn't know if she was ready to go inside.

While she waited, a pair of nuns came out of the building.

One was older, closer to Agnes's age, Fia thought. She guessed the other was in her midthirties, maybe forties. The two women didn't seem to be walking with any purpose, like they would if they were mission oriented. Rather, it seemed like they might be stepping out for a break or private conversation as they strolled away from the door.

"Here goes nothing," Fia muttered and climbed out of the car.

"Excuse me, Sisters?"

They turned to face her, and the elder one, who had darker skin and dark eyes, responded first. "Yes, my child?"

"I was hoping someone here could help me. I'm looking for a girl I grew up with in an orphanage around here."

Fia had come prepared with the basis of a story, electing ultimately to let the story grow organically, and began weaving one lie out of a variety of truths. She told the nuns she had lived with Terra until she was adopted from Father Donovan's home.

The younger of the two women took the photo from Fia's hands and studied it. Fia pointed over the top. "That one is me. This is the girl I'm looking for. Even if you could tell me whether she's still in the city."

The nun shook her head and passed the photo to her elder. "I am sorry. When did you say this was?"

"The photo was taken about ten years ago." Fia hoped she wasn't lying to the wrong nuns.

The elder of the two returned the photo. "I do not recognize your friend. But have you spoken with Father Donovan?"

Fia shook her head. "That's why I'm here. I was told he spends a lot of time here, after his home closed. I took a chance." Now she was hedging her bets on the hope Father Donovan was, in fact, in another state, trying to keep four teenagers safe from an unknown threat, and not actually inside this building. Because if he was inside . . .

The two nuns exchanged worried looks, stopping Fia before she could finish the disastrous thought she had started. Again, it was the elder of the two who addressed her first. "I am sorry, my child. Father Donovan has not been here in a number of days. I must say, I asked if you had spoken to him as much for my own peace of mind as anything."

Fia did her best to look disappointed and concerned. "Is everything okay? Is he sick?"

The elder nun's demeanor shifted, and her tone rose from deep concern to cheerful, bright confidence. "No, dear, he is not ill. It is not common but also not unheard of that a man of his level of dedication would, perhaps, offer to take a young runaway back to their home without stopping to tell everyone his plans."

"Ah, yes," the younger woman added. "Do you know who he might have told? That younger nun he brought by here. What was her name? Annabel?" Her face lit with excitement over the revelation.

"Annabel?" Fia asked, now genuinely interested. Maybe this wasn't a wasted mission after all.

"Father Donovan said she was here from New Mexico, I believe, and had done a great deal of work with the transient community there. She was on a new assignment and looking to get back into the same kind of work here."

"Did she say what prompted her change in scenery?"

"I don't remember that coming up," the elder nun replied. "Sister Ruth?"

The younger nun, Sister Ruth, shook her head. "I can't say I remember anything either."

"Is she working with Father Donovan?" Fia pressed. She

felt like she had found a lead but wasn't quite sure what it was yet. She was definitely fishing in murky waters. "Is he with a new church? Another group home?"

"I believe," Sister Ruth replied, "he has mostly been focused on community outreach, not directly through any church specifically." She waved her hand toward the building. "He's doing a lot here with displaced adults, as well as trying to get a new home for teens up and running."

"He has done a little work through Saint Anthony's," the elder added. "Perhaps someone there would have better answers for you."

Perhaps, but the someone you're thinking of bled out in his demon chamber. Fia nodded and stepped away from Sister Ruth and her companion. "Thank you for all your help."

Before they could say anything, she hurried back to Max's car. Inside, she dropped the photo into the compartment in the center console and gently fingered the silver drum charm that hung from the rearview mirror on a delicate silver chain. "I'm going to make this right, Max. I promise I will make it right."

She pulled out her phone and called Scott, hoping she wouldn't distract him from helping Zari with Max.

She started talking as soon as he connected the call. "Where are you?"

"I have offered to mind Zari's business while she tends to Max."

Fia took a moment to process this information. "That was not what I expected, but okay. I'm going to come by. I just had a couple of interesting chats I want to run by you."

Fia pulled into the space outside Zari's shop, relieved to see the street otherwise empty.

"Mother Agnes said you took off without a word," Scott said as she passed through the doorway.

She huffed, shaking her head. "Of course she did. That's part of what I needed to talk to you about. I left because Agnes was mediating a brawl between Rebecca and Annabel."

"Sister Annabel returned?"

"She told you I left but not that?"

"She was asking if you had come back here. It was a short conversation."

"I guess Annabel has been lost in the woods since she disappeared. She said she doesn't remember much. One of the men we locked up—the one you didn't find dead on the side of the road—knocked her out, and the woman—wait, what happened to Heidi?"

"Heidi?"

"The woman with the accent, the siege leader."

"You learned her name?"

"What? Oh, no, it was—she's Scandinavian? Never mind. What happened to her? Annabel indicated it was just the other woman and the man, although she thinks she heard a gunshot after they ran her and Max off the road. I guess she could have been in the car with them."

Scott waited a moment before replying. "That sounds like something else to add to our investigation. But more urgently, what did you want to discuss?"

Fia ran the last couple of hours through her brain, weighing their importance. Agnes had, as far as they knew, destroyed the monitors connected to the surveillance equipment, so while it was concerning, she chose to table that for the time being. She decided to start with Annabel's return.

"When we pulled into the driveway, the front door was open. We found Annabel inside, pretty out of it, with a serious goose egg. Rebecca and I both kind of . . . I guess we attacked her. Agnes sent her to take a shower, and when she was finished, Rebecca suggested we take her down to the basement." Scott cocked an eyebrow, and Fia nodded. "Rebecca was basically interrogating Annabel, really raking her over the coals. Even if I were still convinced Annabel was involved, I felt like Rebecca's reaction was a little extreme."

A look of concern passed over Scott's face. "I may know why Sister Rebecca reacted the way she did. Fia, this is not my secret to tell, but I think it is important that you know—"

"I was talking with Agnes in her office regarding something she had found in the house, and when I came out, Rebecca was in the bathroom with Annabel—Agnes wanted Rebecca to keep an eye on Annabel—and I overheard something. I was going back to ask Agnes about it when they came out. That's when we headed downstairs. Does . . . does Rebecca have a kid?"

Scott nodded slowly. "That is, ultimately, why she is here."

"One of the kids in the safe house?" Fia ran through a quick math problem in her head. "The twins?"

"No, not the twins. Levi."

"That means . . . when we were talking about the fire, you mentioned a younger teen after I left. Rebecca?"

"Yes. Her father had known Mother—then Sister— Agnes years before, even before Rebecca was born, I believe, and he sent Rebecca to the convent to carry her pregnancy to term."

"And that's why she's a nun."

"Pardon?"

"I knew she had taken her vows out of obligation. To stay with her kid, right?"

"Yes. She had an agreement with Mother Lucy and the rest of the nuns at the time that if she took her vows, she could stay with Levi."

"But not as his mother?"

"I was not part of that conversation, but as I understood it, the agreement between Mother Lucy and Sister Rebecca's father to let her stay was that she give up parental rights."

"That sounds horrible."

"Yes."

"Who else knows?"

"In the house at this time, I believe only Mother Agnes and Sister Cecilia."

"So not Annabel?"

"I don't believe she or Sister Theresa would have been offered that information."

"Well, she knows now."

"I guess so. What was said?"

"Rebecca was accusing Annabel of knowingly putting her child—'my child,' she said—in danger. Annabel said she didn't know what Rebecca was talking about; I guess that was true? Unless she was covering."

"Levi's parentage has been a closely guarded secret. I do not see any way Sister Annabel would have found out."

"I don't know. Rebecca sounded pretty certain Annabel knew what was going on."

"That is, I must say, something you will have to address with them. You said Rebecca was interrogating Annabel in the basement when you left?"

"No, Rebecca was threatening to beat Annabel's face in when I left. She was interrogating her before that." Fia took a deep breath, realizing she was about to admit she might have been wrong in one of their previous conversations. "You suggested the fire may have been an inside job. You said my group had all left by then, recently, but maybe someone came back?"

"That is my recollection, yes."

Fia nodded. She laid out what she had learned—about the cell, about Terra—hoping her confusion wasn't making it too hard for Scott to follow. "Rebecca said Terra was gone; Annabel said she was here. You don't know?"

"That explains how Sisters Annabel and Theresa knew of you, does it not?" Fia shrugged, a gesture of defeat more than anything. "You were wondering, concerned about the idea of a reputation. This is better."

"I suppose, yeah. If Terra had come back here after . . . do you think she's still here? Do you think that's who—part of the reason I took off, snuck off, while they were busy was I remembered something. I hadn't thought about it in years, but when I left the convent, I took a photo. One Sister Cecilia had taken of us in City Park. I didn't want to remember much about my life there, but they were my siblings, for all intents and purposes. It's been in my gun safe since I built the dumb thing."

"Oh? And what . . . ?"

"I came back to get it. I swung by that shelter, the one where I saw Annabel after she had brought the snake down to animal control." A deep wrinkle formed in Scott's forehead. "What? What are you thinking?"

"I'm not sure. What did you learn there?"

"Not much. At least they didn't call me out on my lie."

"Lie?"

"I told them I knew Terra from the house where Mercy and the others were."

"Fia, I don't know if—"

"It was a harmless white lie. I figured I wasn't supposed to tell them about a clandestine convent in the woods where children learn to hunt condemned souls."

"That's not . . . I accept some deception is necessary. I am simply not certain *that* is the lie you should have chosen. If they were familiar with the youths in Father Donovan's care . . ."

He motioned for her to continue. Fia watched his face, waiting for the *then* to his *if*. When he didn't offer one, she picked the story back up.

"They seemed a little concerned about Father Donovan's sudden disappearance, then swept it under the rug. Some excuse about 'a man of his devotion' and returning a homeless teen to wherever they had run from. But they did suggest someone at Saint Anthony's might know something. Is that cause for alarm?"

"I have no reason to believe anyone other than Armando Ariaz and the man you have seen with him have been involved—"

"I can't believe that. He had *shackles* in the church basement! Not in a secret room or one of the subbasements I'm learning are staggeringly common around this town. They were just in the main basement. I went out the door, up the stairs, and straight into the sanctuary. They were just there, for anyone to see. I assumed you went down there to collect the body after I stabbed the bastard."

Scott recoiled slightly from the force of Fia's final statement. "I did. And I saw the restraints."

"And still, you don't think the whole operation is corrupt?"

"I checked the cabinet you thought had been moved. It is entirely feasible, given the false back on the cabinet and its incredible heft, that only those who needed to know were even aware it could be moved."

Fia considered this. As much as she wanted to condemn Annabel and anyone else with ties to Saint Anthony's, Scott had a point. But if Annabel wasn't involved with Ariaz, what was her connection?

As Fia chewed on this question—thankfully, without assistance from the angel—Zari pushed through the curtain separating the shop from the apartment behind it. "Fia, *chérie*, I did not expect you back so soon. I am afraid I still cannot allow—"

"No, Zari, I know. I just came to talk to Scott."

"Something else has changed since you left here earlier today."

"Yeah. But it can wait. You're busy."

"Max is resting. And I admit, I need a moment to breathe as well. I came up to gather a few more provisions. Talk while I gather?"

Fia nodded and started a slightly abridged version of the story she had told Scott.

"Uhlpir." Zari addressed the angel as casually as she did Fia. "Is there anything you could offer Fia or the sisters that would be more necessary than tending my shop?"

"Are you trying to get rid of me?"

"I thought perhaps you could verify Sister Annabel's story. I appreciate your help, I do. But it is not necessary if you can be of help elsewhere."

"I believe her story," Fia said abruptly. The other two looked at her, startled. "I'm still not sure she is inculpable, but I'm not sure she wasn't stabbed in the back either. Would serve her right if she had been." She muttered the last statement under her breath, but that didn't stop it from reaching Zari's ears.

"Fiammetta, that is—"

"I just mean *if* she was responsible for summoning the demon horde—betraying our organization from within—having her own people turn on her would be karma, right?" Fia searched frantically for a way to change the subject. "Have you made any progress with Max? Do you know . . . ? Can you . . . ?"

The end of the question evaded her. She didn't know if *heal him* was right, if he even needed healing.

"I am piecing together some of the time he was under the demons' influence. He has memories of a small woman with heavy blonde hair; does that mean anything to either of you?"

Scott shook his head. "I do not recognize the description offhand, and in my capacity as a priest—"

"And human," Fia added.

"And human. In my capacity, I am not permitted to see any of the sisters without their head coverings."

"You're omniscient," Fia blurted out.

"Yes, but I maintain the boundaries of my mortal disguise."

"And that's why—actually, I do have an idea about a woman with blonde hair. Dark blonde, that dishwater color but maybe sandier? That night the host almost . . . the soul I lost because I didn't know . . . there was a woman. I think she was the anonymous caller to nine-one-one. She had a ponytail like"—Fia touched her middle finger to her thumb in a circle—"high on top of her head but hanging halfway down her back. I never saw her face, though. I think that same ponytail picked Ariaz up one time I caught him stalking me."

"*Chérie*, do you think there might be more details you could access through hypnosis?"

Fia shrugged. Considering what she had seen in the photo, she wasn't sure her memory would be reliable now, but she was willing to try. She decided to keep the photo to herself for the time being. To avoid biasing anyone else.

"Anything is possible, I guess. I might have seen more of her face than I realize. But if it's not someone we know, is it going to be helpful?"

"You don't know which of your memories will help until it does."

"Can't argue with that. Can you . . . ?"

"*Oui*, come with me." Zari led Fia through the curtain behind the counter, leaving Scott in the main room of the shop.

Zari's card room looked exactly like the tourists would expect it to. A large live-edge table took up most of the space. Spread across the top was a deep-red silk cloth, anchored in the center by an immaculately clear globe of glass—a "crystal ball" as far as anyone else knew. Along one wall, a credenza held an altar covered in raw crystals and hand-carved wooden figurines.

Fia sat in one of the two chairs at the table. Zari pulled the other around so she could grip Fia's hands. The process for Zari to hypnotize Fia was different from what she would use to hypnotize a stranger. The two women had been through all this before, and Fia knew the steps without Zari's guidance. Because Zari was looking for specific information and wanted to see if what Fia remembered lined up with Max's memories, it was better for her to be in control.

With a few controlled breaths, Fia focused her attention on the parking lot where she had nearly hit the woman with her scooter, distracted as she had been by the sound of her heart beating in her ears.

At the front edge of the lot, opposite the front door of the restaurant, stood a charging station for electronic bike rentals. As Fia rode the scooter toward the one-way street headed south, a sign stood to the left, nearly two stories above the street, declaring this space to be the home of a diner. Fia wasn't sure if that sign predated the establishment she had just left, though the rusted iron and chipped brick of the industrial building made it look even less like a diner than a restaurant with a full-fledged executive chef.

The woman crossing in front of her scooter was coming from the building. She had come up behind Fia to cross in front of her. Just as Fia had remembered consciously, she held a cell phone against her left cheek— the cheek closer to Fia—blocking Fia's view of her face.

She was small, about the same size as Fia, slender but toned, like someone who had earned her figure instead of being naturally thin. Like someone who trained habitually. The thick, heavy ponytail rested against her back, unmoving, as she walked.

Like Scott, Fia had never seen any of the nuns with their heads exposed.

Except outside Saint Anthony's Cathedral. The woman she had seen engaged in something intimate with Armando Ariaz, the one with the braid.

Before Fia knew what was happening, Zari was speaking to her softly, drawing her out of the hypnosis. Fia apologized. "Did I say anything even a little bit helpful?"

"It is perhaps what you didn't see that interests me the most, *chérie*. It seems this woman took great strides to hide her face from you. Tell me about the faces of the nuns."

"You've seen—"

"I want to know what stands out to you about them."

"Annabel has that Midwest farmer's daughter thing going: the freckles, the dark blue eyes. The freckles make me think red hair. Not like mine but not like this woman either. That demon in the house—but it was a veiled demon. I can't be certain." She took a deep breath, trying to recenter her thoughts. "This woman I keep seeing, her hair is . . ." Fia looked around the room, at a loss for the right word to describe the color.

Zari rose from her chair and opened a drawer in the credenza. She plucked from it a handful of stones and brought them to the table, spreading them out in front of Fia. "I apologize for not having swatches of hair for you to choose from, but are any of these close?"

Fia looked at Zari, eyes wide with surprise. She had not expected the woman to bring her rocks to help her pick out hair colors. But when she looked closely at the offerings, she was even more surprised to find one that was exactly what she needed. She picked up the smooth, opaque stone and turned it in her fingers. It was a warm shade of creamy brown, like sand.

"The tiger jasper." Zari took the stone back from Fia and examined it herself. "Powerful as a gem, less notable as a hair color. Unfortunately, I think we are stuck with blonde."

"Yeah, I figured."

"Tell me about Rebecca."

Fia picked up another stone, rough and raw but translucent, the color of rich honey, and offered it to Zari. "Amber?"

"*Oui.*" Zari took the stone and studied it before returning it to the table. "What about this stone speaks to you, *chérie?*"

"Rebecca's eyes are this color." She touched a lighter area of the gem.

"Very good."

"And she has dark eyebrows. So, probably not blonde?"

Zari gave Fia a half nod that Fia read as Zari agreeing her assumption was probably true. "Not necessarily, but I believe the odds favor that assumption."

"So that leaves us with nothing."

"Not nothing—"

"What are you doing here? No! Get away! Don't touch me!"

Fia barely recognized Max's baritone as it cut through the curtain from the shop floor. What was usually warm and smooth now sounded like crushed ice—jagged, cold, and shrill—edged with panic and rage.

Zari leaped to her feet, nearly upsetting the heavy wooden chair, and was through the curtain in only two strides. Fia hesitated to follow; the tone of Max's question had created a wall she wasn't sure she wanted to break through. If that was his reaction to Scott, she didn't want to imagine what his reaction to seeing her would be.

Unable to resist, she found her feet slowly and followed Zari. She didn't want to make things worse, but she had to see what was happening on the other side of the curtain.

Zari stood between Max and Scott, facing Max with her hands extended to him. Max's eyes were wide and rimmed with deep purple shadows, the irises all but consumed by dilated pupils, black where they should have been the color of warm chocolate. Zari chanted quietly, only loud enough for Fia to know she was forming words. As she spoke, Max lowered the rough-edged chunk of green malachite he had picked up, presumably to defend himself, letting it drop to his feet. In another couple of seconds, he wilted toward the floor.

Scott moved with inhuman speed to catch Max before he reached the floor, gathering him up like a small child. He turned with his bundle back to Zari, his clear blue eyes drawn and sad.

"I am so sorry," Zari whispered. "He was sleeping. I did not expect him to wake or come up the stairs. It is clear we still have work to do." She motioned for Scott to carry Max back into the apartment and turned back to Fia.

Before she could speak, Fia raised her hands in defeat. "You don't have to say anything. I'm gone. Don't know where I'm going, but I'm going."

"Fiammetta, please don't—"

"No, Zari, I see he's really broken. I will do what I can to fix this, while you do what you need to do."

"Fia, I think it may be better if you were present while I continued my soul work with Max. It is possible the demons could replicate your face but not your energy. Perhaps if he is able to feel you close by—"

"Please, Zari. I-I can't. I am responsible for . . . I need to . . ." Fia turned and fought the urge to sprint for the front door of the shop.

TWELVE

In the driver's seat of Max's little white coupe, Fia pounded her fists against the steering wheel and screamed, an animalistic noise that might have come from the soles of her feet. She brought the little car to life and turned up the stereo. The track she had left it on before going inside ended with an intricate drum solo. Max had pointed it out to her, telling her that song might have been the one he was proudest of.

She let him play through his solo, then hit the button to start it over again from the beginning and pulled away from the curb.

She had no idea where she was going, but she needed answers. Seeing the feral fear in Max's deep eyes, his already-pale skin ashen from dehydration and lack of sleep, among other factors—it was more than she could take.

Zari insisted that none of what had happened had been Fia's fault, but Fia couldn't believe that.

The demons had been summoned because of her. She had drawn Max into her world.

If she had never brought him home . . .

Home.

She cranked the wheel at the next intersection to follow the streets north toward her apartment. She needed to take a shower, change clothes, and get back to the safe house. The more distance she put between her and Max, the better off they both would be.

At least for now.

As she crossed into her neighborhood, marked by colorful, elaborate murals on the sides of art galleries and converted warehouses, the hair on her arms prickled. She gave the streets a quick survey, looking for anyone or anything out of place.

Seeing nothing, she eased the car into the garage, and instead of ascending directly to her level, she spun once around the street level, then once around the second level.

"It's your nerves. This whole thing has you on edge. Maybe after your shower, you should have a nap."

Fia pulled the car into the top level and slammed hard on the brakes. Her jaw seemed to unhinge completely at the sight spread out before her.

A dozen or more creatures—their bodies covered in exoskeletons the color of obsidian, with long, sharp claws and teeth—had gathered around a human corpse. They had devoured enough of it that Fia couldn't see, from inside the car, whether she was looking at a man or woman. She climbed out, leaving the engine running and the door ajar, and moved toward their smorgasbord.

Blood had pooled on the ground around them. One of the little demons was trying its damnedest to extract it from the asphalt. In her shock, Fia found herself wondering if it was having any success.

Blonde hair flew like a strange snowstorm, and as Fia grew closer to the frenzy, she saw what—or who—the demons had found to feast on.

The Scandinavian woman from the siege. The Scandinavian woman who had also been stalking her around the city. Now she lay in a dismembered, disemboweled heap on the floor of Fia's garage.

"Fuck," Fia whispered.

The demons took no notice of her as they finished their meal. As they had before, they left only inorganics—which Fia was surprised to see wasn't much—and melted back into the shadows. Fia stepped closer and stared at what was left: a dark stain, bits of plastic, and the pull from a zipper.

"I guess that answers . . . a few questions." Fia kicked at the zipper pull, harder than was necessary, sending it skittering across the asphalt. Then she headed back to the car. She guided it the rest of the way into one of her parking spaces and headed inside.

Fia hurried through the open main room of the apartment, not wanting to linger too long on the pile of drum equipment in the front corner. She passed into the large bathroom, stripping free of the clothes she had been wearing for nearly four days, leaving them to mark her path across the tiles. Reaching into the large glass shower—which could have been a room in and of itself—she cranked the lever all the way to hot. Once the glass enclosure had filled with steam, she climbed in, the water turning her pale skin a bright, angry red almost immediately.

As she had done so many times before—and more times in the last six weeks than she cared to think about—she let the water pound the stress of the day down the drain. With the water pouring over her skin, she closed her eyes and drew deep breaths into her lungs.

In through the nose, out through the mouth.

She let the words run over and over in her brain until her head began to clear. She watched images of Max's bruised and terrified face mix with the grisly scene on her garage floor and swirl down the drain.

After what was probably close to half an hour, Fia switched off the water and stepped out of the shower, drying herself as she passed through the short hallway into the bedroom. She shimmied into a clean pair of jeans, a red tank top, and low-cut black sneakers, gave the bed a longing look, and turned to leave the apartment.

With her hair still damp, she returned to Max's car. She pulled down the little drum kit pendant he kept on a chain around the rearview mirror and clipped it around her neck before starting the engine. She was headed back to the mountains to check in with the nuns, but before she could pull out of the parking space, Uhlpir glittered into shape behind her. Once he was fully corporeal, she watched in awe as he assumed his human form, and Scott folded himself into the passenger seat of the tiny car.

"When were you going to tell me?"

"About?" Fia asked, genuinely confused. He turned in the seat and waved at the space behind the car. "Would you believe it just happened and I was on my way back to the shop?" Scott remained silent, his eyes trained on hers with the strength of a laser. "No? I wasn't sure what to say. Another host must have come here looking for me and expired before I got here. I rolled up on the little vulture-piranha demons eating her body."

"Her?"

"I guess whatever show the blonde woman put on for me worked?"

"Show? Blonde woman? You know the identity of the woman Zari—"

"Oops. No, not that. The other blonde. Heidi. From the attack."

"Was that who . . . ?" He glanced back again before shifting focus. "Actually, that ritual was what I wanted to talk to you about. I have been thinking about the bounties you have received since the explosion in the cave—"

"I think it was a setup. That one, at least. I think one of them sent it to me to get me to that rooftop, to see what they were going to do." She paused, considering her next thought carefully. "Thing is, I think the demons, the ones sent for me, are a subplot. A side quest. I don't think the blonde woman . . ." Fia glanced out the back window, letting the sentence fade.

"The blonde woman what?" Scott prodded after a long moment. "You mean . . ." It was his turn to pause. "I think it may eliminate some confusion if you at least continue to refer to the woman who attacked the safe house by your chosen nickname. Heidi, was it? What were you going to say about her?"

"I don't know. And unfortunately, I can't ask her now. But this cult of worshippers—I think whoever is responsible for the demons is part of their group, but they're not necessarily part of hers."

"The blonde woman?"

"What? No. I mean, maybe. I think there are two conspiracies colliding into one. Someone is gunning for *me* specifically, and I think they are part of a bigger group of people who worship Irzelen. I think they—she, whoever is after me—is part of their group, but the group . . . isn't working with her?" Fia pressed the heels of her hands into her temples.

"You are less certain of what you have suspected was going on."

"I was sure it was Annabel. I'm still not sure it's not. Just getting stabbed in the back is not absolution. But then she tells me she knew Terra. That Terra was the one who told her about the fire in the convent. Which means Terra . . ."

Fia reached into the center console where she had put the photo of herself with her teen comrades and handed it to Scott. She tapped the ponytail. "That's Terra. Do you think—"

"The other blonde? The one Max mentioned under hypnosis?"

"I don't know. I didn't tell Zari about this because I didn't want . . . but now I'm not sure."

"It has been seven years—"

"Probably closer to eight or nine since the picture was taken."

"Do you think she would still be wearing her hair like that? You cut yours off shortly after leaving. And even so, a ponytail is an extreme reason to hang someone without more proof."

"I know. But how do I find out? I don't have time to look for her *too*."

"Have you asked Mother Agnes?"

Fia shook her head. *You know I didn't.* "I came straight here. Shit, I came here, got the picture, went to talk to the nuns at the outreach center. I went to talk to you, Max freaked, and I came back here."

"You've had a busy afternoon."

"Do you think we should head back to the mountains?"

"I am still needed at Zari's. I just came to make sure you were okay after—are you okay?"

"Is Max okay?"

"He will be. I think."

"Onward and upward, then, I guess. Want me to drop you off?"

"It's out of your way. I can get back on my own." He climbed free of the car and vanished before Fia could even put the car back into gear.

THIRTEEN

Fiammetta, I am glad you chose to return."

Fia had come into the safe house through the garage to find the nuns she had left assembled in the kitchen. Agnes and Annabel sat facing each other at the steel table. Rebecca stood against the wall several feet way, her expression sullen, her arms crossed tightly over her chest, and the knuckles of her left hand wrapped in a white cloth.

Fia guessed, from the scene, that Rebecca was protesting Agnes's apparent insistence they treat Annabel like a human and not like the family dog that had gotten into the chicken coop. Upon closer inspection, Fia noticed a new wound on Annabel's face, a split lip she hadn't had when Fia left, likely the reason for Rebecca's bandaged hand.

"I wasn't . . . I just had to find something back at my condo." After a long pause, she took a breath deep into her lungs and held it, handing the photo to Agnes. "Sister Cecilia took this of us on one of her field trips. I talked to Zari while I was back in the city, and she said Max had mentioned something under hypnosis about a woman with long, dark-blonde hair. And someone has been following me. Do you know where Terra is? Can we get in contact—"

"No." Agnes's response was so quick, Fia flinched. "Apologies, Fiammetta. I have, unfortunately, not maintained a connection with Terra."

"What about Meredith?" She pointed at the other girl in the photo. "Do you know where she is? Can we . . . ? Maybe she knows where . . ."

Another thought entered Fia's racing mind, making her feel frantic and desperate. *What if it's Meredith? Meredith hated me even then. Maybe she dyed her hair to look like—*

Stop. Fia pushed the thought aside, realizing that everyone was focused on her face, which she guessed was shifting and twisting as her brain worked.

"May I see?" Annabel asked quietly, reaching toward Agnes, who obliged, handing over the photo.

Fia scolded herself for revealing why she was focused on Terra. She realized, too late, she could have used the photo to test Annabel's story, like police photos. *Do you see the person who told you about the fire at the convent in this photo?*

Annabel studied the photo for a long moment before meeting Fia's eyes. "You said someone has been following you?"

Fia shrugged. "Or maybe she thinks I'm following her. She's connected to the priest, though. Or was."

"Was?"

Fia turned to Agnes. "She doesn't know?"

"I didn't think it was relevant."

Fia directed her next statement to Annabel, putting as much force as possible behind it, hoping for a reaction. "I killed the priest. Ariaz. He's been giving me creepy vibes, like the guy I . . ." She displayed her scarred hand to avoid finishing the sentence. "So I tried to get him to act on it, and when he did, I stabbed him. I meant to put it in his leg or somewhere nonfatal, but I think I hit a kidney or something instead."

Annabel recoiled, but her face didn't reveal what Fia had hoped it would. The nun was shocked, of course, that had been Fia's intention in her delivery. But instead of anger over Fia having murdered her lover, Fia thought she looked more sympathetic. Annabel's next words supported this theory.

"Fia! I'm so sorry. That sounds deeply intimate; you must still be reeling."

Fia sighed. "Unfortunately, he's not the first guy I've killed in self-defense. Can I even call that self-defense? I lured him in with the intent of stabbing him."

"It is over and done with now, Fiammetta," Agnes replied, her voice strangely cold, like the steel table beneath her folded hands.

"That it is, Reverend Mother. Do you have something more you'd like to say on the subject?" Fia wasn't certain she was prepared for the answer, but she also fully expected not to get one.

"It may have been prudent to have brought this . . ." Agnes paused. Fia assumed the nun was searching for a word, though Fia couldn't even try to guess which. "Ariaz back here for interrogation. He may have had information—"

"With all due respect, and I honestly mean that, he is not—was not—an information kind of guy. He was a no-answer answer kind of guy, cagey, arrogant. I don't think you would have gotten anything from him he didn't want you to have."

"And we have no way of knowing that now."

"Hey, I'll make you a deal. The next time a raving psychopath has me chained in the basement of a church, I'll let him know he's wanted back here for questioning. Does that work for you?"

Fia stood from the stool she had perched on, toppling it in her haste. She righted it, the edges of her ears burning, and paced away from the table toward the back door that led to the garden and the forest beyond it. She stared out the window at nothing for a long moment, waiting for her pulse and breathing to slow. When she felt calmer, she turned back to face the others.

"So you don't know where Terra ended up?"

"I do not have any way of reaching her," Agnes answered flatly.

Fia cocked an eyebrow. There was something strange in the nun's choice of words, even for Agnes. Agnes seemed to be putting a lot of effort into selecting just the right words to answer Fia's questions without revealing a secret, but Fia didn't have the energy to figure out what Agnes wasn't saying.

Fia looked at her phone, checking the time. She wished she had taken that nap, and now it was too late.

There wasn't much more she could do without talking to Max. And she couldn't talk to Max. At least not yet. But she also doubted she would be able to sleep. She rubbed the heels of her hands against her forehead.

"Fiammetta, do you need to take a break? You have barely slowed since the siege, that I have seen."

"No," Fia lied. "I'm fine. Maybe some coffee?"

True to form, Rebecca pulled herself away from the wall she had been holding up and began digging in the commercial-size refrigerator. "I think we could all use a meal."

Before Fia could answer, her phone vibrated with an incoming message. *Where are you?* A text from Scott.

"Hold that thought," she told Rebecca as she typed out her response.

I apologize for dragging you back so soon, but Zari would like you here, if you are up for it. You have had a long couple of days.

Fia replied that she was on her way, told the others where she was going, and left them behind as she headed back to the city for the third time that day.

Fia pulled in behind Zari's shop, heading for the apartment. She raised her fist to knock on the painted green door but changed her mind. Instead, she pushed through the door into the warmth of the kitchen. It wasn't so much a physical warmth, though that had been true in Fia's first days here, as an emotional warmth. Fia thought it was the first place she had ever really understood the difference between house and home.

Not wanting to fill the air with her voice, she paced through the ground floor of the apartment, searching for the others. Finding no one, she eased down the stairs to the basement, where she found the priest standing sentinel at the door to Zari's bedroom.

"I'm here; what's up?" she whispered, trying to make her voice as indistinguishable as possible.

"Zari believes she is breaking through, but she needs your help."

"Only just breaking through?" Scott nodded. "Shit, what does she need?"

Zari emerged from the room and embraced Fia without a word.

"Scott said you needed my help?"

"*Oui.* I feel like I am making progress, but then he slips backward again. I do not know enough about him or the people in his life to make sense of what he's saying."

Fia swallowed hard. She didn't think she could help either but guessed she was better than any other option Zari had. "I'll try. I don't know much."

"I will still need you to be as quiet as you can. Speak up if it is appropriate, but otherwise . . ." Fia nodded, laying a finger over her lips. "Then follow me."

Back in the small space beneath the floor, Fia took a moment to look around in a way she hadn't before. What she had thought was likely a crawl space had been set up as a sort of sanctuary. Fia wondered now if Zari had carved the space out when she moved in.

It was no larger than a few feet in any direction. The walls were made of carefully stacked stones packed with clay. The floor was cool dirt, and the floor joists were visible overhead.

Along one wall stood trinkets and idols, similar to the altar in the shop, but the magic present in this space prickled the hair on Fia's arms.

Just as he had before, Max lay flat in the dirt, his intricately decorated flesh exposed and pale in the light of half a dozen candles. Zari had surrounded him with various stones, raw from the source but smooth from being touched, each lying only a couple of inches away from him. Fia recognized a few of them—opal, amethyst, the smoky quartz Zari had built into the bracelet Fia wore—but a few she didn't. Lying in the hollow of Max's collarbones was a small piece of turquoise, and in the center of his forehead was a nugget of white howlite. Fia knew each gemstone and crystal was meant to aid Zari's work, but she didn't pretend to fully understand any of it.

"Where should I . . . ?"

"I have a theory that while the demons can replicate faces and voices, even speech patterns they usurped from Max's memories, the specific aura of a person would be harder to replicate. This is because the aura is not a fixed property. Your aura does not feel the same to me as to Max. The demons would have to replicate how you *feel* to him, and that would be much more complicated for beings you have said should not be able to shift in the first place."

"I didn't; Irzelen did."

"All the more evidence to support my theory. Because of that, I would like you to lie as close to Max as you can without touching him."

Fia surveyed the ground around Max before stripping down to her undergarments. She stretched out in the dirt and scooted closer to Max until she could feel the heat of his skin.

Zari sat behind Max's head, her legs folded into a lotus pose to allow her to also be as close to him as possible without touching him. She reached out and tapped a closed fist against Fia's shoulder, indicating she wanted to give something to her. Fia reached back with her palm turned up, and Zari pressed a cool, metallic-feeling stone into her hand.

"Hematite for you, Fiammetta. It will aid in your concentration throughout this, keep you connected to the earth, and absorb negative energy. If you start to feel anything strange, please get rid of the stone. Too much negative energy will cause it to explode."

Fia snapped her head up, turning a confused look toward Zari. Zari merely waved for her to lie down, as if she hadn't just told Fia she was holding a volatile object that might cause her severe injury. Fia stared at Zari for a long moment before deciding she wouldn't get any more information and returned her head to the dirt.

From her position on the floor, Fia couldn't see much of what was going on beside her, but she could see Zari's hands moving, swirling inches above Max's head and shoulders. It was a long time, though, before Zari said anything directly to him. When she did, it was to encourage him to tell her more about the woman with the long hair.

"She didn't want me to see her. She kept her face hidden from me. Sometimes behind her hair, once in a mask. Usually, she just kept it turned away or in the shadows."

Someone he knew? Questions started passing through Fia's mind before she was ready. *But if the demons were corrupting his memories, making him see people who weren't there, why was she hiding?*

Fia squeezed the crystal in her hand and pushed the thoughts down so she could focus on Max's words.

"Max." Zari made her voice soothing, as if she were recording a meditation track. "Tell me about the person who hurt you."

"First?"

Fia turned her head to look at Max. *What does he mean by that?* She watched him for a moment, then turned questioning eyes back to Zari.

Zari nodded and took Fia's hint, putting voice to Fia's thoughts.

"The woman from the safe house," Max replied, "with the broken ribs. With the needle."

That matched Annabel's story about the abduction. Fia rubbed her thumb firmly but idly against the smooth stone, bringing up the details Annabel had offered. "Did she drug you?" She whispered the question loudly, hoping to disguise her voice enough to not startle him. His temperature rose, and the hair on Fia's arms, which had finally relaxed, stood again at attention.

"Dark, it's so dark. I feel like I'm falling through . . ."

He trailed off, maybe in search of a word, maybe losing track of the thought altogether. Fia squeezed her stone again, resisting the temptation to grab Max's hand.

"Falling through what, Max?" Zari asked after a moment.

"Gel? Some kind of goo. It's liquid enough to fall through but not like water. And then concrete. Bricks. Chains."

"You said she hurt you first. Who was next?" Zari asked quietly after giving him a moment to finish.

"Annabel."

Now Fia's temperature was rising, until Zari's voice cut through. "Remember, *chérie*, we do not know what is real and what is imaginary. You are quick to blame young Sister Annabel, and if I am not mistaken, that began when I turned the High Priestess for you." Fia wasn't sure if the voice was in her ears or her mind, so she kept silent.

"What did Annabel do, Max?"

"Cut my foot. So easily. Like she was cutting a steak."

Fia dug her fingers into the dirt. Scott had mentioned a deep wound on Max's foot, suggesting he could heal it without too much trouble. Still, rage burned in her throat. *Who does that? Slice someone's foot?* She had to remind herself that everything done to Max had been done to hurt her indirectly. Ariaz had told her as much. *The only real way to hurt you is to hurt someone you are meant to protect.*

He hadn't been wrong.

Of course they would have done heinous things to Max. The more they hurt him, the worse it would be for Fia. She ground her teeth and returned her focus to Max.

"You are certain it was Sister Annabel?" Zari asked.

"No," Max replied softly. "I was. I was so sure. I kicked her. It was a reflex. I kicked Desmond in the face when I was a kid for tickling my feet. Broke his nose. Mom was so angry."

Fia's brow furrowed, but Zari seemed pleased. "Max, that sounds like a real memory. Can you tell me about Desmond? Is that your brother?"

"He plays guitar. He's a DJ. On the radio. Annabel knows him too."

That doesn't sound right. Fia pushed the thought toward Zari.

"How does Annabel know your brother?"

"We were kids. She knew us when we were . . . the time I got sick. My appendix."

"Zari?" Fia whispered. "I don't think that's real."

"No, *chérie*, nor do I." To Max, she said, "Tell me what happened to your appendix. How old were you?"

"It was my tenth birthday. We were on the roller coaster, and I threw up. And I couldn't stop throwing up. Annabel was at the party. She was with me on the coaster."

"Max, was Annabel with you when you had surgery?"

"She was with me on the coaster. I threw up on the sidewalk."

"Max, who else was with you when you got sick?"

"Desmond. It was my birthday, and Des's too."

"You have the same birthday? Are you twins?"

"Des is older. We had our parties together when we were little. I got sick when I was ten. That was the last year we had our parties together."

"Max, do you talk to your brother often?"

"Enough."

"Does he know about Fia?"

"No."

"Max, why do you think Annabel was at your party?"

"I remember she was there. She cut my foot, and I don't know what made her so angry. We've known each other so long. She was there when I got sick."

Fia's temperature rose again, burning in her cheeks and at the edges of her ears. It was bad enough they had corrupted his memories of her, of Scott, of whoever else, but to meddle with his childhood . . .

She passed the hematite back and forth from one hand

to the other and inhaled slowly. She kept the breath in her lungs, counting to ten, before releasing it just as slowly.

Zari stayed the course, asking Max who else was at his party besides his brother and Annabel.

"I-I don't . . . it wasn't my birthday. It was the weekend before."

"Tell me more." Zari's voice changed, and Fia caught the same sense of excitement. The memory was changing, maybe for the better. "Tell me what happened when you got sick. Where were you?"

"The old coaster. The wooden one. It's not there anymore. I was in a car by myself. When I got off, I threw up. All over my broth—his girlfriend. I threw up on his girlfriend."

"What was her name?"

"Betty? Bernie? She was my first."

"First?" Zari made no effort to hide the confusion in her voice.

"Des wasn't home. His girlfriend. I was there by myself. Des was somewhere with Mom and Dad. Annabel came over—"

"Max, what happened to Betty?" Zari grabbed the reins and pulled back, dragging Max away from drifting back to the nun.

"Betty? Beth? Bella?"

"Max, who was your brother's girlfriend? You got sick and vomited on Desmond's girlfriend."

"Bella. But that wasn't . . . Desmond was gone with Mom and Dad. His girlfriend came to see him. Crashed the car."

Fia's head swam as she listened to Max try to put together a linear thought. She could only imagine how it sounded to him. She tried to focus on the tone of his voice more than the words, to pick up where he sounded confident and where he sounded more confused, hoping it would mean something later.

"Max, was Annabel at your birthday?"

"Annabel? No, I think Bella was Isabelle. I called her Izzy because she hated it." He punctuated the statement with a giggle. Fia searched her own memories to find a time Max might have mentioned his brother. If he had, he hadn't talked about the difference in their ages. She wondered how old Desmond had been at the time Max was remembering.

"Was Annabel at your birthday? When you got sick?"

"No." His simple declarative statement was almost forceful. Fia thought that was a good sign. Zari must have, too, because she encouraged him to continue talking about Bella. "I threw up all over her. She never talked to my brother again. He didn't talk to me for two weeks. Then we got in a fight, and we were fine."

"Did you fight with your brother a lot?"

"I kicked him in the face for tickling me. Mom was angry. I got in trouble for breaking his nose, but it was his fault. It never grew back right."

"You don't like people touching your feet. What happened when Annabel cut your foot?"

"I kicked her. In the chest. Father Scott was angry, but I didn't hurt her as bad as I hurt Desmond."

"Scott? Father Scott saw you kick Annabel?"

"He was there. He brought me water when I asked for it."

"Is that why you were so frightened when you saw him upstairs in my shop?"

"He didn't hurt me. The nuns hurt me. He just watched. I think he hurt Fia, though. He took her out of the room, and when he brought her back, she had bruises on her face."

"Fia was there?"

"They kidnapped her too. But then they turned her against me. She came back one time and kicked me. In the ribs."

"When did Fia get there?"

"I don't know. The woman with the broken ribs gave me a shot of something in the arm. When I woke up, Fia was there. It was dark, but I could hear her voice."

"You didn't see Fia in the room with you?"

"Not at first."

"Max, could you *feel* Fia in the room with you?" He didn't reply. "Max? Do you understand the question?"

"I heard her voice. She was in a shadow."

"Do you feel her near you now?" More silence. "Max, is Fia here now?"

Lying beside Max in the dirt, Fia felt a scalding fever sweep over his body. He began to shiver, gently at first, and then shivers graduated to shaking, and shaking to convulsions. Fia sat up, moving away from Max, quickly and abruptly enough her back slammed against the rock wall. She grunted from the force and drew her knees into her chest.

Zari had calmly placed her hands on either side of Max's neck, offering him some stability as he seized. As Fia watched, the muscles of his stomach contracted, undulating violently. Zari quickly turned him onto his side, in time for him to vomit in the dirt.

He hadn't had anything to eat since the last meal they had shared on the drive back from Kansas, so the vomiting was more pantomime than anything else. A trail of spit dripped from Max's lips, and a faint acrid scent drifted into Fia's nose.

The seizure subsided, and Zari returned Max to the ground, keeping his head elevated on her shins. "I believe that may be where we stop for today," she said softly. "*Chérie*, you are welcome to sleep in the guest room tonight, if you would like."

"Do you need me to?"

"I do not need anything more from you. If you would like to return to your own bed, you may be more inclined to rest there. I would recommend sleeping in your bed rather than returning to the mountains."

Fia nodded. She wondered if Zari really meant, *Stay away from Sister Annabel until you have more information,* but she let the question fall to the side. She redressed before climbing up out the trapdoor.

"Fiammetta, could you ask Father Scott to come back in here, please?"

FOURTEEN

Something pulled Fia from a deep and dreamless sleep. She tried to reach for her phone to check the time, but her arms refused to comply, as though they weighed one hundred pounds each. She tried to turn her head, but only her sleep-bleary eyes moved, and she could just see the blue LED lights of the clock on her dresser. Three thirty-two became three thirty-three as she watched. Her vision cleared, along with the fog in her mind, and she became acutely aware of what had awoken her.

The soft, fine hair along her neck and arms stood on end, and the sound of too much electricity filled the darkness of her room. Though she couldn't move to turn on a light, she didn't need to. She had grown all too familiar with the buzzing feeling that came with the presence of a divine being.

Her eyes adjusted to the darkness, dilated pupils letting in more and more light as she focused down the length of her nose toward the foot of the king-size bed. Soon she could make out a hulking shape, a light-absorbing black against the heavy charcoal gray of the room.

What she couldn't see was anything besides the mass.

Where there should have been the outline of her dark wood dresser against the red-brick wall, there was only charcoal gray. To her left, the hallway to the bathroom was the same gray. To her right, the blackout curtains covering the balcony door were gray. Even where she knew the curtains had been separated ever so slightly, where light should have shone through from the city outside, there was only gray. But ahead of her, at the foot of the bed, was a black mass.

She studied the mass more closely, and what looked like a head and shoulders took shape. As she pieced together what she was looking at, the paralysis lifted. She pulled herself up into a sitting position, drawing the covers up over the loose-fitted sports bra she had chosen to sleep in. She caught sight of the being's wings, slack against his back.

With a heavy sigh, she broke through the buzzing air. "Irzelen? Is that you?"

A pair of shimmering gold-yellow eyes glowed in response, and she reached for the bedside lamp.

No. The voice boomed inside her skull with such force, she thought her head would burst. "No light," he hissed.

"Oh. Okay. What . . . ? How did you get . . . ? You know what, no. I don't want to know. What do you want? Why are you here? Don't I have to invite you in? How . . . ? No, I think that's all my questions. I'm actually glad you're here, though. I think I need your help."

"You are distracted from your mission."

"Not distracted. I am definitely not. I'm trying. It's not like I can simply ask people, 'Hey, did you summon a demon horde to kill me?' Humans aren't bound to honesty the way . . ." She thought about the rest of that statement before doubling back and starting over. "Do you have to tell the truth? Is that part of that divine law you keep spouting?"

"You are thinking of faeries."

"Faeries are real?"

"Please try to focus, Miss Drake. I think you well know by now that the divine are not bound to do anything regarding mortals. Especially not telling you the truth. Perhaps if we were, you would have fewer problems. Your angel, on the other hand—that is not why I am here. I asked you to perform a task for me that I am incapable of performing myself, and you are no closer to finishing it than when I first approached you. Perhaps I should simply leave you to them. Once they have disposed—"

"No, listen, look, I'm closer." Fia breathed, drawing back the reins on the desperation in her voice. "I'm close. I am. And I'm motivated. I am motivated like you wouldn't believe."

"The fate of your lover."

Fia cringed at the sterile way Irzelen used the word *lover*. "Ick. Please don't say—but yeah, yes, they really did a number on—"

"Kill him."

"Come again?" She had come to expect an abrupt lack of couth from the demon, but even that didn't brace her for the impact of his declaration that she should simply murder Max.

"Kill him. The only way to rid him of the demon shadow in his mind is for you—or anyone, it does not matter; your practitioner may be better equipped—to kill him."

Fia stared, wide-eyed, at the demon through the darkness. Now fully adjusted to the scant light in the room, she could see he was folded like an accordion, crouching at the end of her bed, his knees to his chest, his tail resting against his heels. She was even starting to make out the blue-gold iridescent sheen of his fibrous wings. Everything about this being, from the translucency of his wings to the black chitin covering his body, reminded Fia of a giant insect. Even the buzzing, though unmistakably electrical in the way it made her feel, reminded her of an apiary.

She didn't know how to answer. So she repeated his proclamation back to him.

"Yes. The only way to break the bond between the mortal mind and the demon shadow left on it is by killing him. Honestly, Miss Drake, you act as if you haven't done it a thousand times over. It seems you have even gotten comfortable slicing and dicing those demons—"

"Hundreds," Fia corrected, though she wasn't sure why. She guessed his estimate of one thousand was either hyperbole or the differences in their realities. Zari had suggested years might seem like only a blink to the immortals; perhaps the number of souls Fia had returned to Irzelen's charge had blurred, until three hundred may as well have been one thousand. "But that's different," she continued. "As for the demons, I only—"

"Is it? Isn't all human life said to be precious?"

Disgust dripped from his words as if they were something putrid and rotted. It was the first real indication Fia had gotten of the contempt he held for humanity, beyond his declaration that Ariaz and his ilk were nothing more than pests. Before, his disdain had come through in shallow, lifeless words, as if he were talking about hating broccoli or mushrooms. This, applying the word *precious* to humans, sounded like it made him physically ill to even think it, let alone utter it aloud.

"The difference," Fia started again, "is that the hosts I have—"

"Destroyed?"

"*Neutralized* were beyond repair."

"I assure you, Miss Drake, the longer the demon shadow

remains on the mind of your lover, the closer he will become to that same prognosis."

Fia thought about that for several pounding heartbeats. *Kill him.* The words echoed in her mind.

"It is the only way, Miss Drake. The bond must be severed through the death of one entity or the other. Your practitioner is powerful, but even she cannot kill the demon shadow—"

"Wait, hold up. The shadow is . . . the shadow is alive? It's not just a residue left behind by the actual demons? Does that mean . . . ? What does that mean?" Fia's head throbbed. She took a mental step back and started over. "There is a shadow in Max's brain, a physical entity, like some kind of demonic tadpole? Is it solid? Will it . . . ? Is it going to grow?"

"It will grow. Without intervention—and I only offer you this advice to bring your attention back to where I need it; if not for my predicament, I would let him perish—without intervention, the shadow will become corporeal, feeding from your lover. Likely, eventually splitting him in two. Your practitioner has proven herself a powerful sorceress time and time again, but it is clear that if she has not already rid him of the entity, she will not. The only choice left is to sever the bond they are creating. And the only way to achieve that is mortal death."

"What about an angel?"

"She is most certainly not strong enough to kill—"

"No! I mean, could the angel kill the shadow without killing Max?"

"You are referring to your guardian, Uhlpir? He would face severe consequences, and he is far too righteous to consider ending a life, even that of a demon, even for you."

"What do you mean, even for me?"

Irzelen ignored the question, continuing without pause.

"No, Miss Drake, the only way I see to solve your most pressing problem, so you may return your focus to *my* problem, is mortal death. Kill your lover, and he will be rid of the shadow."

The demon punctuated his statement by vanishing. Unlike the times before, when he had taken flight in phoenix form, this time he merely blinked from existence.

Fia's eyes snapped open, revealing the empty darkness of her bedroom. Above her, the ceiling fan spun in its hypnotic circle, cooling her feverish skin. Slowly, she rose from the mattress and looked around. Everything was where it belonged. She could see the edges of her dresser, a shade darker than the dark of the walls, no more than a silhouette. She could see a sliver of vaguely amber-gold light between the curtains over the balcony door.

She lowered her feet to the floor and moved cautiously to the foot of the bed, her phone clenched in her hand, though she didn't know why. She didn't think she could use it as a weapon, and she wasn't holding it the right way to use the flashlight. She rectified the second problem and set the little LED light aglow, aiming it at the floor where the demon had sat on his haunches, still taller than she would have been standing beside him.

There was nothing on the hardwood to indicate he had been there. She wasn't certain what she had expected to find—burn marks, claw marks?—but she was relieved not to find anything.

"It was a dream. A stupid dream," she scolded herself, switching off the flashlight. She crossed the room and pushed the curtains aside to open the balcony door. She stepped through onto the concrete platform, the material rough against her tired feet, and leaned her bare stomach against the railing.

On the roof of the neighboring building, which was not quite even with where she stood now, an enormous humanoid being stood motionless for several long moments before spreading translucent blue-gold wings and shooting straight up into the sky.

FIFTEEN

"Do you think it would help to elevate his arms and legs? You know, let gravity do its thing?"

Fia had spent most of the following morning at the public library, for the first time since her teens. In preparation for killing a man to destroy a demon, she had wanted information a little more reliable than the internet. Once satisfied she had everything she needed, she had returned to Zari's early in the afternoon, a stack of papers she had printed from medical journals clenched in her fist.

Early in her research, she had discovered an article regarding the consequences of drowning in extremely cold water, such as might occur when someone broke through ice into a frozen lake. This late in the summer, not even the glacial lakes would still be frozen enough to achieve Fia's goal, so she had refocused her research energy on figuring out how to replicate the conditions in Zari's iron-and-porcelain bathtub.

She had given Zari the original catalyst article first, before sharing any of her plan, hoping to get Zari's honest thoughts. Though she had expressed all the same concerns Fia had had at first, it didn't take a lot for Fia to convince Zari it was their best option.

"Irzelen said if someone with your skill hadn't gotten that shadow out yet, this was probably the only way. How would he know what kinds of skills you have?"

Zari had chewed on Fia's question long enough Fia thought she wasn't going to answer.

"I cannot honestly say, *chérie*. You know I would not deceive you, and I have never spoken with the demon, that I am aware of. I believe it is quite—perhaps *complimentary* is the wrong word—a testament to your station that he has chosen you, not only to complete this task of his but to connect with you on multiple occasions."

Fia wasn't sure she could take any of what was happening as a positive, even if she was one of an elite group of mortals graced by the divine. Not just the demon but Uhlpir as well. At the end of the day, she had still pissed someone off badly enough for them to appropriate an army of demons, subsequently angering the head demon. Irzelen had only approached Fia because she was the target and, therefore, the two of them had a mutual stake in breaking the thrall this mortal had on the horde.

Now, seated at the table in Zari's kitchen, Fia was trying to sort out the best way to follow Irzelen's advice, hoping against the shimmer of doubt that her conversation with him had not been merely a dream. She hoped that he had, in fact, given her this suggestion rather than her subconscious having conjured it up on its own. She *had* seen him fly away from the neighboring roof, but she felt like she had made enough mistakes leading up to this point; she didn't need to go looking for more.

Fia asked Zari again if elevating Max's limbs above his heart would help with what they had both read.

Zari read over the article again, pulling her finger along the page. "I am not a doctor, *chérie*, but I cannot see how it would hurt the process. How do you propose we accomplish this?"

Fia wrinkled her face, carving deep trenches through her forehead, and considered the question. She had what she thought was a plan, but she had also hoped Zari would offer her own plan that would either corroborate or replace what Fia had cooked up. She shifted the subject, hoping she could prompt Zari to offer her own ideas.

"Do you think we should call Scott? He might be able to—"

"I think this secret is best kept between us, *chérie*. And I think you do as well."

"In case it doesn't work."

"In case it does. How do you think Father Scott will respond to this idea?"

"He'd probably insist there was another way."

"*Oui*, and do you believe there is another way?"

"Kind of. We could keep at the soul work, but for how long?"

Zari nodded. "For how long, indeed. And with no guarantee we would not have to resort to this in the future anyway. I am inclined to agree with you, Fiammetta. The demon is strictly invested in retrieving what he believes has been stolen from him. He is not interested in the destruction of life, beyond that of the summoner."

"Yeah." The word felt small but heavy, like a filler Fia was using more to acknowledge Zari's words than to agree with them. After all, it wasn't a question of agree or disagree. Fia knew, in her gut, this was the answer.

Zari circled back to address Fia's question with more certainty. "No, I believe it is best we keep this between the three of us for now. In the time I have spent with Father Scott, in both his human and angelic forms, I have determined he is quite attached to you. And that his interactions with Irzelen are perhaps more intimate than you might realize."

"Irzelen said something like that too. That Uhlpir wouldn't risk killing the demon shadow in Max's mind, 'even for me.' Do you know what he might have meant?"

Zari shook her head. "I cannot guarantee it is a question he would answer, but it is one you would have to take to him. It is not something he has divulged in our time together."

After a long pause, Zari suggested, "Perhaps filling the bathtub with ice and water?"

"That sounds like a lot of ice."

"*Oui.*" The word from Zari, even in another language, sounded heavier than when Fia had spoken it. There was something Zari wanted to say. That she couldn't bring herself to say it concerned Fia almost more than anything else they were doing.

"What is it, Zari?"

"I am worried for you, Fiammetta."

Zari closed her eyes and took a breath deep into her lungs, making her chest heave as she filled it. She held it for a moment before releasing it, relaxing every muscle in her body. Fia watched Zari's body slack with the exhalation of air.

Then Zari regained her posture, straightening her back and lifting her chin. "You have taken innocent lives and come away from it mostly unscathed."

"Life," Fia corrected. "And I wouldn't call him innocent. The hosts were different."

"This will be different. This will feel different."

"How?"

"That is for you and you alone to know. I cannot describe

the feelings I felt in words. I can only access them in my memories. You, too, will have those memories."

Fia pondered the woman's words, along with others she had heard from Zari in the past. She spoke delicately. "Zari? Have you . . . have you done something like this before?"

"Not this, no. But I have intimately ended a life that needed to be ended. There are better ways—pharmaceuticals are effective and painless, but they are slow; a gun is quick, if it gets the job done, but it is messy—but suffocation or drowning is different. I cannot explain it further than that."

She paused briefly before changing the subject. "I believe if we were to, as you suggested, raise his arms and legs above his heart and then lower his temperature rapidly with ice, we could simulate the body's response to being plunged into a freezing lake. Hypothermia first, then drowning."

"That sounds . . ."

"Horrible?"

"Unfortunately perfect." The women sat in silence, watching one another's faces, for another long moment before Fia stood, smoothing her hands over the thighs of her jeans. "I guess we should get started. Do we need more ice?"

Zari nodded. "There is a convenience store nearby where I get the ice for the icebox. I think three, maybe four, bags will be good."

Fia grabbed the car keys off the table and left the way she had come.

A couple of blocks from Zari's, she pulled into the lot of a convenience store and checked the freezer where the ice was kept. Locked. *Of course.* "I need some ice?" she said to the man behind the counter when he asked if he could help her.

"How many?" he grunted.

"Four. And this." She tossed a chocolate bar onto the counter.

"Ten eighty-two," he reported.

"Yeesh. Candy's expensive, like they think that will stop us from buying it or some—Sorry, here you go." She handed the man a ten-dollar bill and fished another single out of the stack.

The man counted back her change and grabbed a giant key ring from below the register. He motioned for her to walk ahead of him.

They loaded the bags of ice into the back of the car, and she thanked the man. She tossed the chocolate on top and headed back.

As Zari watched, Fia placed the chocolate in the icebox. "For Max," Fia explained. She hadn't really known why when she had grabbed it, but it had felt right in the moment.

Zari nodded and followed Fia back out to the car to haul the bags of ice inside. With one bag in each hand, Fia motioned for Zari to go ahead of her, following the woman as she carried the other two bags down the spiral staircase.

In the basement, they left the ice in the bathroom. Fia poured one bag into the claw-foot bathtub and started the cold water running at half speed. She smashed the other three bags on the tile floor and tore them open. Propping them against the tub, she followed Zari into the bedroom, where Zari descended through the trapdoor in the floor.

"Do you need . . . ? Can I help?" Fia whispered.

"No, *chérie*, for this, I think we will only be in each other's way." After some scuffling and labored exhalations of *humph* from Zari, she reemerged with Max over her shoulder. "Now you may be able to help," she told Fia. "I need only for you to guide him to the floor."

Fia crouched down to nearly eye level with Zari. With a hefty shrug, Zari lifted Max's torso from her shoulder and let him fall back into Fia's waiting hands. Fia tried to lower his shoulders to the floor but lost her balance and fell with him. She landed on her butt with his head and shoulders in her lap. She stifled a gasp, though she wasn't sure why. If anything were going to break the trance Zari had him in, it would have been the fall, not her escaping breath.

When he remained still, she released the breath she had taken in and reached out to stroke his hair. She hesitated, her hand inches from his head, a sick feeling in her stomach. *He doesn't trust me,* she thought, lowering her hand to her side.

She met Zari's eyes as the woman lifted herself back out of the subbasement. What little Fia could see of the space was now dark, and the aroma of extinguished candles rose behind Zari.

Zari nodded, a gesture Fia took as encouragement. She hesitated again, more afraid to touch Max than anything she could remember. And again, Zari gave her a deep nod.

With her breath trapped in her chest, certain her heart had stopped the moment she fell to the floor and hadn't restarted, Fia rested her hand against Max's temple, where the purple-black bruise had faded to shades of yellow and green. She laced her fingers through his hair, combing them back toward herself.

Max shuddered, and Fia jerked her hand away, turning wide eyes to Zari, who was now crouched beside her.

Zari reached out, looping her arms under Max's, and pulled him into a bear hug. She lifted him to his feet, then pulled him off them again to carry him like a too-old child into the bathroom across the hall.

Fia followed, her hands shaking and tears threatening at the edges of her vision. *He doesn't even trust me when he doesn't know it's me.*

By the time she reached the bathroom, Zari had already laid Max on his back in the claw-foot bathtub, legs and arms propped up on either side. "I advise against restraints. He may fight you—I hope he fights you—and I don't want to cause any more physical damage than has already been caused."

Fia nodded, still afraid to speak. She knew any level of panic she caused Max in this moment would soon be erased, but she couldn't bear to see him in that state again.

"Ice," Zari coached, nodding at the bags. Fia handed her one and kept another for herself. They each picked up a bag and, in unison, poured it out over Max's torso. As the second and third bags were emptied, Fia was ready with the fourth.

From a cabinet, Zari produced one of the most truly modern things Fia had seen in this house-turned-curio-shop: a touchless thermometer. She cleared ice away from a small plot of real estate on Max's chest and aimed the device at one of the gray-and-black orchids.

"Ninety-eight. I suppose I should have checked his normal temperature before starting. You will check his radial pulse for me, to get a base? Then check again when he becomes hypothermic: ninety-five or ninety-four. We will see how quickly his temperature drops." She tried the device again. "Ninety-seven two."

When the thermometer beeped the desired temperature, Fia checked Max's pulse a second time. It was faint, but she could still feel it. "Should we wait?"

For a long moment, Zari said nothing. Then: "Please check again."

This time, Fia could barely find the spot on Max's wrist where she knew his pulse point had been. She shook her head, and Zari stepped back out of the way, letting Fia climb into the tub with Max.

Fia swallowed hard on a heavy lump in her chest and filled her lungs with air.

She turned the water up to full power and put her hands

against Max's shoulders, pushing them down into the water. "I'm so sorry," she whispered as the break in the surface sealed over the sharp angles of his face.

The trance broke, and Max's eyes gaped, meeting Fia's, flashing wildly with fear and panic. He was small and wiry, but he still outweighed Fia by twenty, maybe thirty, pounds. He began to thrash against her, and she pushed all she had against his chest to keep his nose and mouth from breaking the surface.

Deciding she didn't have enough strength in just her hands, Fia leaned forward, resting her elbows against his shoulders and putting her own face in the water. She drew her head back, took another breath into her lungs, and laid her chest on Max's, her forearms locked across his collarbone.

He continued to thrash, and her arms and chest ached from the cold. Just as she was certain she wouldn't be able to hold him any longer, he stopped moving. She collapsed against him, her lungs burning from holding her breath. She lifted her head free of the water, which now spilled over the side of the tub onto the ceramic tiles below, took another deep breath, and laid back down, her limbs heavy and her eyes closed. She needed to hold him like that for a minute or two, to make sure the shadow had time to leave . . . however it might do that.

She wondered if it would leave or just die. If it left, would it pour out his ears, nose, and eyes in a cloud of black smoke and fade into the shadows of the bathroom?

The red darkness behind her eyelids shifted and faded, until swirls of brilliant blue and blinding white had replaced it. Her once-heavy limbs now felt light, and she felt as if she were floating. The smell of spent matches and rotten eggs mingled with something sweetly floral.

Orchids.

SIXTEEN

Fia's lungs burned, and she coughed, hard enough she thought she might vomit. Searing white light flooded her brain. She sat up so abruptly, she slammed her shoulder into the edge of the claw-foot bathtub.

Her heart pounded in her ears. Her eyes darted back and forth, assessing her surroundings. Ceramic tiles in cream and shades of blue stretched out beneath her. Directly ahead of her was the cylindrical base of a pedestal sink, the wall behind it covered in wood-finished wainscoting.

Between Fia and the sink, Zari crouched low, her shirt wet and her face drawn with worry.

Fia coughed. "Where's Max?" She tried to stand but slipped on the wet tiles.

"He is still in the ice." Zari pulled Fia to her feet. "Your research suggested reviving you was more important in the moment. If you are . . ."

Before Zari could finish, Fia climbed into the bathtub, which was still filled with ice, though considerably less than before. Zari had drained the water, leaving the nude Max where he had been. Fia straddled Max's hips and leaned close to his face.

Though she couldn't remember the last time she had considered the steps, Fia ran through checking Max's vitals, hoping for the opposite signs than she would ordinarily hope for. She checked to see if he was breathing—he wasn't—and listened for his heartbeat—it had stopped.

"Fiammetta, should I help you move him?"

Fia looped her arms beneath Max's, hauling him up against her chest. She worked to stand, holding him against her, grateful she still wore her sneakers for some traction. Zari moved quickly, first stabilizing Fia as she swung her right leg over the side of the tub, then lifting Max's legs to keep Fia from dragging them behind her.

The two women laid Max on the floor, and Fia dropped to her knees beside him. More old memories of first-aid training in the convent came back to her. She stacked her hands, right over left, lacing her fingers together. With the heel of her left hand against Max's sternum, she used the force of her dominant hand to press deeply and firmly into his chest.

"One, two, three . . ."

She called out her counts as she pressed down, putting all her weight into the compressions. When she reached thirty, she pinched Max's nose with the fingers of her left hand and used her right hand to pull down on his jaw. Covering his mouth with her own, she blew—once, twice—before returning to his chest.

She had repeated the pattern several times when Zari leaned down on the other side of his body. "Fia," she said softly.

"No!" Fia shouted before starting the compressions again. She counted to thirty before telling Zari she wasn't giving up. She shifted to breathe for Max again, and Zari picked up the compressions, calling out her own count as she did.

"*Un, deux, trois . . .*"

When Zari reached *trente*, Fia breathed again.

This time, Max coughed hard, filling Fia's mouth with water. She lifted his shoulders from the floor, turning him so he could cough up what was left, before backing away until her shoulders hit the wall. She continued trying to get away, sliding up the wall as she watched Max's shoulders heave. The sound of his cough, wet and abrasive, as though he were coughing up wet sand, made her cringe.

She caught a glimpse of herself in the mirror.

Parts of her hair were still wet, clinging to her forehead or standing out from her scalp. The whites around her green eyes were lined with threads of bright red, and her flushed cheeks glistened with tears.

Fia glanced down to see Zari behind Max, who was still coughing, holding his hair back away from his face. Fia fought to keep her feet in the room with them, pressing her back against the textured paint of the bathroom wall.

When Max had stopped coughing, he turned his face toward Fia. He jerked backward, knocking Zari off-balance, causing them both to fall back against the bathtub. Max scrambled to find his feet, his eyes wide and dark.

Fia succumbed to the will of her feet, turning from the frightened man, only to find Zari had locked the three of them in the room. The old door still required the use of a skeleton key to open it once it was locked.

"Zari, please let me out."

"No, *chérie*. We came here to do a job; we must finish it. Please look at me." Fia stood fast, her hand still on the doorknob as she pressed her forehead into the wood. "Fiammetta, please turn back to look at me. Look at Max."

"I can't, Zari."

"You can. And you will." Zari reached an arm across Fia's chest, gripping her by the arm and turning her by force. "Have I ever been unkind to you, Fiammetta? Have I ever forced you to do anything that would harm you?" Fia shook her head. "Have I ever forced you to do anything of which you were incapable?" Fia shook her head again. "Then turn around and look at this man who adores you. Why do you think he fears you?"

"Look at him! He's a rabbit looking at a coyote. How can you ask me—"

"No, Fiammetta, that is not what I am asking you. I do not need to know what evidence you have that he fears you. I want to know his reasoning. What is in his mind to make him fear you?"

Fia turned her eyes to Zari's, a wave of confusion passing over her. She didn't understand the question. Or maybe she just didn't understand the difference between the two questions. "What are you asking me?"

"He fears you, that is certain. But what brought him to that place? Why does he fear you?"

"I don't know."

"He fears you because the demons manipulated him to fear you. The demons were able to manipulate him because he cares for you, because you are important to him. Go to him. If your experiment was successful, you will be able to reach him now." Zari stepped aside, giving Fia a firm shove.

Regaining her footing, Fia took one hesitant step forward.

"Go," Zari urged.

Max had squeezed his nude body between the end of the bathtub and the wall, and he sat shaking on the floor, his knees to his chest, his eyes on Fia as she inched closer.

A click behind her caught Fia's attention. She spun to find Zari had taken the opportunity to sneak out of the room, relocking the door behind her, leaving Fia no choice but to try connecting with Max.

She eased her way to the end of the bathtub and sat cross-legged, far enough away from Max that he could see she wouldn't be able to touch him without effort.

Before she could get settled, Max lunged, driving Fia back into the tile floor. Between dilated pupils and rage, his dark eyes were nearly black, and he ground his teeth. He squeezed her arms, digging his fingers into the bone, and lifted her up to slam her back again.

She braced herself, but the impact was sudden enough that her head still hit with a crack that made her vision swim. She pushed back against him, trying to free herself from his grip, but he was fighting with superhuman strength.

He lifted her again, but this time she was prepared and let her shoulders take the brunt of the impact.

She wrapped her legs around his and rolled their bodies so she was on top, but he easily threw her off. She hit the wall with a grunt and struggled to regain her breath. She had only a second to regroup before Max was on her again. He hauled her to her feet and swung her away from him, away from the wall.

Unable to maintain her footing on the wet tiles, she slipped, smashing her shoulder into the edge of the sink. As she went down, she grabbed uselessly at the wall, finding a towel instead and dragging it to the floor with her. Max was on her before she could recover, gripping her by the sides of her head.

Before he could hit her head against the tiles, she wedged her forearms between his and slammed them open, breaking his grip. She shoved him back, swinging hard, her fist connecting with his mouth. He reached up, touching his fingers to his lip to check for blood, before diving at her again. She had barely managed to find her feet when he hit, driving her back into the old wooden door.

The door creaked beneath their combined weight, and Fia shoved Max off her again. This time, he slipped in the water on the floor, falling back into the edge of the bathtub. He grabbed it, securing himself, and used it to push himself back into a standing position.

Fia let him advance on her again, ducking low as he got close and plowing her shoulder into his stomach. He grunted at the force of the impact but recovered quickly. Wrapping his arms around her waist from behind, he pulled her off her feet and dropped her face-first onto the floor.

He placed a wet foot on the back of her neck, holding her down. Pivoting, he swung his other leg over her and sat on her back. He lifted her by the chin, wrenching her head back and leaned in close to her face. She growled. Working her arms under her, she lifted both their bodies, dumping him off.

His back and head hit the wall, and he fell to the floor. Fia climbed on top of him, grabbed him by the shoulders, and pinned him down, but he was stronger and easily wrenched his arms free. He tangled his hands in her hair and pulled her down, pressing her mouth into his.

Fia pulled back, confused, and met his eyes. Something had changed. She was still looking into wide, dark pupils, but realization had washed over him. She let him pull her shirt over her head and lowered her torso into his. She could feel the heat of his body against hers, and she accepted another rough, ravenous kiss that pinched her lips against her teeth. It hurt, but she pressed into it.

He pawed at her jeans, but the wet denim refused to slide against her skin. She reached between their bodies to help, pulling the garment off her hips and down to her thighs. With his feet, Max pushed them free and rolled their bodies with his hips so he was once again in control.

He finished stripping her, tossing her underwear to the side. She wrapped her legs around his back, pulling him down, encouraging him to give her all his weight.

He was rough and hard against her. With each thrust of his hips, she slid back several inches, until she was able to brace her hands against the wall behind her. Max did the same, gripping her wrists, and pushed her until she thought he was going to tear her in two.

She cried out, wrenching her arms free of his grip. She pulled him deeper, deeper into her, clawing at his back and hips. He kissed her neck and collarbones, down one side and up the other, before pressing his mouth into hers to muffle the scream she knew he knew was pending.

It was over almost as suddenly as it started. Max fell against her, panting, tears covering his handsome face. She wrapped her arms around his shoulders, tangling her fingers in his soft hair, and kissed the top of his head before sleep overcame them.

Seventeen

hen they woke, Fia checked the door to find Zari had
unlocked it at some point. She crossed the hall to Zari's
room, hoping to find where Scott and Zari had left Max's
clothes when they stripped him. Clothes in hand, she turned
to go back to the bathroom, only to find Max standing in the
doorway. Startled, she let her eyes drift over his body before
offering him his shirt.

He took it, looked it over, and handed it back to her. "I
can't . . ." Fia took the shirt, trading it for his boxer shorts.
"I'd just as soon throw it all in the garbage." He slipped the
cotton undergarment over his hips and reached for the jeans
she handed him. "They feel . . . I guess I probably have to
wear something, right?"

Fia froze, not certain if she should say something or nod.
After two days of him lying nude in the dirt, she didn't think
Zari would be bothered, but he pulled on his jeans anyway.

"Shoes?"

Fia looked around before shaking her head. "I guess they
must have been in . . ." She shrugged. "I don't see shoes."

Max looked down at his bare feet and wiggled his toes with a sigh. "Okay." He glanced toward the ceiling. "What is that smell?"

"Dinner. You must be starving." To tell the truth, Fia was too. "I got you something. It's upstairs."

The kitchen smelled of roasted pork, and Zari sat at the table, waiting for them. Three places were arranged with plates and glasses, and a pitcher of iced tea rested in the center.

"Fia, Max," she greeted them softly. "Max, how are you feeling?"

Max rubbed at his temples. "I'm really not sure. I feel foggy."

Zari nodded and stood from her chair. "Where are my manners? I have tiptoed around in your psyche for a couple of days, but that does not excuse me from a proper introduction. I am Zari, a friend of Fia's. Please, sit. Dinner is nearly ready. Pour yourself some tea if you would like."

"She's mentioned you. I was supposed to come by here and meet you, but . . ."

"I would have liked to have met you under different circumstances, but I think it may have been serendipitous that I did not. As it was, Fia had an ally with whom you were not acquainted. Do you remember any of the last few days?"

"I think I remember everything and nothing at the same time. Is that possible?"

"*Oui*, I think that is very possible. I think that is to be expected. Much of what you might have remembered before I brought you here had been corrupted."

"Corrupted? How?"

Zari's face twisted, and she hesitated. "If you really want to know, we will tell you, but I think the less you remember, the better off you will be. Fia can fill in the blanks if you need her to."

Max replied with a twist of his own face. "For now."

The three of them sat in silence for several long moments before Zari rose from her chair to tend to the roast. "Pork and potatoes," she explained. "Max, I hope you are a meat eater. You have not had anything for a few days."

"Maybe that explains the fog."

"Some, perhaps."

Max stood. "Let me help." Fia shook her head, already knowing Zari would decline his offer.

"No, no. I have everything under control. Please, *chér*, just rest, relax. You are more exhausted than you may realize."

Max returned to his chair.

"I offer to help all the time," Fia whispered. "Or I did as a kid. She never lets anyone help."

"I can hear you, Fiammetta."

Another few minutes passed, and Zari returned to the table carrying a stone roasting pan filled with potatoes, carrots, and slices of pork. "Help yourselves, please."

They ate in silence, Max shoveling in food the way Fia had the first time she ever sat at this table. He had eaten better than half a plateful of food by the time he slowed enough to engage in some light conversation.

"Zari, your accent."

"*Oui?*"

"You are from Haiti? Your French, though—it's proper French."

"Is there a question in that?" From anyone else, Fia would have expected the question to sound annoyed or insulted. From Zari, though, it was merely encouragement for Max to continue. Her tone was soft, cheerful.

Max blinked, pursing his lips. "I guess, why? I don't mean to be so blunt, but anyone I've ever spoken to—I have a cousin, an expat, living down there—they speak a different French."

Zari smiled. "Kreyol. Yes, it is different. African influences on the language spoken by French colonists, I believe."

"I'm sorry, I don't mean to be rude."

"Not at all, Max. My education was . . . unusual. Many in my village spoke Kreyol as well as, as you say, proper French. I learned both. I elected to speak French as I had more encounters with whites, in New Orleans especially, and the farther north I came."

Fia studied the deep angles of Max's face. Lines of empathetic concern trailed across his forehead and into his eyes.

"In Haiti, whites were tourists. They had no prejudice against me because I belonged. Everyone they spoke with— shopkeepers, housekeepers in their resorts—spoke Kreyol. Higher positions, concierges perhaps, would often speak French to them to be more accessible. But villagers and common folk—from us, they expected to hear Kreyol.

"In New Orleans, the Creole is not always met the same way. People living there understand and accept it. Visitors have different ideas. Visitors think it is the sound of an uneducated swamp dweller, an image not made better by popular media."

"So you speak French instead of Kreyol to blend in?"

Listening to Max and Zari, Fia felt a wave of embarrassment for having never asked. She had accepted, without question, Zari's scattered use of French as normal. She guessed that was the point Zari was making: the farther away she moved from Haiti, the less people expected her to speak Kreyol.

Zari placed a hand softly over Fia's, meeting her eyes with a gentle expression. "You did not know to ask, *chérie*. Max has had the experience of native speakers. He recognized the difference."

Now Fia saw a different look of concern on Max's face. "Zari, can you . . . ? Fia didn't say . . ."

Zari smiled, placing her other hand over Max's. "*Tu es franc*, Max; it is nice. That is another question Fiammetta has always wished to ask but never felt it would be proper. It is true; I can occasionally read the thoughts of others. I think it is more that I am a good interpreter of expressions and body language—and that Fiammetta makes her faces very loudly— but I think sometimes I do hear the words you are thinking. Alas, it is no more than a parlor trick."

They finished their meal quietly, with Zari asking Max casual questions about his life. Fia listened, trying to determine if Zari's questions were out of genuine interest, checking into his memories, or a combination of the two. Ultimately, she guessed it didn't matter; Max seemed to be doing much better than he had even earlier in the meal. The more Zari kept him talking, the more relaxed his posture became. As they cleaned up their plates, Fia felt like she was back with the Max she had taken home following one of his band's concerts, before he was exposed to demons and phoenixes, monster-hunting nuns, or anything about her world.

She wished he could be that Max.

With the table cleaned up and the leftover roast prepared for storage, Max stretched his arms over his head, yawning. Zari leaned into Fia, speaking softly.

"I think it may be good for Max to go with you. Sleep at your apartment. All I have here is the children's beds. He has slept there without trouble, but now that he is not afraid of you, I think he will be more comfortable with you. I would say take him to his own bed, but I am not confident he should be alone."

"He has roommates too. If something happened, they might freak out."

Zari nodded. "Are you comfortable taking him to your place?"

"I think so." Fia watched Max wander off from the table for a moment before turning back to Zari. "I didn't find shoes?"

Zari shook her head. "He was not wearing them when we brought him out of the basement. I would say they are buried beneath Mother Agnes's destruction."

"I figured as much. I'll have to figure something out."

"You can call Father Scott if you need help. Or you can bring him back here. You know where there is a key?"

Fia nodded. She had never felt comfortable using the key in the past, but if she needed help in a hurry, she knew she might finally have to.

"Max, are you comfortable going home with Fia?"

Max, who had taken interest in one of Zari's tchotchkes, spun back to the women, his eyes wide with surprise. "I-I don't see why not."

Fia shrugged. "I guess it's back to my place, then." She stepped around Zari to retrieve the chocolate she had bought from the icebox. "Thank you. For everything."

Zari replied with a gentle smile, pressing a kiss to Fia's forehead.

Max eased his car into the space once held by Fia's SUV and cut the engine. "What happened to the Scout?"

"It's a long story."

"Is that why you were driving this? Is it my fault?"

Fia's nerves prickled, and her muscles tightened. She

didn't blame him for what had happened to her and her car, but the response had been involuntary. Max spoke again before she could answer.

"I'm sorry all this happened."

"Max, none of this . . . if anything, I'm the one who owes you . . . I think I'm going to be apologizing for years, though I wouldn't blame you if—"

"If I hadn't stormed out . . ." He reached across the console and squeezed her hand. "Let's just go inside."

Inside the apartment, Max stopped short. "Max? Are you . . . ?" Fia let the question fall short as she watched Max cross the open space to the stacks of cases in the corner.

He picked up the largest of the cases, one of the hard leather ones, and examined it quickly before setting it aside. He reached for the long, narrow bag propped against the wall and unzipped it. Fia watched quietly as he pulled the silver stands from the bag, one by one, and set them up to his side. When he opened one of the smaller nylon bags, Fia quietly picked up one of the metal bar stools and moved it closer to the center of the room, climbing atop it.

With a quick glance at the forest of stands, Max grabbed one, splayed out a set of arms, and rested the snare drum on it, giving it a test thump with a knuckle. He opened another hard case, this one flat and wide, and pulled out one of the brass discs. With the cymbal tucked between one arm and his still-bare chest, he pulled another of the stands closer. He seemed to be falling into a rhythm, spinning a wing nut at the top of the stand, loosening it quickly. He palmed both the nut and the felt pad beneath it, slipped the cymbal onto its post, fitting it snugly over a second felt pad, then replaced the first pad and nut from his palm.

Each step seemed, to Fia, to be smoother than the one before, and Max had his kit assembled in a matter of minutes.

He took his place on the throne, the snare drum fitted snugly between his knees. After a few subtle tweaks, he slipped a pair of sticks from a bag he had hung off the floor tom and tapped them cautiously on each of the instruments. Seemingly satisfied with the arrangement, he began a steady cadence on the closed high hat, alternating offbeats between the snare and bass drums.

Fia felt a strange calm wash over her as his hands flew from one drum to the next, filling her apartment with meaty thumps from the bass drum and crisp reports from the snare. Soon he was adding bright, melodious cymbal chimes and looked completely at peace.

Fia had let herself get lost so deeply in Max's euphoria that when he stopped suddenly, the silence raised gooseflesh over her arms and shoulders. He tucked the sticks back into the bag, stood up from his throne, and climbed out from behind the kit. He walked right past Fia without even pausing, heading straight for the bedroom. After a second, Fia followed, realizing in the stillness how exhausting the day had been.

Fia woke as the bed shook. In the dark room, she reached for the bedside lamp, but Max thrashed toward her, and she dodged to avoid his fist. Hoping it was the right decision, she grabbed his swinging hands and pinned them to the bed, climbing on top of him.

"Fia," he muttered, sounding panicked. "Let her go! Where are you taking her?"

She moved her hands from his wrists to his shoulders, holding him down the best she could while trying not to hurt him, and leaned in toward his face. "Max," she whispered gently. "Max, it's okay. I'm right here." She leaned back, resting on his thighs, and pulled his torso into hers. She stroked his hair, pressing his head into the curve of her neck. "Shh, I'm right here. I'm fine. You're fine."

She didn't know whether she believed her own words, but she did her best to make him believe them.

He relaxed some, letting her comfort him and melting into her chest, before shoving her away with inhuman strength and screaming with the full force of his lungs. Fia tumbled back, hitting the floor with a thud that knocked the breath from her lungs. She gasped for air as Max did the same.

Fia clambered to her feet and darted to the side of the bed. Max's eyes were open, and he was fighting to breathe. She reached out slowly, hesitantly, and rested a hand on his shoulder.

He jerked away from her, scooting to the other side of the bed. Even in the dark, Fia could see his eyes flashing like a threatened wildcat's. She shrank back, dropping her hands to her sides, feeling lost.

She didn't think she needed help from the others, not enough to call Scott, but she didn't know what she did need. Slowly, she stepped toward the balcony door, choosing to open the curtains instead of turning on a light. She watched as Max came out of the nightmare, panting, his chest heaving. His breathing slowed, though not as much as Fia would have liked, and he released his grip on the bedsheets. His eyes, which she had thought were at risk of simply ejecting their orbs, narrowed, his eyelashes once again obscuring the edges of his irises.

The light from the streets outside cast long, dark shadows on the room and transformed Max's frightened face into something twisted, unnatural. Fia moved back to the bed, climbing up slowly, and reached out to him. "Max? Max, can you hear me?"

"Oh my god, Fia, I-I watched them pull you out of that room, dragging you. You couldn't even get your feet under you. I screamed for them to bring you back, then there was a noise like a gunshot." Tears poured from his eyes, glittering on his cheeks in the scant light from the window.

"It's not real, Max. It's not real." She felt tears on her own cheeks as she pulled him into her for a second time. "It's not real; I'm right here. I'm okay. I'm okay." She repeated the statement until she wasn't sure if she was trying to convince Max or herself.

When she woke again, she was still sitting mostly upright with Max wrapped in her arms. He had, at some point, wrapped his legs around her, and they were twisted together in a grotesque pretzel. She attempted to straighten, only to be greeted by a screaming protest from her back.

Fia worked as delicately as she could to untwine her body from Max's without disturbing him. The sun had come up over the prairie far enough that it was shining in the balcony window. She considered closing the curtains and leaving Max in the dark but decided that was too much movement and might disturb him. Instead, she slipped out of the room and into the bathroom and started filling the oversize bathtub, with only the amber-colored motion lights inches above the floor to light her way.

She stripped out of what little she had been wearing and climbed into the hot bath, flipping the switch to turn on the massage jets. She leaned back, letting the water splash around her and the air bubbles pound against her aching muscles.

"Fia?" Max's voice was soft, gentle. She opened her eyes to find him standing at the edge of the bathtub, nude, his face dark with shadows. She scooted out of the way so he could climb in with her, and he wrapped himself around her as he did. "Am I going to be okay?"

EIGHTEEN

Fia refilled the bathtub, wanting to stay wrapped in Max as long as she could. The water had always been calming to her, and she felt like he was getting the same energy from it.

When they were both sufficiently pruned, they climbed out, dried off, and returned to the bedroom to dress. Max looked at the clothes he had to wear and grimaced. She had thrown his jeans in the wash before going to bed the night before, trying, more than anything, to get the dirt of the basement out of them, but he told her they still felt weird.

"Do you want to go get something else from your house?"

Still staring at the jeans lying on the bed, where he had put them when he had taken them off again, he shook his head. "Can you get them for me? I can't put those on, and I don't want to leave here without them."

Fia watched him for a moment before nodding. "Of course. You're going to be okay here by yourself? Do you want me to call Sc—"

"No! No, please no. I'll be fine. Just need some pants."

Fia grabbed the credit card she kept stashed in her dresser, checked the size on the discarded garment, and leaned in to kiss Max gently on the cheek. "I'll be quick."

She headed out of the apartment, on her way downtown.

The open-air mall was the closest to her neighborhood but still a fifteen-minute drive under the best circumstances. She slipped into a parking garage, going to the top level out of habit. She rode the elevator back down and hopped onto the free bus, riding it to a section of the mall consisting of several small stores and half a dozen restaurants. Once off the bus, she looked around, gauging where to go to find something for Max. She ultimately decided on a trendy young adult store she had shopped at once or twice.

On her way out of the store, she shifted course and ducked into a nearby candy store, thinking she'd grab another treat for Max. Realizing she didn't know what he might like, she grabbed a mixed box of chocolate truffles and one each of the cookies and got back on the bus to the parking garage.

When she got off the elevator, she stopped dead in her tracks. Leaning against the back of the little white race car was Sister Ruth, the younger nun from the outreach center. When Fia started walking again, so did the nun.

"Fiammetta."

"Do I know you?"

"No, but I know you."

"I've got chocolate. Can I at least throw that in the car?"

"Please. I am not here to cause trouble. I just want to talk."

Fia gestured toward the car. "Then let's talk."

"You came to our outreach looking for answers that we did not give you."

"I kind of got that impression."

"Sister Abigail did not know what to make of your lie."

Fia puffed a laugh out through her nose. "So you knew."

"We have worked with Father Donovan for many years. We knew the young children in his care before he was forced to close his home. Neither you nor your friend were part of that group. You are too old."

Fia waved to the other side of the car. "Get in, Sister, please. Take advantage of the air-conditioning. Let me drive you back to the outreach center." Sister Ruth looked the car over and, after a moment, accepted Fia's offer.

"How did you know who I was?" Fia asked, turning the key in the ignition.

"As I mentioned, we have worked with Father Donovan. Which means we are also familiar with Mother Agnes and Father McGregor."

"Do you know . . . ?" Fia didn't know how to finish.

"What they are involved with? Yes, I do. We do."

"Just you and . . . did you say Abigail?"

Sister Ruth nodded deeply. "Yes, just Sister Abigail and me. As far as anyone else knows, Father Donovan works independently, disconnected from any organized church. His story is that he worked as a parish priest for several years, until he felt he could do more good on the streets, working directly with people who didn't come into church. And all of that is mostly true."

"I can see that. What is his connection to Saint Anthony's?"

"Straight to the point. Father Donovan, and his newest young companion, Sister Annabel, had been trying to encourage Father Ariaz . . . how much do you know about Armando Ariaz?"

"I know he's dead."

Sister Ruth's face drained of color, her dark eyes wide,

aghast at the abrupt delivery of Fia's announcement. "He is, indeed. But before that, what did you know?"

Fia pulled out of the parking space, heading toward the ramp out of the garage. "I know he is, or was, involved with some—shit." Fia braked as she rounded the corner to the next level and nearly collided with a large dark mass. "Sorry, Sister, but this guy . . ." She let the apology trail off, realizing the demon in her path had frozen time, leaving Sister Ruth frozen as well. "Right, that's how we're doing this." Deciding it didn't matter, she left the engine running and climbed out of the car. "Irzelen?"

The demon, who had been encased in his own wings, unfolded but remained in a crouched position. "Miss Drake, what have you learned since last we spoke?"

"Was that real? Were you really in my bedroom?" When he didn't answer, she continued. "I did what you told me."

"You ended your lover's life?"

"I did."

"But you brought him back."

"That wasn't a question. Yes. I did."

"Mortals. You still seek immortality after so many millennia. I admire the tenacity, if not the intelligence." He drew his long claws over his chin, stroking it thoughtfully. "That is not what I asked you, however."

"You asked what I learned. I'm not sure what you want to know."

"Did killing your lover reveal anything to you? Are you any closer to returning my property?"

Fia shook her head. She guessed it wouldn't do any good to lie. "I may have taken a step backward."

Irzelen nodded toward the car. "You have met someone new? Does she have anything to offer you?"

"I don't know. You froze her before I could find out." She thought of Max back at the apartment, waiting for her. "When you freeze things around me like this, does everything get frozen? Because I left a naked man in my apartment, waiting for me to bring him pants."

"Human modesty," the demon scoffed. "Yes, if we need time stopped, we can stop everything."

"Do we notice when you do that?"

"You are straying from the point, Miss Drake."

"But now I kind of want to know this."

"Perhaps that is something to take up with your angel when you are not on a time-sensitive mission. The clock is ticking, Miss Drake. The longer my demons exist on this plane, the more control they will have over their mortal summoner."

"But death is death, right? I should be able to kill them no matter what?"

Irzelen shrugged, an astutely human gesture of dismissal. He didn't know the answer to Fia's question, nor did he care to find out. Fia had been tasked to return his demons to him. How she did it was of little consequence to him, but he had asked her to do it in case it required a mortal death.

"Max had a nightmare. He's convinced I had a hand in his abduction—"

"But you did."

She started to protest but couldn't follow through. "Yeah, fine, I did, but not in the way he thinks. He thinks I was there, with him in the dungeon. That I had been abducted too and they turned me against him. I think that's his working theory, anyway. How do I know if that shadow is gone?"

"You killed him?"

"Yes."

"By human standards or truly dead?"

"What's the difference?"

"Mortals believe death is the cessation of heart rhythms. Death—true death, when a mortal soul is free to leave the body—happens a little later than that."

"I think truly dead. I don't know how long, but Zari had to get me out of the water first—"

"Your practitioner is a powerful sorceress. I trust she knows the difference between human standards of death and divine standards. Surely she allowed your lover—"

"Stop. Saying that. It sounds creepy coming from you. You or Uhlpir, either one. You make it sound so clinical."

"You would prefer mate?"

"God no! Lover it is. Yeah, I'm learning that Zari's got a few more tricks up her sleeve than I realized. You said before you should just leave me to the demons. Why haven't you? Why are you letting me figure this out when it's clearly taking longer than you would like? And while we're talking about time, you've been around for, like, a million years. Why are you getting so fussed over a month?"

"Uhlpir."

"Sorry?"

"Your angel. We have . . . history. I have never seen him so invested in a mortal charge as he is with you."

"History? You know him from before this?"

"We have had, as you might say, a bit of a cat-and-mouse game going for centuries in mortal time."

"That's . . ." She ran through a laundry list of adjectives before settling on, "Weird."

"I think, Miss Drake, that it is time for me to take my leave and put your timeline back in order. You might want to get back in the vehicle so your new friend doesn't think anything is out of order."

With the bone-shattering crunch Fia was growing used to

as part of his shape-shifting routine, the demon became the much-smaller phoenix and flew free of the garage. Fia did as he suggested, climbing back into the car, but not before Sister Ruth asked, "Miss Drake, is everything okay?"

"Peachy. Did you see anything in the . . . ?" She waved her hand toward the front of the car. Sister Ruth shook her head. "I thought I hit something. What were you saying, about Ariaz?"

"Was I? Oh, yes. Being associated with Mother Agnes and Father McGregor, I assume you are privy to some of the seedy underbelly, if you will, of our city."

"Sister, I am up to my belly button in underbellies. If what you are trying not to say is that Armando Ariaz is a demon worshipper and partially responsible for overrunning the city with demons dressed up like humans, I am already fully on that train."

Sister Ruth looked at her hands clutched in her lap. "I should have known. What I have heard of you must be true, then."

"What have you heard? I apparently have a reputation, despite having worked very hard to stay anonymous in most areas of my life."

"You are one of the best hunters the church has seen. Your kill rate is phenomenal."

"I think you can thank Father Scott—Father McGregor—for that. He just kept dropping them, quite literally, on my doorstep for a while. As soon as I was finished with one, another would appear. He claims that all stopped after . . . after I left him in a cave."

"The demon nest north of the city."

"Sister, can I trust you to be completely honest with me at this point?"

"I can try. I can only tell you what I know."

"Of course. But I got the impression you knew more than you were telling me about Terra."

"Ah, I was afraid it would come to that. Miss Drake, I hate to be the one to tell you this, but I am afraid your friend is dead."

NINETEEN

hat do you mean? I don't . . . I mean, what happened?"
Fia had not expected that to be what the nun told her.
She had expected something unpleasant as soon as she had
seen the woman leaning on the back of the car, but for her to
just unceremoniously announce that Terra, Fia's childhood
friend, was dead had taken Fia by surprise.

"I don't know all the details," Sister Ruth explained. "But
as I understand it, she was cornered by one of her bounties
and killed in the process."

"Sister Annabel—who you said has worked with Father
Donovan—said she had met Terra before coming here. Do
you know where this attack took place?" Her instinct was to
test Sister Ruth's knowledge, but she didn't know enough
about Annabel or about Terra's life after leaving the convent
to really challenge the woman.

"If I am correct, I think a small border town in New
Mexico."

Fia nodded. That sounded right based on what Annabel
had recently revealed. "Do you know anything else?"

"I must apologize, Miss Drake. I do not. I cannot imagine the Reverend Mother would not have more details, though. Are you still in contact with her?"

Fia rubbed at her temples. She had a strong feeling Sister Ruth was right, considering how cagey Agnes had been when Fia asked how to get in contact with Terra or someone else who might know how. She guessed this was another conversation she needed to have with the old nun.

"I am sorry, Miss Drake."

"Huh?" She blinked at the nun, taking a second to realize that the nun was misinterpreting her reaction. "No, Sister, that's not—thank you for telling me. I thought she might have been in danger, but I guess . . . either way, I can stop searching for her."

Fia pulled into the lot outside the outreach center, letting her newest ally out at the door. As Sister Ruth climbed out of the car, she took one more opportunity to offer Fia her condolences. Fia replied with a half smile and waited for Sister Ruth to get inside before pulling out of the lot.

"Max?" Fia called out when she got back to the apartment. The silence that answered was heavy and eerie. Fia laid the clothing bag on the bar, put the chocolate in the refrigerator, and tried calling Max again.

This time, the answer came in the form of glass shattering in the bathroom.

Fia ran to see what had happened and found Max in front of the sink, looking bewildered. The floor glittered in the bright lights that surrounded empty wall where a mirror had once hung. Max was staring at his hands, which were covered in blood.

"Max? Are you . . . ?" She didn't finish the question. She knew he wasn't okay. She placed a hand gently on his shoulder.

He turned wild eyes to her, and she flinched, remembering the last time he had looked at her that way. Instead of attacking her, though, he spoke, his smooth, deep voice thready and cracking. "Fia, what was that thing?"

"Thing?"

"In the mirror. I saw something. I came in to brush my teeth because I don't know when I did that last—I'm sorry, I was going to use your toothbrush—but when I turned on the light, there was something in the mirror."

"Something like . . . ? What did it look like?"

"It was me, my face, in the low . . ." He waved a hand toward the floor, indicating the motion lights. As he continued, Fia pulled him back toward the shower to get his bare feet out of the broken glass. She eased him down onto the bench at the back of the shower.

"I turned on the bright lights around the mirror, and the face changed. Something dark, black, like an insect . . ." A wave of realization passed over his face. "That thing in the alley that night, that thing that dropped you onto the asphalt. It looked like that but smaller. Fia, Zari said you'd tell me what I needed to know. What do I need to know?"

"Let's clean you up first, then we'll talk." Fia looked at the glass on the floor and back at Max's feet. "Let me clean up the glass first. Don't move. I'll be right back." She started out of the shower and then turned back, grabbing Max's hands and pulling them straight up. "Elevate the wounds?"

He nodded. "Sure. Sounds right."

Fia crunched through the glass and out to the kitchen to find a broom.

Once she had the glass cleaned up, she pulled Max out of

the shower and led him to the sink. She helped him wash off the blood—which was already clotting and partially dry—assessing the wounds underneath the mess.

"Not as bad as it looks," she said, pulling a tube of antibiotic cream from a drawer. "What do you think?"

Max studied his hands as if they were something he'd never seen before. "I think they look okay."

"Better to keep them clean anyway." Fia pulled a roll of gauze from the same drawer and wrapped it firmly but loosely around the bulk of the wounds, which were spread primarily over his knuckles. "Did you punch the mirror?"

Max shook his head. "I can't . . . I don't remember. I saw that thing, that black thing with the sharp teeth, and then the mirror shattered."

Fia looked around to see if she could find any other clues. She thought he might have used something as a fist pack to intensify the blow, but she didn't see anything. She also didn't see her toothbrush, which he had said he planned to use.

She finished wrapping Max's hands, taping the gauze in place over the ointment, and led him out of the bathroom. "I bought you some things," she said, handing him the bag of clothing.

He reached in and pulled out a pair of boxer shorts. He examined them before setting them aside and pulling out a pair of jeans. He held the jeans up to his hips, twisting to look at how they fell, then set them with the shorts. In the bag were another pair of jeans, more underwear, and a couple of t-shirts, which he held up to his chest.

"Thank you, Fia. You didn't need—"

"Shh," she said, taking the shirts from his hands. "As much as I love this,"—she waved a hand toward his nude body—"you're going to have to get dressed again at some point. And I'm on board with you not wearing the same clothes you wore while . . . so you at least needed something to wear back to your own house."

Max's face fell. "You don't want me to stay here?"

"No! I mean . . . that's not . . . god no, Max, I want you here. As long as you want to stay here. But don't you want your own familiar things? Your own toothbrush?"

"Oh, I guess, probably." He picked up the clothes he had piled on the counter. "We should wash these."

Fia took the stack of new clothes, pulling off tags as she walked, and threw them in the washing machine before returning to Max. "Do you want anything to wear in the meantime?"

"I think I might try sleeping a little more." He turned without waiting for her to respond and headed back toward the bedroom.

Fia considered following him but decided against it. She didn't know what he wanted from her—and she wasn't sure he knew either. She picked up her phone and found Scott in the contacts.

"Can you come by here?" she asked when he picked up.

"Is something wrong?"

"I don't really know. I just need . . . can you just come by?"

"I'll be right there."

Fia disconnected the call and threw her phone unceremoniously onto the leather sofa. She stepped out onto the balcony in time to see Max draw the curtains over the bedroom door. She leaned heavily on the railing and looked out over the city to the south.

She soaked in the serenity of a silent skyline, of knowing the noise and chaos it concealed. It wasn't quite like the skylines of other major cities. Where Chicago or New York might stretch across the full panorama, Denver was isolated to a handful of ultra-tall buildings reaching their fingers above the medium-tall buildings. From here, she could see the swooping edge of the football stadium and the narrow cylinder of the tower drop ride at the amusement park that sat in the heart of the city.

She felt a slight tingle of electricity and pulled her attention from the far distance to the building next door. The angelic form had materialized on the low roof where the demon had been not thirty-six hours before. Scott was tall; Uhlpir was taller, better than seven feet. While Irzelen was broad and bulky, Uhlpir was slender, boasting much the same body type as Scott: tall, lanky, and all arms and legs. The angel's wings could obscure a school bus without much effort, and Fia had seen them stir dirt and gravel for a couple dozen feet in all directions with the slightest movement.

Uhlpir locked eyes with Fia, and she pointed to the street below.

Down at street level, Fia hiked her butt up onto a concrete planter box, drawing her legs into herself. Father Scott leaned against the box beside her.

"What's going on?"

"We killed him."

"Pardon?"

"Zari and I—well, I drowned Max. In the bathtub. At Zari's."

"Fia! Are you—"

"He's okay. I think. It was Irzelen's suggestion. You said I might need him. And he showed up, told me if the demons had been monkeying around in Max's brain . . . so I killed him. Then I brought him back. But he's still—I suppose nightmares are to be expected. And hallucinations?"

"Are you asking me?"

"Kind of." She quickly ran through everything that had happened, starting with her witching-hour conversation with the demon, trying her best to tell the story in order without leaving anything out. "And now he's upstairs asleep. At least, I hope he is. He said he was going to try. He closed the blackout curtains in my room, and then you showed up."

Scott sat silently, long enough Fia started to worry she had done something wrong. "Irzelen told you to kill Max?" The tone of his voice sent a shiver across Fia's exposed flesh.

"Yes?"

"And Zari went along with it?"

"She wasn't excited about it, but she saw the logic."

"Fia . . ." He let whatever he was going to say drift away on the breeze, but Fia had a feeling what was coming wasn't going to be nearly so light. "You should have come to me first. There are things—I could have helped you do it safely. You could have seriously injured Max with this stunt—"

"Stunt? You said—"

"Did you think about the potential for brain damage?" His voice remained level and cool, but Fia almost wished he were shouting.

"Actually, that's all I was thinking about—"

"And what if it hadn't worked? You should have come to me."

Fia drew back as the edges of Scott's words sliced through the air between them. But she didn't know if she wanted to fight back or walk away. She hadn't liked the idea Irzelen had presented to her, but she hadn't had anything better either. And after all the time Scott had spent with Zari and Max, she had guessed he hadn't either. And she told him as much.

"It's done now. And I think it worked, but he's still—"

"If he's still seeing the demon, there's a very good chance it didn't. Fia, you are working without a net, and you desperately need one. I cannot believe—"

"Hey, stop yelling at me. I handled it. Isn't that what you keep telling me when I ask about stuff? 'It's been handled.' There are dead bodies rotting—or did you feed them to the piranha demons?"

"Irzelen told you this was not the first time he and I have met?"

"He did. Is that something I should know about? He said you've never gone to the mat like this for any other human."

More silence from the angel in priest's clothing.

"Scott—Uhlpir, is there something else I should know?"

"I honestly don't believe there is." His tone was still short, but Fia thought it was softening. He was angry, and she guessed she understood. She would have been, too, if the roles had been reversed. If she were honest, she probably would have been more than angry. "I'm sure you can imagine Irzelen and I have had interactions throughout the millennia—"

"No, this wasn't 'have had interactions.' This was history. He said you had history. What kind of history? I thought we weren't keeping secrets anymore." She sighed, knowing that had never been true. They might have all agreed not to keep secrets, but between Terra's death and Rebecca's child, she knew the agreement hadn't been anything more than words.

"It is really not all that he suggests. I have been working in this capacity—guarding hunters—for . . . years. Decades. I have lost track. We have had what might be more than our fair share of run-ins. Compared to what he might have had with other angels, especially."

"He said 'cat and mouse.'" She wanted to press and find out what that phrase meant in the current situation, but she decided she was better off bashing her head on the bricks behind her. "Why does he think I'm special? Why does everyone keep telling me that? Why do *you*? Why did you bring me that bow back then?"

"You are a skilled hunter, one of the best—"

"Forget it." She climbed down from the wall and started for the door. "You're not going to tell me anything real, so just forget it."

"Fia, please—"

"No. I'm done. I'm going back upstairs to make sure Max is still sleeping, or at least not breaking any more mirrors."

"Is that what you wanted to talk to me about?"

"Partly. I just needed to talk. To someone. But yeah, I need to know what he's seeing. If these hallucinations and nightmares are normal. If he'll ever get past them. If I did the right thing, listening to the demon's advice. And for the record, it was Zari's suggestion we keep it from you. I asked if we should get your help; she said no."

"Do you think he's ready to see me?"

Fia shrugged. "I think his memories of what happened in that dungeon are mostly gone. He knows he was there; he knows something horrible happened. But I think he's done consciously thinking we were all there, beating him up and torturing him." She paused, feeling her confidence fade. "I think."

"If you don't mind, I'd like to come up and see him."

"I hope he's sleeping."

"That is fine. I am not looking for conversation. I just want to assess the damage for myself. Seeing is believing, right?"

Fia led Scott back upstairs to the apartment. Before leading him into the bedroom, she tossed Max's new clothes into the dryer. "He doesn't want to wear the clothes he was wearing when he was abducted. I can't say I blame him, but it seems like a strange thing to fixate on."

Scott nodded. "It is a psychosomatic reaction. He doesn't remember much of what happened, but he remembers the clothes he was wearing."

"Something like that. Let me check on him before you come in?"

"Of course."

Fia kicked out of her shoes and padded through the bathroom, into the bedroom. The room was dark, almost as dark as a moonless midnight, but she could make out the shape of Max against the white of her sheets. She inched closer, around the foot of the bed, until she could see that he was asleep—soundly, she thought. She peeked back out into the main room of the apartment where she had left Scott and beckoned him to join her, flipping on the bathroom light as she made her way back.

Fia climbed into the bed, lying so she faced Max. She whispered to him.

"Don't wake him," Scott coached. "See if you can get him talking without waking him. I think it may be less traumatic that way."

"Max?" Fia whispered again.

He murmured a soft reply.

"Can you hear me?"

"Mm."

Fia looked at Scott without moving too much, urging him into the conversation. "Max? Can you tell us what you remember about the people who abducted you?"

He told Scott a similar story to the one he had told Zari under hypnosis. Unlike that story, however, his words were now choppy, sleep garbled. And this time, Annabel had been left behind. "Knocked out, maybe they killed her. Woman, ribs, shot."

Scott glanced at Fia questioningly.

"He told us before that the woman we had in the holding cell, the one with the broken ribs, injected him with something," she explained.

Scott nodded and pressed on. "What do you remember after that?"

Max muttered something Fia couldn't make out. Now that her eyes had adjusted to the dim light from the bathroom, she could see his eyes darting back and forth behind his eyelids. The pulse point on the side of this throat danced as his heart began to pound. She turned worried eyes back to Scott, wondering if they should stop and take a break for a while.

Scott either didn't get the message or didn't agree. "Max? What did you see in the mirror?"

"Mirror."

"Yes, Max, the mirror. You told Fia you saw something and that's why you broke the mirror. Can you tell me what you saw?"

"Black. Insect? Not my face." Max's breathing grew shallow, rapid, like a pant but more frantic. Sweat beaded on his forehead and in the deep creases of his chest.

Scott placed his fingers against Max's temples, muttering something that sounded to Fia like humming. The only indication she had that he was forming words was the movement of his lips. The familiar divine buzz filled Fia's head. But Max fell silent again, his breathing slowing to normal.

Scott stayed there like that, his expression and posture that of someone trying to find a specific bird in the forest, for several long moments.

"Well?" Fia asked when Scott released Max and stepped back away from the bed.

"It is going to take some time, but I think he is recovering. He saw a demon—one of the summoned horde—in the mirror earlier, but it was a memory, not a remnant. Though I would have discouraged it had I known your plan—"

Fia raised a finger to hush Scott and pointed to Max, who was quiet and still again. She gestured for Scott to follow her back into the living room.

"You told me," she said once they were somewhere she didn't think they'd wake Max. "You told me not to ask Irzelen for help finding Max because *you* thought I might need his help with something bigger. *You.* You told me to wait. Now you are telling me I was wrong for taking the advice you basically predicted I was going to need?"

"No, Fia, that is not what I—I would have discouraged you from your plan because of the harm it could have done to you. To both of you. What would you have done if you had not been able to revive him? What if you had caused real damage? How did you know how—"

She cut him off, ignoring all but his first question. "But I was. I did. He's fine. You just said so yourself. He's going to need some time, but he's fine."

The lines of concern in Scott's flushed face deepened as Fia spoke.

"What? Why are you looking at me like that?"

"I sincerely hope you are right, Fia. For both your sakes."

Twenty

Fia closed the door behind Scott, flipping the deadbolt, and crossed back to the center of the room. She stood staring at Max's drums for a long time, deciding what to do next. She didn't want to leave him alone, but she didn't want to interrupt him if he was finally resting.

She circled around behind the kit and pulled her fingers over the vinyl of his throne. She did the same to the pouch of sticks hanging off the large drum on the side. She touched a toe gently to each of the three pedals in succession, pushing at them softly, operating them without making any noise. Her stomach tightened, a feeling she was beginning to equate with guilt, and she stepped back out into the open floor.

Fia folded her legs in under herself, lowering herself to the floor, placing her nose level with the top edge of the bass drum. She drew in a deep breath—*in, two, three, four, five*—and let it go—*out, two, three, four, five*. She did that several more times, training her eyes on the little window in the front of the drum and letting them blur out of focus.

Meditation had never been something she was good at. Zari had taught her techniques when they had first met, when Fia was a teen. In those sessions, Zari had explained that what worked for her would not necessarily be what worked for everyone else, and vice versa. As she grew older and gained more control over her life, music had truly become Fia's meditative technique of choice. The concert where she had met Max had been a way of decompressing after getting caught and nearly strangled by a bounty. Music and sex had been her meditation for years.

In this moment, however, she didn't feel like either was appropriate. So she focused on more traditional techniques.

Something must have worked because the next thing Fia knew, the alarm on the clothes dryer signaled the end of the cycle, startling her out of her trance. With a heavy, exasperated sigh, she exploded from her lotus pose, splaying herself across the hardwood floor on her back, limbs outstretched. Her head hit the floor with a thump harder than she had meant for it to, and she groaned. "Ow. Damn it." She rubbed at the point of impact, then let her head rest back on the floor and her arm flop back to its respective side.

She had only been there a few seconds when she peeled herself up off the hardwood and padded into the kitchen. She dug one of the chocolates from the box in the refrigerator, sniffing it in a futile attempt to identify its contents, and took a bite.

"Plain," she muttered.

She gave it another look to see if she could pick out the remaining plain truffles from the assortment. It was a simple little dome with tone-on-tone chocolate drizzle across the top. She popped the rest of the candy in her mouth, wondering how many of each flavor were in the assortment. She flipped the box over, hoping for a key or even just a list of varieties, but instead found just nutrition facts—*Nutrition facts on candy: absurd*—and a list of ingredients, paired with a warning that *This product was processed in a facility that may have processed nuts, milk, or shellfish.*

"Shellfish? Well, that's unsettling," Fia said aloud before returning the box to the refrigerator.

She crossed the expansive great room to the modern-style black-and-silver sofa. For all its leather upholstery and ninety-degree angles, it was a remarkably comfortable piece of furniture. She sat and looked out through the floor-to-ceiling window and door that led to the balcony.

It had only been about seven weeks since the night a phoenix had smashed through the balcony door, interrupting Fia's first night with Max. She felt like it had been seven years.

Even though she had a full view of downtown from her balcony, seated on the couch inside, she couldn't see much more than a few scant clouds spray-painted across an azure canvas. After a few minutes of watching puffs of white drift across her vision, Fia let herself tip over onto her side, drawing her legs up into her torso and resting her head on her arm. In another few minutes, she was asleep.

She woke to a hand in her hair. Bleary-eyed, she turned toward the source. Max had apparently woken sometime after she had laid down and had pulled his new clothes out of the dryer. Now dressed in jeans and a simple black t-shirt, he crouched at the end of the sofa, reaching over the arm to stroke Fia's hair.

"Hey," she croaked out in an unreliable voice. Clearing her throat, she sat up and tried again. "How did you sleep?"

"Dreams." He sighed, joining her. "Lots of dreams." He curled his legs up onto the seat of the sofa and leaned into her, resting his head on her shoulder.

"Do you remember any of them?"

He shook his head. "I don't think so. At least no one died."

"Well, that's positive. Are you hungry?"

"I probably should be. What time is it?"

Fia checked her phone. "Three thirty."

"What do you have?"

She shrugged. "It's been a few days since I've really even looked in the refrigerator." There was something simultaneously comfortable and uncomfortable about discussing what was for dinner. Under normal circumstances, their conversation probably would have been normal. But under the current circumstances, it felt forced, awkward. There was an elephant in the room, and she didn't even know what breed it was to be able to address it.

"Max, are you . . . ? How are you feeling? Really."

He sat up, twisting to face her. "Strange. Disoriented."

"I can understand that."

"Fia? What happened to me?"

Fia swallowed hard. He deserved to know. Something.

"I don't know, Max. I mean, I wasn't—you left the safe house after the dust settled. Annabel said she picked you up off the side of the road and was bringing you back when someone ran you—ran her off the road."

"I remember that." He nodded, his eyebrows knitting together over his nose. "I hadn't gotten far on foot, about halfway back to the paved road. Sister Annabel showed up in that big, gold land yacht. She had to go all the way back to the asphalt to turn around. On the way back, we passed a black—blue—dark-colored SUV. Annabel got kind of . . . I guess, panicked, saying there was no reason for anyone to be on that road, that it was essentially all part of the driveway?"

Fia nodded. "I guess. I'm not sure of the particulars of their property boundaries, but it seems to dead-end in that flat outside the house. You didn't see the SUV when you left?"

Max shook his head. "I was fuming. I honestly thought I was walking back to the city. I'd probably be getting back here right about now if it hadn't been—but then, I'm not sure I was much better off the way it played out."

"Do you remember anything else?"

"Sure. Annabel got twitchy, like a rabbit or something, some little prey animal trying to get away from the predator. She just kept checking the mirrors after we passed that SUV. I guess they went all the way to the asphalt to turn around too because it was several minutes before they showed up in the rearview. But once they were there,"—he snapped his fingers—"they were right on us. Annabel tried to speed up, tried swerving to miss them, but ultimately, they were bigger and faster. The driver smashed into the back driver's side fender of the car. We were going fast enough the car spun in the gravel. The nose dipped over the side; I thought we were going down into the ravine. I think I would have preferred that outcome."

"Maybe," Fia agreed. "Then what?"

"Annabel was scrambling. She was bleeding; she hit her head on the window, I guess. Couldn't get her seat belt unfastened. I got mine fine and was reaching to help her when I heard a gunshot. I looked back through the back window but couldn't really see . . . but it looked like . . . that woman the big dude fell on, the one who probably got a few broken ribs for her trouble? I think she's the one who drugged me."

Fia nodded again. "You said that, and the guy knocked Annabel out?"

"I think—I thought, even before—they had a different air to them. Like maybe they were hired muscle, with no dog in the fight, just in it for the money. And I think they were . . ." He tapped his middle and pointer fingers together.

"Married?"

"Together, somehow. Married, friends with benefits. Something. I just didn't get the impression—and then I think they killed another . . . was it the blonde woman?"

"Blonde woman?"

"Their platoon leader, the scary one."

Fia shifted, not certain she was ready to tell Max what had become of Heidi. "No, it was one of the other men. After you left, Rebecca and I took—in the basement, there's a—they have a prison cell, apparently for just this reason. Rebecca and I took that blonde woman and three others—two men and the woman with the broken ribs—and locked them up."

"Who let them go?"

Fia shrugged. "The door was locked; Rebecca checked and double-checked the lock before we returned to the surface. And I checked it again before I left."

"Did Annabel have time before she left to find me?"

Fia nodded reluctantly. "While Rebecca and I were downstairs, Annabel was outside in the garden. Scott said something about 'tending to the dead.'"

"Theresa?"

"Theresa was—oh, you mean . . . yeah, I think Scott . . ." She hesitated. She not only did not know how to finish that sentence but couldn't tell Max what she thought had happened.

"So Annabel and Rebecca both had an opportunity to set the prisoners free?"

Fia stared into Max's eyes for a long moment, thinking about what he had asked and what she saw in his face. He seemed fine. He seemed like Max—logical, zealous Max. She asked him again if he was feeling better.

"I think so. I'm still tired. And achy. And bruised. And confused. But I think I feel better." She started to answer his question about who had opened the cell door when he changed the subject. "Fia, where are my shoes?"

She blinked several times, startled by the question. "I don't know." She still wasn't sure how to tell him they were underneath the basement of a now-collapsed demon lair. "I can run out and grab you some new ones? I didn't know what size before." She was on her feet before she had finished the question.

"Fia, where are my shoes?" This time, the question felt more like a challenge.

Fia's shoulders fell, and she returned to the sofa. "Your shoes are buried under a house Mother Agnes blew up."

Max tilted his head first one way, then the other. "Why did Mother Agnes blow up a house?"

Fia once again found her feet and headed for the kitchen. "Max, do you remember the night I told you about . . . what I do?"

He stood and followed her, taking a seat at the bar. "Yeah? What about it?"

She pulled a bottle and glasses from a cabinet and set them on the bar. "This is that kind of story."

She poured each of the glasses half full of whiskey before rounding the corner to sit on the stool next to Max. She tapped her glass against his and took a healthy gulp. He followed suit, sipping at his own drink instead of gulping.

"Why did Agnes blow up a house?"

"I have to start by saying, I don't know what happened to you. I know that after that woman drugged you, they pushed the car off the side of the hill, down into the ravine. Annabel got a pretty decent concussion, I think, and spent a good . . . I don't know, thirty, thirty-six hours stumbling around in the woods looking for her way back to the safe house. They must have thought she'd go in the creek and drown. I don't—but they took you to a house around Capitol Hill and locked you in this weird subbasement. I think it was maybe a storm cellar or bomb shelter."

"Who? Why?"

"I don't know, and to hurt me."

Max's usually pale face drained of any color it had. "To hurt you?"

"I told you about the demons. How someone was trying to use them . . . I guess they figured out the demons weren't getting the job done, so they decided to come at me from a more human angle."

He took a deep breath, followed by a deep swallow of whiskey, and waved for her to continue.

"And I think they—the human, whoever is behind all this—tried torturing you but couldn't stomach it? Maybe. It looks like you got knocked around a little, and that cut on your foot—"

"Cut?"

"Scott said you had a—you said under hypnosis that someone cut your foot. You kicked them in the chest."

Max twisted on the stool to bring his left foot up so he could see the bottom, then contorted the other way to see the right. "Shit." He turned so Fia could see.

Running the width of his foot at the top of the ball, just below his toes, was an angry red streak. It wasn't a fresh wound; rather, it looked like it was in the early stages of forming a scar. The state of the wound brought up a question.

"That wasn't there before? The . . . the demons corrupted your memories, made you think things about people that weren't real. They had you convinced you and Annabel had known each other as children. And that Scott and I were responsible for hurting you. Did they corrupt your memory of what happened to your foot?"

Max shook his head. "No, that absolutely is not something I would have forgotten. I would say that is a new cut. Or I would say that if it didn't look like it was already scarred."

Magical healing leaves scars. Fia's eyes drifted to her own scars.

Aloud, she offered what she hoped was a serviceable answer. "Maybe when the demon cut you, it also . . . healed the wound? Maybe cauterized it?"

"Maybe. You would know better than me about what a demon could and couldn't do in that respect."

Fia sighed. "I know virtually nothing about demons. Except that they don't belong here, so when they come here and shift to a human form, weird shit happens."

"Weird shit?"

"They kind of resemble zombies."

"Like the guy after the ball game."

"Like the guy after the ball game. Max, I'm so sorry I got you into all of this."

"I don't remember giving you much of a choice. In fact, I'm pretty sure you told me to get lost and I couldn't take a hint. So it's as much on me as—"

"No, Max, you didn't know why I was telling you. I should have made you stay away."

"You couldn't if you tried." The corners of his mouth curled up, the smile reaching his eyes, and he winked at Fia. He put away the last of his whiskey. "Hey, do you want to come with me to get some shoes? Maybe a toothbrush?"

"From your house?"

Max's mouth twisted sideways, and he shook his head. "Just get some new stuff." He looked down at his feet. "Well, you might need to get the shoes."

Fia nodded, sliding off the stool. She, too, downed the remainder of her whiskey and then rinsed out the glasses. Max returned the bottle to the cabinet. "Let me grab my shoes," she said, skirting around him.

He wrapped his arm around her waist and pulled her back. He pulled her hips against his, gripping her butt firmly, and kissed her mouth. "I think I'm going to be okay."

She nodded, kissing him again, and headed for the bedroom.

She reached to flip on the light, but something caught her attention.

A soft glow in the far corner of the room.

It was a perfect shade of white but hazy, more like glow-in-the-dark than electric, and the glow was faint, fading. She stepped around the foot of the bed toward the glow, though she was sure she knew what it was.

When she reached the corner, she crouched toward the glow and reached out her hand. Where she expected warmth, she felt nothing. *It's not humming either.* She pinched the feather—pure white and the length of her extended fore-arm—between two fingers and lifted it from the floor. As she had done before with another just like this, she twirled the feather between her thumb and pointer fingers.

Unlike the other feather, this one faded from a white glow to white and then to gray before turning to ash and crumbling to the floor.

TWENTY-ONE

What are you doing out here?"

Scott's voice broke through the serenity Fia had found in the garden behind the safe house. Garden, she thought, was a gross understatement for this area of the safe house grounds. The courtyard garden was hidden away and almost completely secluded. There was even a tunnel leading from the house made of tree branches that had grown into each other.

The bench she sat on was one of two on opposite sides of a small stone courtyard, where creamy white limestone and red brick spiraled into each other in the center of the twenty-foot-wide round space. Around the borders were vining plants—grapes, cucumbers, squash, and tomatoes—that created an archway leading to the shed. Each row of plants moving away from the vines and back toward the house was shorter than the one before it. There were beanstalks and berry bushes, rows of leafy greens, carrots, and potatoes, and those were just the things Fia and her brown thumb recognized.

Fia's seat faced the place on the cobblestones where Sahir, a spiritual man from India, had given Max a tattoo that had, in all likeliness, saved his life. The tattoos were blessed with ritual magic that protected against possession by condemned souls. They also—surprise—protected the bearer from being harmed by demons. Not completely, but judging by the burn on his chest that had left the tattoo unharmed, Fia, and the others, had deduced the added benefit.

After finding what she could only feasibly call a dead feather in the dark corner of her room, Fia had tried everything she could to keep Max from seeing her shaken. She didn't know what it meant, and she wasn't sure she wanted to know, but now, facing Scott—facing Uhlpir—she was all but certain she was keeping what she had found under her hat.

She had taken Max to a couple of different stores to get what he needed: deodorant, a toothbrush, and most importantly, shoes—a leather version of the simple black-and-white high-top sneakers that bore the name of an old sports hero from before either of them was born. Once they had everything he needed, Max had finally decided he was hungry, and Fia had been too. They had found a small hamburger bar, and halfway through the meal, Max had asked if they could come back up here to the safe house.

They had taken their time driving up, even pulling into a rest stop to watch the sun set over the mountains. Part of Fia had wanted to chase the sun, to just keep driving west, passing the turnoff to the safe house and leaving it all behind. In the cabin of the little car, with just her and Max, it had felt like what she imagined normal should feel like.

Max hadn't been privy to her fantasy and had prodded her when he thought she was going to miss her turn.

Agnes had greeted them at the door, explaining that Rebecca and Annabel had already turned in for the night.

"That's fine," Fia had said with a nod. "I think we're here for rest more than anything."

With that, Agnes had stepped aside, allowing them to make their way to the bedroom on the ground level, assuring Fia as she breezed by that she had taken care of "the issue" in the room. Fia had cringed, realizing she herself had *not* taken care of the problem; that there were still cameras somewhere in her apartment.

Max had been in the room only seconds when he stripped out of his clothes, down to only his shorts, and climbed into the enormous bed. He had encouraged Fia to join him, and she had done so with little hesitation.

But while Max had fallen asleep within minutes, Fia had lain awake in the dark, staring at what she could see of the ceiling, for the better part of an hour. She had eventually slipped free of the bed, leaving Max sleeping alone. Gathering her clothes, she had dressed in the bathroom before heading outside.

She had come out to look at the stars but had found herself in this fairyland instead, and she had sat staring at the ground where the ritual had been performed only days earlier.

Days.

It felt like a lifetime ago.

Scott took a seat beside her on the bench.

"Couldn't sleep."

"A lot of that going around."

"So I hear."

"How is Max?"

"Sleeping. Ironically." She sniffed a laugh through her nose. "It's funny, in a way. When we first came up here, he couldn't sleep because it was too quiet. Now, I think this is the first time since we rescued him that I've seen him really sleep, without sedative, without . . . without magic. He was breathing steadily, slow and deep, when I left and hadn't moved in twenty or thirty minutes."

"That's good."

"It is. But he's kept me awake so much lately, I guess my body has just decided this is how it is now. We don't sleep anymore."

"You'll sleep."

"Thanks."

He lifted her hand from the bench between them and squeezed it softly with both of his. "You'll sleep. You are in dragon mode. When Max feels safe, you will sleep."

She stayed silent, chewing on those words. It really had come to that. Everything she did now was to protect him. She wasn't sleeping, because she needed to make sure he was.

She still hadn't grown completely comfortable with the thought by the time Rebecca eased into the garden. Her dark features were pale with concern. "Fia? I'm glad I found you. I think you need to come inside."

"Why? What . . . ?" She didn't finish the thought. Something was wrong with Max.

Back inside the vast cabin, Fia could hear Max's voice coming from the stairs. She followed the sound. Halfway to the top, Max knelt on one of the steps. Two above him sat a bucket and a bottle of bleach. And he was scrubbing furiously at the step in between.

"So much blood." He kept repeating the sentence as he scrubbed, almost keeping time. "So." Scrub. "Much." Scrub. "Blood." Scrub.

"I just found him like that," Rebecca said. "I woke up and heard something strange. Given everything else we've gone through, I was worried. I came out, and there he was, scrubbing at blood on the stairs."

"Didn't you say you got that cleaned up?" Scott's voice was soft and worried.

"Yes. Yes, I did," Rebecca confirmed.

"So. Much. Blood." Max's gentle, warm baritone voice was strained with panic.

"He's having a nightmare," Fia offered.

"Has he been sleepwalking?" Rebecca asked.

"I wasn't sure. I was gone when he smashed the mirror. He was awake when I left, but—I honestly don't know." She thought about the explanation he had given, about brushing his teeth, but not finding a toothbrush in the mess.

"Do you think you can steer him back to bed without waking him up?" Rebecca's voice was also strained.

"Yeah, I'll try. You go back to bed. Scott, you too. I . . . I'll take care of him." Fia climbed the stairs and knelt beside Max, resting her hand on his, stopping the scrubbing motion. "Hey, leave it. Come back to bed."

He turned to look at her, his brown eyes wide. "Fia? I can't get the blood out."

"Max? Are you awake?"

"There's so much blood. It's all over. I can't get it out." The deep angles of his cheeks shone wet in the scant light from the foyer.

"You know what? Forget it. I'll tell you what we're going to do."

"I have to clean up this mess. I can't look at it. I can't—"

"Max, let me tell you what we're going to do. Tomorrow, in the daylight, we're going to go get a board, and we're going to bring it back here. And we're going to replace that step. Don't even worry about the stain. We'll just get rid of it."

His frightened expression softened briefly as he studied

her face. "No, I have to clean this up. I made this mess; I have to clean it up." He resumed scrubbing.

"Max, you did make that mess, but you made it saving my life." She pulled the scrub pad from his hand and put his hand to her chest. "You feel that? My heart is beating because you made that mess. Come back to bed with me."

He stared at her for a long moment before acquiescing. He let her pull him to his feet and guide him back down the stairs. Scott waited for them at the landing, and once they had passed, he climbed up to gather Max's cleaning supplies.

Fia guided Max through the foyer and into the dark hallway that led to the room they had claimed as their own. Inside the comfortable darkness, he sat on the edge of the giant bed closest to the door, and Fia made her way around to the window side. When she reached her destination, she saw his shoulders shaking in the moonlight. She pulled him back to lie against her as gasping sobs sputtered from his chest. He rolled onto his side, pressing his back into her, and she let him cry, pulling her fingers through his long hair, unsure what else to do for him in that moment.

Soon they were both asleep.

They woke to a crash coming from the kitchen. "Stay here. I'll go check," Fia whispered, resting her hand on Max's chest. She climbed out of the bed, half expecting him to ignore her request and get up to join her. When she glanced back over her shoulder, though, she found him with the covers pulled up to his chin, his dark eyes wide with panic. She sighed.

We need to find somewhere he can heal.

She slipped out of the bedroom and headed into the

kitchen, where the crashing sounds persisted. Once through the swinging door, she saw Annabel and Rebecca entangled in a full-blown brawl. She surveyed the scene. A cast-iron pan lay on the floor in front of the stove. A chef's knife lay halfway to the other side of the counter. One of the steel stools that normally sat under the raised table in the middle of the kitchen was overturned, and the table itself was crooked. Even the enormous commercial refrigerator was slightly off-kilter.

The two nuns were in the empty space between the island counter and the back door, Rebecca astraddle Annabel's torso, her forearm across Annabel's throat. Annabel was pawing at Rebecca's face with one hand, punching at her side with the other, and doing her best to cough under Rebecca's weight.

Fia was on them in just a few strides, her arm around Rebecca's waist, hauling back in an effort to remove her from the scuffle. Rage and adrenaline made the little woman nearly impossible for Fia to budge.

As she struggled, someone else reached in to help. She looked up to see Agnes prying Rebecca's arm free of her prey. It took both of them, but Agnes and Fia finally got the women separated. Agnes helped Annabel to her feet and shoved her toward the door that led to where eight children and Sister Cecilia used to keep their quarters.

Taking Agnes's cue, Fia pushed Rebecca toward the door into the rest of the house. Walking ahead of Fia, Rebecca reached up to straighten her wimple. Back in the hallway, Fia asked Rebecca what had happened.

"She's crazy!" Rebecca snarled. "Annabel tried to kill me!" She hoisted her robe until she could show Fia the wound above her left hip, presumably left by the knife Fia had seen on the counter.

"She stabbed you?"

"She tried. I guess I have better reflexes than she expected. I think the robe helped some too."

"Why would she—"

"Because she's a psychopath! Clearly, she murdered Theresa and kidnapped Max, and now she's trying to kill me. I don't know why."

Fia pressed the heel of her hand into her forehead. She didn't like that Rebecca was screeching like a banshee right outside the bedroom where she imagined Max had stuffed himself into the armoire by now. Or jumped out the window.

"Fiammetta, may I have a word?" Agnes said, poking her head through the doorway. "Alone."

Fia's brows met in the middle as she turned her confusion from Agnes to Rebecca and back again. "Yeah. What the hell is going on around here?" She followed Agnes back into the kitchen, where Agnes grabbed Annabel by the arm on the way to the back door.

Agnes jabbed a finger into Annabel's shoulder, urging her down the stairs into the basement. Fia brought up the rear as they descended. In the basement, Agnes guided Annabel to the holding cell at the back of the space. After Fia had come in behind them, Agnes closed them in.

"Sister Annabel, I am afraid I have no choice but to ask you to leave."

"Reverend Mother, I—"

"I think it is best for everyone involved if you are no longer associated with our organization. Fiammetta can help you pack if you would like." Agnes's tone was calm, though not the scary calm Fia expected. The elder nun sounded almost sympathetic, kind. The crease in Fia's forehead deepened until she thought her eyes might collapse in on themselves. She reached up to smooth it out.

"You're not going to . . . ?" Annabel's voice sounded as shocked and confused as Fia felt.

"I will make arrangements to get you into the city. The sisters of Saint Mark's will be expecting you. You are familiar with Sisters Ruth and Abigail?"

Fia felt the crevice in her forehead return as she struggled to understand what was happening. "Reverend Mother, if I may, why did we have to come down here to have this conversation if we're just going back upstairs—"

"Fiammetta, I wanted to have this conversation in private. Sister Rebecca's emotions have taken control of her faculties; she is *reacting* instead of acting. I did not want to invite another scuffle between them. And this is the most secure place in the house."

"I am not going to pretend to understand any of this. You are letting Annabel *go*, after she—"

"I think there is a great deal more to what took place in the kitchen just now than either woman is going to admit."

"I already told you what happened," Annabel said.

"You gave me your side of the story, Sister Annabel. I am now going to go upstairs and get Sister Rebecca's side."

"And believe her. Whatever she says, you'll believe her. You already believe her, and you haven't even talked to her. Otherwise, you wouldn't be sending me away."

"Sister Annabel, please. I have made my decision regarding the safety of everyone involved. Please do as you have been asked." With that, Agnes turned and left the cell and the basement.

"What happened?" Fia asked, curiosity getting the better of her. "Rebecca told me you—"

"Tried to kill her."

"Yes."

"Yes, I did. You didn't, so I did."

"What?"

"You were told the way to break the connection between the demons and their human summoner was by killing the summoner. How do you think Rebecca and Father Scott escaped that explosion if she hasn't been working with the demons all along?"

"Shit." Fia's reaction was more about Annabel questioning the story she had been fed than about the nun's logic, but Annabel wouldn't know that. The story *had* been fishy, but Fia had assumed Uhlpir had used a touch of divine magic to convince everyone—including Rebecca—it had been the truth. Now Fia wondered if Theresa and Annabel had shared the same theory.

"Right. So I did what I thought—"

"Come on. We're supposed to be packing." Fia grabbed Annabel by the elbow, pushing her toward the door. Once aboveground, she pushed Annabel toward the double French doors that led into the back side of the foyer, closer to the stairs leading to the nuns' quarters.

"Fia, why are you—"

A strangled gasp cut Annabel's question short. Fia jerked her head around toward the sound to see Max, his face gray, his mouth gaping.

"Max!" Fia left Annabel standing on the first step and crossed the granite floor to where Max stood frozen. "Max," she whispered close to his ear. "Come on, let's get out of here."

She tried to steer him back toward the hallway, but he shoved by her. He crossed the foyer in two long strides, driving Annabel into the wall with enough force to rattle the expansive windows in their frames.

"Max! What—"

Max slammed Annabel's shoulders into the wall a second time, interrupting the nun's attempt to speak.

Fia moved to step in but stopped when she heard a deep animal sound coming from his chest. The growl bloomed into a full wildcat scream, and he lifted Annabel from the wall, only to slam her back again.

"It's a different story when I'm conscious and can fight back."

Fia grabbed him by the elbow and pulled his arm back, breaking his grip on one of the nun's shoulders. "Max, let her go. Don't—"

"Are you defending her?" he snarled.

"No, Max, I just don't . . ." She stopped and stepped back, letting go of his arm. "No, you deserve this. Go ahead."

"Fiammetta! Sister Annabel, what is going on out here?" Agnes demanded from the top of the stairs. Rebecca appeared hesitantly behind her.

Max gave Annabel one final shove, her head bouncing off the wall, and stepped back, his hands raised in surrender. Annabel slid down the wall to the floor, her eyes swimming in her head. Fia reached down to pull her back to her feet as Agnes descended the stairs. The elder nun grabbed Annabel by the other arm, pulling her free of Fia's grip.

"Get up the stairs, Sister Annabel. I will be up in a moment." Agnes turned her eyes up to Rebecca, still standing at the top. "Sister Rebecca, back to your room now." She turned back to Fia as the younger nuns disappeared. "Do you mind telling me what is going on here?"

With a deep breath, Fia gave Agnes a rundown of everything Zari had found out from Max about his abduction. "So he still thinks Annabel was there."

"Max." Agnes's tone softened as she studied Max's face, still creased with dark, angry shadows. "You are certain it was Sister Annabel in the basement with you?"

"I'm not sure of anything, but I couldn't stop myself. I saw her, and—" With a pained cry, he grabbed the sides of his head, dropping to his haunches and curling into himself.

Fia dropped down to his level, her face close enough to his she could feel him breathing. "Max, let's get you out of here."

"Fiammetta, are you going to be okay?"

"I'll be fine. Are you really shipping Annabel out of here?"

"I think it is for the best."

"Just into the city? Sister Ruth . . ." Fia looked at Max, who had finished sitting on the steps and now held his head between his knees. "I need to talk to you, but . . ."

"Please take care of Max first. There will be time to talk after."

Twenty-Two

Fia pulled the little race car into the space in front of Zari's crystal shop. Max had fallen asleep, albeit restlessly, shortly after they left the safe house. For the rest of the ride, he had shifted and jerked, mumbling, moaning, even talking, though Fia hadn't really understood any of what he was saying. What she had recognized as words had been garbled, even vaguely foreign sounding. She watched him for another moment, debating whether to wake him and take him inside or bring Zari out to him.

She didn't have long to wonder. Zari stepped out of the shop, striding down the sidewalk to the side of the car. Fia rolled down the window, and Zari leaned in.

"What is wrong?"

"What isn't? He just attacked Annabel and then, I guess, got a splitting headache. He slept on the way back here, but not . . ." She waved a hand toward him to indicate his current state. "He's been like that for the whole ride."

Zari watched for a moment before telling Fia to wake him and bring him inside.

"Do you think we broke something?" Fia asked.

"I would like a minute with him to find out what we are looking at."

"Right. Of course." Fia gave Max a gentle shake, though it didn't take much. He jerked upright hard enough Fia thought he might propel himself straight through the windshield. "How's your head?" she asked once he stopped scanning his surroundings.

"Pounding."

She got out of the car and walked around to the passenger door, opening it to help him out. "Zari wants to talk to you inside."

He fell into her arms, letting her pull him from the car, and leaned against her as they walked up the sidewalk to the shop entrance.

Inside, Zari looked them over. "You both must be exhausted. Please . . ." She flipped the sign on the door from *Open* to *Closed*, locked the door, and gestured toward the stairs at the back of the shop.

"Upstairs?" Fia asked.

"*Oui*, we will have more room, and I do not think this warrants my ritual space."

They climbed the stairs to a space Zari had filled with back stock and a library of occult references. She gestured for Max to have a seat in one of a pair of leather armchairs. "Fia, I apologize that there is not another chair for you up here, but if you would like to take this opportunity to make use of one of the beds—"

"No, I'm staying. I'll hang out over here." Fia grabbed a small section of floor near the storage area, hoping that would keep her out of the way if Zari needed a book, and sat.

"Very well." Zari combed through the library, locating the book she wanted with little effort. She opened the book, flipping through only a couple of pages before settling on what she wanted, and quickly ran her finger over the page. Taking the other armchair, she pulled it around so she faced Max. She leaned in close and locked eyes with Max, holding the stare until Fia could see Max's eyes lose focus. His eyelids began to flutter in place, then he blinked several times, quickly. Each time he blinked, he grew further from completely re-opening his eyes, until one blink, they simply remained closed.

"Max, what do you see?"

Fia twisted her face, thinking the question was far too vague to be effective, but Max launched into a detailed description of a basement that sounded to Fia more like a dungeon: concrete walls and floors, chains built into the walls, one spotlight in the center of the room casting heavy shadows anywhere it didn't shine.

"They want me confused. They want to make me feel crazy. She's back to give me another shot, something heavy; I can feel it in my veins, like school glue. I can feel it filling me up; I think my veins are going to split open. And then the light fades to a foggy black, and I sleep."

"How many times do they do this?"

"I lost count. Five or six, maybe eight. I wake to see Annabel with a knife. Scalpel, bright silver, reflecting the spotlight. There's nothing beyond the spotlight. It shines in my eyes, and everything on the other side is black. There are voices in the dark. Annabel sounds . . ."

He trailed off before starting on something new. "I'm waking up again, and I think I must be dead. There is something—a lot of little somethings, like small dogs—clawing at my body, eating me alive. I can hear the skin ripping in their teeth. I can smell the blood. I am just going to lie down here, let them finish . . ."

Fia's stomach turned as Max's story trailed off again. She realized that Zari had done something different this time, something to put Max back in the dungeon, back in the moment. He wasn't remembering; he was living. He wasn't pulling details from memories; he was seeing them firsthand. And relaying them to Zari as if he were back there, reporting the whole scene live.

"I'm fine. Everything is fine. None of it was real. I'm fine." He patted his chest where Fia had seen the seared claw marks. "Except for this. The tattoo protected me? It burns, but I think I'm fine."

"Where is Annabel, Max?"

"She's here. She comes in, in between. She gives me the drugs."

"What does she look like?" Fia asked quietly, not sure whether she was supposed to but hoping she wouldn't pull Max out of his state.

His face twisted as he considered. "She looks like Annabel. Blue eyes, freckles."

Picking up what Fia was pushing for, Zari asked the question a different way. "What color is her hair?"

His face twisted again, this time into something like revelation. "She's wearing her head covering." He waved his hands around his head. "Normal clothes, a white t-shirt, blue jeans, but also her head covering."

"Does that seem unusual, Max?"

"I don't know. Shouldn't she always wear it? That's the rule, right?"

"She's breaking a lot of rules, though. Do you think it is unusual that she would break so many rules but follow that one?" When he didn't reply, Zari tried again. "Why are you focused on what she is wearing? Is there anything special about it?"

"No. A white t-shirt tucked into blue jeans. White sneakers. Like mine, but canvas."

Fia tugged at the tail of her own untucked t-shirt, desperately grasping at any detail that might be a clue. *Tucking in her shirt is not a clue. It means nothing. A lot of people still tuck in their t-shirts.* But Zari had asked about anything special, and Max hadn't mentioned it the first time. *Maybe he thinks it's something?*

"And her wimple?"

"Is that what—yes, her hair is covered. And her neck. And her ears."

Even if Max didn't think it was weird, Fia definitely did. Zari was right; Annabel was breaking so many rules, why continue wearing the wimple? Unless . . .

She filed the rest of the thought away for later.

"Who else is there, Max?" No response. "Is Annabel the only other person with you?"

"I think so. There are other people—Fia, Sister Rebecca, Father Scott—but I think I am imagining them."

"What about the woman with the long hair?"

Max began to shake, his breathing quickening with each new breath. He dug his fingers into the arms of the chair and scooted his feet over the floor as if he were trying to get away from something.

"Max, what about the woman?"

"She . . . she is in charge. She is calling the shots. She is angry that I refuse to give up. She wants me to die. But she wants me to suffer while I do. I won't give up. I won't let her—she controls the demons, tells them what to do. From the shadows. I don't see her face, only her hair. Once, she has a mask. I can see her hair but not her face. It's a costume mask, plastic, no features, no paint. Just the mask. And the ponytail. High, tight, sleek ponytail."

Zari pulled away from him, scooting her chair a few

inches back. "Thank you, Max. I think that is enough for now."

"Really?" Fia asked. "Just like that, you're done?"

"More importantly, Max is finished. I think he has had enough for today. We may try again tomorrow. Max, you can wake up now."

Max's eyelids parted slowly, and he looked around the space before turning his glance back on Zari. "Where am I?"

"What do you remember?" Zari asked him softly.

"Fia?"

"I'm right here." Fia pulled herself off the floor and moved quickly to crouch beside Max's chair.

"Did I attack Sister Annabel? I think that's the last thing I remember." He rubbed hard at his forehead with the tips of his fingers, grimacing. "I think I blacked out. I saw you talking to her, coming in from outside, and something snapped. That's the last thing I *really* remember."

"Max, anything you did—"

"Annabel and Rebecca got into a fight—another fight," Fia said, interrupting Zari. There was no point in sugarcoating what had happened. "Agnes asked me to help Annabel pack to send her away." She refused to tell Max just how far Agnes was sending Annabel. He didn't need to be mollycoddled, but he also didn't need to know that Annabel would still be in the same city. "That's what you saw. I was taking her upstairs to get her things together."

"Did I hurt her?"

"I think her feelings more than anything. Might have given her a bump on the head."

Max ran his hands over his face and through his hair, pulling it up off his neck. Zari stood and stepped behind him, taking the bundle and tying it into itself. Then she quietly returned to her chair.

"Max," Zari asked after a moment, "do you doubt Annabel was responsible for what happened to you?"

Max shook his head, a gesture that looked more like frustration than negation. "Zari, do you think it would be okay if I laid down for a while?"

Without a word, Zari was on her feet again, guiding Max out of the chair with a gentle hand on his back. Fia watched until they were out of sight and picked up the book Zari had used earlier. It was still open to the same page.

"Hypnosis techniques for the immediate retrieval of traumatic memories," she read aloud. "Note that these techniques should only be used in extreme cases where other, gentler methods have been unsuccessful, as they may result in new trauma."

Fia fought off the impulse to be angry that Zari hadn't used this before, reminding herself that Zari had tried her best to avoid causing more damage to Max's psyche. She closed the book and laid it on its back on the shelf where Zari had found it, then pushed Zari's chair back into its rightful place before descending the stairs herself.

The afternoon went by slowly. Unable to sit still, Fia left Max sleeping in the basement of Zari's apartment—he had chosen to sleep in the lower bunk in the guest room—and Zari tending the store, and went walking around the neighborhood.

She passed by the building where, at sixteen, she had deep-fried her own arm while punishing a pedophile named Ted. Poe McGinty, another girl living on the streets at the time, had healed Fia's burns with her tears, crying on the ruined arm as Fia watched raw, oozing tissue transform into scale-shaped scars.

The diner had never recovered from the ghost of what had taken place there, and after years of sitting vacant, it had been renovated to house a real estate office. The motel that had stood behind the diner—where most of the sex acts Ted had brokered took place—had been torn down, and the lot now stood empty.

Fia sat on a broken curb, narrowly missing the exposed rebar, and stared at the empty space for what felt like an eternity. By the time she regained her footing, everything from the lower half of her butt down was prickly. She shook her legs out, trying to reinvigorate the blood flow, and headed back toward Zari's.

She entered through the apartment, figuring the front door was locked by now. She found Max cresting the stairs out of the basement and asked how his nap had been.

"Okay. Not good, but I feel a little less foggy. I'm hungry, though."

"That is good to hear, Max." Zari stepped through the curtain from the shop. "I had planned on cleaning up a pot of chili I made the other day; would you two like some?"

Fia smiled. "Green chili?"

Zari returned Fia's enthusiasm. "Of course."

Fia turned to Max. "It's really good."

Max nodded. "I would love some."

"Tortillas?" Fia asked, hopeful. Even after so long away, she had never gotten over a homemade tortilla with her green chili.

"You would expect anything less?" Zari teased.

"Zari makes her own tortillas," Fia explained to Max. "They're delicious."

Max pulled a chair out from the table and gestured for Fia to sit before joining her. "Fia, do you think, after we eat, we can go back up to the safe house?"

Fia started, surprised. "Absolutely, if that's what you think you want to do. Zari?"

"I think it is a good sign that you want to return, if you think you are up for it, Max."

"Hearing Rebecca and Annabel brawling in the kitchen was . . . awful, but if Annabel is gone . . ."

"As far as I know, Agnes's plan was to get her out as quickly as possible. When she asked me to help Annabel pack, Agnes said she had already talked to Sister Ruth—"

"Who is Sister Ruth, *chérie?*"

"Oh, sorry, I didn't—she's one of the nuns I spoke to when I was looking for Terra, from the outreach—"

Fia stopped, remembering she didn't want Max knowing Agnes was only sending Annabel as far as the city.

"I think Sister Ruth was meeting Agnes and Annabel somewhere to take Annabel the rest of the way out of town." The lie tasted bad. Omission was one thing; outright lying wasn't fair to Max. But neither was the anxiety that he might run into his captor on the street somewhere.

"If she's gone, I think I'll be fine. I would like to go."

TWENTY-THREE

Fia slipped quietly out of the bedroom, closing the door softly behind her. "You brought Max back here?" Scott's voice in the early morning stillness made her jump.

"Christ! I oughta put a bell on you."

"Do you think this is the best place for him? After last time?"

She shrugged. "He wanted to try again."

"And Zari?"

"She said he's the only one who can know for sure. So here we are. What happened after we left, after Annabel . . . ?"

"Agnes has had Rebecca on a short leash. Neither of them has told me exactly what happened."

"Welcome to the mushroom club, where we're kept in the dark and fed bullshit. Annabel told me—what did they tell you?"

"Sisters Annabel and Rebecca had an altercation. Agnes said they both agreed Annabel started it."

"Started it. Sounds like a pair of high school kids brawling in the hallway. Annabel—she decided the reason you and Rebecca were able to get out of the cave alive was that Rebecca was connected to the demons. From that, I assume she's had it in for Rebecca ever since, maybe trying to do what Irzelen recruited me to do."

"What do you think?"

"Obviously, I know her theory is wrong. And maybe her theory was a ruse. To throw me off, not knowing what I know. I thought maybe I'd talk to Rebecca. See if Annabel said anything to her before trying to stab her. Have you seen her?"

"I have not. I have actually been away since late last night. Probably since just before you got here."

"Cool. I'll track her down. This is a big place but not that big."

Scott nodded. "If you need me, I will be out at the training grounds. I promised Mother Agnes I would move a few heavy things in the storage building out there." He traded places with her, patting her on the back as he walked away.

Fia decided heading for the kitchen first wasn't the worst idea. There, she searched the oversize refrigerator for something she could put in her empty belly. She finally settled on toast with peanut butter.

Once finished, she continued her search for Rebecca. She checked the back hallway, listening at the door of the office but hearing nothing. She passed below the trapdoor to the passage that would spit her out in Theresa's room, considering the shortcut but deciding instead to take the long way upstairs.

The upstairs hallway was silent as well. Though Fia couldn't imagine she and Max had been left alone in the house, it was starting to look as if that might be the case.

She descended into the library, the last place she thought she might find either Rebecca or the Reverend Mother, and came up empty there too. She tracked back through the house to the back door of the kitchen and tried the basement. Satisfied there was no one in the house, she headed for the garden.

Fia took a relaxing breath of pine-scented oxygen deep into her lungs. She didn't feel like she had done much of that since making her decision to leave town. She followed the packed gravel path toward the garden. As she got closer, the air took on the aroma of carefully tended flowers and vegetables, peppers and chives dominating.

As she emerged from the cover of the trees, she stopped short. Fever reached her cheeks and ears, and her stomach turned, pushing the acrid taste of bile into her mouth.

Fia watched the nun quickly, deftly, twist her sandy-brown hair into a long, heavy braid that reached nearly to her waist. She tucked the braid into her collar and reclaimed her wimple from the priest, securing it to conceal her hair. She turned and left the cathedral steps, climbing into an awaiting rideshare.

Kneeling on the cobblestones just a few feet away, her back to Fia, was the woman Fia had seen with Armando Ariaz. Light-brown hair lay thick and heavy against the black of her robe, her headdress lying on the bench nearby.

Fia pulled her scooter through the parking lot. She could hear her blood rushing through her veins, so loud it drowned out the surrounding traffic. As she pulled through the opening to leave the lot, a woman stepped in front of her. She had seen her earlier; she recognized the woman's ponytail, the one that had descended the stairs ahead of Rylan. Now, the woman passed in front of Fia, seemingly oblivious, her phone pressed against her ear. Between her hand and the device, Fia couldn't see enough of the woman's face to identify her.

"The coat hook," Fia whispered, so low she barely heard it herself. "Bitch!" she snarled.

The woman turned to look at her, her tawny face shifting into a bright smile. "Fia, good morning," Rebecca greeted her cheerfully.

Fia ground her teeth, and a low growl formed in her chest, building to a dragon roar. She drove her shoulder into Rebecca's stomach, wrapping her arms around the woman's waist and pushing her back until the branches of a lilac bush scraped her arms and tangled in Rebecca's hair. Fia released her then and swung a fist, connecting with Rebecca's jaw.

Rebecca spat, hot saliva and blood hitting Fia's cheek, and she threw her own punch, aiming for Fia's gut. "So, you finally figured it out," Rebecca scoffed. She wrapped a leg behind Fia's, pulling her off-balance. Fia caught the brunt of the fall with her shoulders, bracing herself to keep her head from hitting the stones. The impact knocked the air from her lungs, though, and as Fia gasped for breath, Rebecca dug a canvas sneaker into her ribcage.

White canvas sneakers.

Fia coiled around the kick, wrapping her arms around Rebecca's leg and rolling away. Rebecca hit the cobblestones with enough force to make her cough. Fia thought she might vomit but didn't slow her attack. She spotted the small garden spade Rebecca had dropped in the initial attack and scrambled for it, trying to reclaim her feet as she moved.

As she closed her scarred fingers around the rubber grip of the spade's handle, Rebecca closed her own around Fia's ankle. Fia turned as Rebecca hauled back on her leg, trying to face the nun. She thrashed uselessly with her free foot, not hitting anything, but the jerking movement was enough to break Rebecca's grip.

Fia crab-crawled away from the smaller woman, her hand finding the spade once again. She held onto it, waiting for Rebecca to advance on her, which only took a few seconds. When Rebecca got within Fia's reach, Fia swung the spade, tearing through the fabric of Rebecca's robe and leaving a jagged red gash in her bicep.

Now it was Rebecca's turn to snarl. Instead of words, the sound that came from her throat more closely resembled that of a threatened animal. She rose to full height and drove her heel into Fia's chest. With Fia on her back, Rebecca straddled her, glaring down from above. Fia moved to bury the spade in her opponent's thigh, but Rebecca stomped down on Fia's arm, sending the tool skittering across the stones, where it finally stopped under the edge of a bush.

Fia jerked her arm free, knocking Rebecca off-balance. She took advantage of the moment and scrambled backward, far enough away from Rebecca that she could regain her own balance.

Back on her feet, Fia grabbed the woman by her braid and wrenched her head back. She pulled Rebecca toward her until their faces were barely more than an inch apart.

"I'm going to kill you."

Rebecca laughed, a mirthless sound, and smacked her own forehead against Fia's. The impact made Fia lose her grip on Rebecca's hair, and as she staggered back a step, Rebecca straightened herself, smoothing a hand over her shirt, then over her hair.

"You won't. If you had it in you, you would have killed Annabel on sight."

"Why didn't you?" Fia asked. "I didn't understand your reaction when she resurfaced, but you didn't *think* she was dead; you wanted her dead."

"Annabel meant nothing to me. She was just a convenient patsy. Then she started figuring things out." She lunged at Fia, and Fia withdrew, a mouse taunting the cat. Rebecca laughed again, amused but nothing more. "Are you *afraid* of me?" She lunged again, and again Fia withdrew. "You are afraid of me. The great Fia Drake, world-class soul hunter, afraid of little ol' me."

Just as Fia had planned, Rebecca lunged a third time, and this time, Fia held her ground. She grabbed Rebecca by the shoulders and swung her around, slamming her back into the small shed at the edge of the garden.

Rebecca coughed and howled in rage more than injury. "You don't even know what this is all about, do you?"

"I can't imagine the reasoning makes sense to anyone but you and your weird cult." Fia punctuated her statement with an upward punch to Rebecca's ribs. She felt one of them crack with the force. She drove another punch into the woman's gut: left, then right, then left again, as if she were twelve years old, working on Agnes's heavy bag in the basement of the convent.

Rebecca timed the punches, dodging one just enough that Fia drove her fist into the side of the shed. Unfazed, Fia grabbed the other woman by the arm, spinning her around. She twisted Rebecca's wrist until the nun involuntarily fell to her knees. Still holding her by the wrist, Fia kicked her in the back, only letting go when she felt the momentum pulling her forward too.

Rebecca scrambled, half running, half crawling, to the other side of the garden. She recovered the spade they had lost in the struggle and held it out in front of her like a dagger. "Did you know there has never been a time I didn't know who you were?"

Fia slowed her advance, morbidly curious where Rebecca's story would take them.

"Of course, no one ever said anything to me. I didn't even warrant a direct comparison. I tried to leave the convent before Levi was born. Terra told me how you had spent days planning your escape. Packing a bag one item at a time so one would notice. Listening to the floorboards, memorizing their squeaks. I tried. Agnes caught me. Nothing happened there that Agnes didn't know about."

Fia tried to scan her surroundings without taking her eyes off her opponent. She quickly gauged the time needed to disarm Rebecca and get her to the ground.

"She let you leave." Rebecca's words were a few degrees cooler than the mountain air around them. "I became a prisoner, and she let you leave."

The final words exploded in a screech, and Rebecca lunged for Fia.

Fia was prepared. She grabbed Rebecca by the wrist, wrenching it until the nun had no choice but to drop her weapon. The spade bounced off Fia's toe, offering only a soft clatter as it hit the stones. Fia kicked it into the greenery and spun Rebecca toward the ground.

Grabbing a small stone, Fia clenched it in her fist and straddled Rebecca as the nun tried to find her feet. Using the stone as a fist pack, Fia hit Rebecca in the back of the head, knocking her flat on her stomach.

She grabbed Rebecca by one arm and hauled back on it, hard enough she felt it separate at the shoulder. Rebecca howled, this time as much in pain as in anger, and swung her free arm, but Fia had the upper hand.

Once Fia successfully had Rebecca on her back, she fell to her knees, pinching the woman's ribs between them, and drove the fist still clutching the rock into Rebecca's face. She didn't aim for any particular spot; she was simply determined to break as many bones as she could.

She pummeled Rebecca with her fists, reaching for the molten core of the earth, trying with each blow to push Rebecca into its depths. Even when the woman's face was barely recognizable, when purple-black bruises had started to form, taking on the pattern of Fia's knuckles in some places, Fia kept striking.

Until someone grabbed her by the wrist.

One rough, calloused hand locked around her scarred wrist, an arm wrapped around her chest, and she was being hauled backward, away from her goal. She struggled, pulling free of the grip to land one more punch before she was lifted off her feet.

Her captor spun the both of them around, putting himself between Fia and Rebecca, who now lay battered on the ground, dark red blood seeping onto the pale stones from a wound at the back of her skull. Fia tried to dart around the person standing in her way, but he caught her and drew her into his chest. He pressed her face into him and spoke softly into her hair.

"Fia, no. She is not worth it. I don't want this." He released her head and, with a long, slender finger, lifted her chin so she had to look into his eyes. Eyes the color of good whiskey burned into her own, tears glistening at their edges. "Fia?"

She growled deep in her chest and struggled to pull away. He clutched her more tightly.

Then the air in the garden began to hum. Everything in sight grew brighter. Max loosened his grip, and they both turned to look behind him.

Uhlpir knelt beside Rebecca's battered body, his wings unfurled but slack against his back. His long, flushed face was gaunt with despair, and tears glistened in his silver-blue eyes. He lifted the young woman from the ground, pressing her into his chest.

The fever returned to Fia's skin, and she wrenched herself free of Max's arms with a shriek, lunging for the angel. Max grabbed for her but missed and stumbled to his knees.

Before Fia could reach her mark, though, she stopped short, shocked by the scene unfolding before her.

The angel leaned down and kissed Rebecca's head. The broken woman turned her face to look at him and moved her mouth to speak. He laid a finger over her lips, silencing her, released her from his embrace, and moved his hands to rest against the sides of her head.

Fia expected to hear a crunch as he effortlessly wrenched the head in his hands, his immortal strength snapping Rebecca's neck like a pencil. Instead, the garden was silent. Even the humming that accompanied the angelic form had ceased.

Uhlpir gently laid Rebecca's ruined body on the stones and rose to his feet. In one giant stride, he stood before Fia, anguish radiating from him in waves. He lowered himself to one knee. Kneeling in this form, he was still as tall as Fia was. He took her scarred right hand in one of his own and gestured for Max to join them, taking his left hand as he did.

Uhlpir bowed to them, dipping his head and shoulders deeply enough they could see his back. He stretched his wings out to the sides. The anger Fia had felt moments earlier as he cradled Rebecca in his arms, certain in that moment that he had known all along what she was, subsided. In an instant, it was replaced with panicked horror.

The pure-white wings dulled, as if someone were turning a dial. Brilliant light became gray, gray became ash, and ash fell to the ground around him. His eight-foot angelic form melted back into the six-and-a-half-foot-tall man who had once taken up most of the twin-size bed in Fia's bunker with just his legs.

He rose to his feet, red cheeks glittering with tears, kissed each of their hands in turn, and stepped past them, headed back for the house.

"Uhlpir, wait."

He stopped but didn't turn back.

"Why? Does this have anything to do with the feathers I—we—found?"

"One of many untruths I have told you, I am afraid. Losing one could be explained; I could have caught it on something and had it pulled free. Irzelen could have pulled one free in our altercation.

"The one you found on your car, however . . . for that, I had no explanation. But I could not tell you when you asked. This . . ." He gestured toward Rebecca's body. "I am claiming my fate."

A cold sadness passed over Fia as the pieces fell into place. "You were dying. That's why I'm different to you. You knew I was your last?" Uhlpir said nothing, confirming her theory with his silence. "Do you know why . . . why Rebecca . . . ?"

"Why do so many humans do what they do? Jealousy. You were a shadow upon Rebecca's life, even before she came here. Arriving during the turmoil of your departure did little to alleviate that. Everything she has done, perhaps since puberty, has been overshadowed by the presence of Fia Drake."

"What happens now?"

He lowered his chin and spoke to his feet. "Another angel will be sent to guide you. Or whoever takes your place. Or both. I, I assume, will live as a mortal, grow old, and die as Scott McGregor."

Fia wanted to say more, but she didn't know what. She felt like he wanted to say more but didn't know what. Max pulled her into his chest as they watched Scott retreat into the house. When the door closed behind him, Max turned and kissed her head.

"What do we do now?"

Fia led Max through the French doors into the foyer. Looking around, she wondered where to begin looking for Agnes. She had started for the stairs, heading for the Mother Superior's office, when she heard the woman come in from the hallway.

"Fiammetta, did Father Scott tell you where he was going?"

Fia shook her head and puffed a small, joyless laugh through her nose. "He said something about personal business. Reverend Mother, we need to talk. There is something I need to tell you and then something I need to show you."

Back in the city, Fia eased Max's car into the space that had once belonged to the Scout and closed her eyes, leaning her head against the headrest. She tried to clear her racing thoughts. For what felt like the twentieth time, Fia ran through what was likely the last conversation she would ever have with Mother Agnes.

Agnes invited Fia and Max to sit with her on the foyer steps. Fia thought the stern, stoic woman looked tired, but not the kind of tired that could be remedied by a good night's sleep. She gripped Fia's hands in her own, taking stock of the cuts across Fia's knuckles. "They call these 'fight bites.' It happens when a punch makes contact with the target's teeth," Agnes explained before Fia could start her story. "I trust you have taken care of our problem?"

Fia lifted her head from the seat, pushing the memory aside, and turned to look at her passenger. For maybe the first time since they had freed him from the demons, he was sound asleep. Fully restful sleep. No murmuring, no tossing—just still, quiet sleep. She watched him for a full minute before something caught her attention.

At the opposite end of the otherwise empty level of the garage sat a pair of motorcycles she hadn't seen before. Pulling the keys from the ignition to keep the car silent, she opened the door and climbed out of the car. She wasn't sure what she expected to learn by simply looking at the bikes, but she crossed the shadowed space anyway.

When Max joined her, she handed him the note she had found taped to one of the seats.

Please do not mourn for me. I have made my peace, and in some ways, I am looking forward to a mortal life. I know that you both will be fine without me, and I have no doubts we will see each other again before it's all over.

Maybe the best thing about mortality is, I know what it means to say I do love you, Fia. You never knew your father, but I hope Father Scott was able to fill that void for you, even if just for a short time.

These are for you. Take a break. See the country. Enjoy each other.

Until we meet again, all my love,
Scott

"He bought us bikes?"

"He bought us bikes."

Acknowledgments

To my Patreon supporters, I continue to extend my deepest gratitude.

Founding Legacies
Patricia Harris
Redbird Stormcrow

Concrete and Chords
Glenda Pearl Kilgore

Mortar and Monitors
Caroline Barnette
Lissa Fone
Robin Stevens

To the musicians whose music is featured in this series and who will likely never read this statement, thank you for the ongoing inspiration.

To Jenny Elliott, for your relentless devotion to and support for artists of all media.

About the Author

What began with a princess captured by a pirate and rescued by a dragon has developed into D. Gabrielle Jensen's lifelong fascination with stories of the unexpected and unexplored. She has dabbled across many styles and genres, but whether through startling, staccato works of pulp horror or the dirt and grime of urban fantasy, she always finds her way back to speculative fiction.

An award-winning bestseller, D. is built from drumbeats and hot asphalt. Even as an imaginative child in the rural mountains of Colorado, she felt pulled to the chaos and clamor of The City—any city, every city. With this in mind, she aims to infuse her work with mortar and music. Her favorite views of any city are from the rooftops and the side streets. She strives to show the beauty of both in her stories, urging readers to walk the streets with her as she introduces them not only to powerful heroines and antiheroines but to the buskers, bartenders, and baristas who make up the fabric of every city.

If writing be her first love, music is the trusted friend D. turns to when that love forgets her birthday. She can sing along with new songs before they've finished playing and set up a drum kit blindfolded. She can't remember a time when she didn't know how to play her parents' vinyl records. She has one Spotify playlist (out of many) that can run for two full days without repeat and an active hatred for paperless concert tickets. She works that love of music into her writing through allusions to lyrics in imagery, characters named after songs and musicians, and behind-the-scenes playlists. She will even write to a metronome if she needs to give a scene just the right cadence.

D. loves things that begin with the letter C—coffee, cats, cities, conversation, concerts—and things that don't—airports, humans, macrophotography, urban decay, macrophotography of urban decay, and the beauty of flaw. She encourages everyone to join her across social media and on Patreon. Strike up a conversation. What are you waiting for?

www.patreon.com/writerdgabrielle

www.instagram.com/writerdgabrielle

www.facebook.com/writerdgabrielle

www.twitter.com/writerdgabriele